Poorly Zeroed

A Net Zero Travesty

By John M. Cape

This is a work of fiction. Names, characters, and incidents are either the product of the author's imagination or are used fictitiously, and any resemblance to any actual persons, living or dead, is entirely coincidental. Any perceived slight of any individual is purely unintentional. Even so, the planet involved is Earth. The various material related to the associated science, policy, energy characteristics, and historical charts are mostly derived from a collection of sources generally classified as nonfiction.

While all attempts have been made to verify the information provided in this publication, neither the author nor the publisher assumes any responsibility for errors, omissions, or contrary interpretations of the subject matter herein.

Singing Bowl Publishing, Houston, Texas
oildusk@aol.com

Library of Congress Control Number: 2021917796

© 2022 John M. Cape

ISBN 10: 0-9787893-2-6
ISBN 13: 978-0-9787893-2-9

Cover Graphic Licensed from Getty Images

Table of Contents

Extract of Absolute Zero Emissions 2050

*"The two big challenges we face with an **all-electric future** are flying and shipping. Although there are lots of new ideas about electric planes, they won't be operating at commercial scales within 30 years, so zero emissions means that for some period, **we'll all stop using airplanes**. **Shipping is more challenging**: although there are a few military ships run by nuclear reactors, we currently don't have any large electric merchant ships, but we depend strongly on shipping for imported food and goods.*

*In addition, obeying the law of our Climate Change Act requires that **we stop doing anything that causes emissions regardless of its energy source**. This requires that **we stop eating beef and lamb** - ruminants who release methane as they digest grass - and already many people have started to switch to more vegetarian diets. However the **most difficult problem is cement**: making cement releases emissions regardless of how it's powered, there are currently no alternative options available at scale, and we don't know how to install new renewables or make new energy efficient buildings without it."*

Absolute Zero Energy Emissions 2050
Research Program Sponsored by the UK Government

Extract of President Eisenhower's Farewell

"In this (the technological) revolution, research has become central; it also becomes more formalized, complex, and costly. A steadily increasing share is conducted for, by, or at the direction of, the Federal government. Today, the solitary inventor, tinkering in his shop, has been overshadowed by task forces of scientists in laboratories and testing fields. In the same fashion, the free university, historically the fountainhead of free ideas and scientific discovery, has experienced a revolution in the conduct of research. Partly because of the huge costs involved, **a government contract becomes virtually a substitute for intellectual curiosity**. For every old blackboard there are now hundreds of new electronic computers.

The prospect of domination of the nation's scholars by Federal employment, project allocations, and the power of money is ever present and is gravely to be regarded. Yet, in holding scientific research and discovery in respect, as we should, we must also be alert to the equal and opposite danger that **public policy could itself become the captive of a scientific technological elite.**"

The Offer

The Offer
FEBRUARY 2032, ARKANSAS

The chain-link gate is already hanging open as Eacher glides his electric scooter quietly into the farm yard. After parking his bike, the crickets and bullfrogs are suddenly silent as he walks onto the dimly lit front porch.

Cappy barks excitedly inside. No need to knock.

Paul opens the door moments later. "Eacher, my old friend. Welcome." Paul lives on a small plot of land in the country he and his only brother inherited from their father. He is around fifty years old, about six feet tall, and very thin, like many. He's dressed in jeans and a long-sleeved wool shirt that hangs loosely over his frame. Planting season is not yet underway, there's no grime under his fingernails.

Eacher follows him into the well-lit dining room, and his wife, Rose, steps out of the kitchen to offer him a drink. He knows she is about five years younger than Paul, but wouldn't guess that from looking at her. Her sun-darkened and wrinkled skin is a grim testament to the high cost of untold hours in the sun.

Eacher takes a quick sip. The water is room temperature, as expected, but surprisingly has no taste, which took some effort. He appreciates the consideration, drains the glass, and hands it back to her.

"Beer?" Eacher sets a six-pack on the table and removes one for himself.

Paul takes two and hands one to Rose.

"Damn, store-bought beer. That had to be expensive."

"You guys are worth it! I need to explore something with you." The room feels like a sauna, and the dry heat from the woodstove is baking everything in the room. Eacher removes his coat and moves toward the living room.

"No problem. We miss you on campus. Do you mind if Rose joins us? We don't get many visitors." Paul said.

"Her insights are always appreciated. She's smarter than either of us!" Eacher watches for her reaction.

"Now you're sweet talking me!" Rose blushes on cue. "Please don't stop!" They grab the sofa, and Eacher takes the loveseat.

Stacks of rough-cut firewood line the wall, and Eacher guesses that it's enough to last the rest of the winter. They've spaced their furniture tightly together, suggesting that they once relocated from a larger residence. As a single man living by himself, Eacher's place, by contrast, is a tribute to minimalism.

"You mentioned that you need to make a decision?" Paul asked as he put his arm around Rose's shoulder.

"Yeah, I'm facing a deadline to respond."

"It involves an offer?"

"Yes, but you'll consider it an odd one."

"Well, let's hear it."

"Yes, tell us more," Rose adds.

"I've just been invited to attend a no-cost training program. After I complete it, I'll get a financial stipend."

"What's the catch?" Paul said.

"Well, as I understand it, I'm to participate in a boot camp for climate skeptics."

"You're kidding me. Right?" Paul looks a little confused. "You've always been so polite and considerate. I can't imagine you as a climate warrior."

"Well, I don't need to be combative to employ the scientific method," Eacher said.

"It just sounds like some type of scam," Rose said.

"I thought so myself when I opened the email they'd sent me. Then I went through an interview and did some legwork on the details. It's a new program, but it seems legit." Cappy is lying on the cushion next to Eacher and enjoys having his ears scratched. He's not as skinny as his owners.

2

"Assuming this proposal is real. Who would pay for it and why?" Rose asked.

"There's a foundation set up by a billionaire that organized this."

"Well, I agree with Rose; something is off. The whole idea sounds absurd. You know that Rose and I participated in rallies that supported Net Zero, and it was a simple plea. Accelerate clean energy and dump fossil fuels, and not necessarily in that order. Neither of us was disappointed when those policies got implemented."

"And that's never bothered you? Even with everything that's happened?" Eacher asked.

"Now, hold on there; we've always agreed to disagree on our politics. I'll acknowledge that living with what we set in motion has caused us considerably more hardship than expected. Still, it was all for a good cause." Paul said.

"See, I knew you guys still see our country in a favorable light," Eacher said. "Most of the other people I know are less enthusiastic about the changes we've all gone through."

"Just trying to do our part," Paul said.

"Well, I wouldn't expect anything less of you two."

"You're saying that some mullet is willing to fund your exploration of hairline cracks in the foundations of climate science?" Paul said.

"Well, that's the idea. Though I think it's more like vast canyons that don't connect." Eacher said.

"Seriously? I've never realized you had such strong reservations about what's happened." Paul said.

"You probably remember that I ended up at your community college after my tenure track at a major university evaporated. My research funding was sparse, and my papers couldn't pass a peer-review sieve. Suffice it to say that my ideas weren't consistent with the version of the science I was supposed to align with."

"Ah, but if your opinions are so much different than settled science, it was a wonder they ever let you on a tenure track in the first place!" Paul said.

"Now you sound like my ex-wife!"

"That's right. When I first met you at our community college, you mentioned you were going through a separation." Paul said.

"She kept telling me to conceal my objections and align with what colleagues wanted to hear. She was right, but I wasn't willing to suppress my professional intuition to obtain tenure."

"In that case, this sounds like an ideal gig for you. You'll get to hang out with people who believe the same curious things you do." She said.

"But, why bother? Net Zero is a done deal. What good can come from this type of commitment?"

"What chance would another opportunity like this come along?" Eacher said.

"It's hard to believe it showed up this time!" Paul said.

"Eacher, I'm not suggesting that your perspectives are mainstream; we both know they're not. Even so, if you think legitimate questions deserve better answers, go find them!" She said.

Eacher glances appreciatively at Rose. "Thanks!"

"So, you might go?" Rose seems amused by the thought of Eacher signing up for this initiative.

Eacher stands up without saying anything and walks toward the window. He just heard a discernable thump in the distance, and the noise was like a baseball bat smacking a grapefruit. He had occasionally driven past the wind turbines on the hills behind this property. However, this was the first time he'd noticed their operating sound inside this house. With fewer leaves on the trees this time of year, perhaps the sound traveled farther than it would at other times. Maybe the wind was more intense, driving them to operate at higher speeds?

Cappy starts barking and Rose gets up to let him out. She looks back at Eacher.

"I don't know." Eacher finally responds. "My employment days are behind me, and I don't need to get involved. I also have to prepare for next winter like everyone else."

Paul stands up and then walks over to Eacher, standing next to the window. He puts his hand on his shoulder. "Whether our opinions agree or not, there's no one more worthy of the opportunity you've described. The past geological studies you've shared with me were professional. No one else on our campus had similar levels of skill or knowledge. Tell you what, do this and come back and tell us what you learn. I don't think it will change our opinions, but we'll try to be open to whatever you want to present."

"If I go, I'll stop by again. I came here expecting that you would convince me this was a bad idea. You think I'm not just going through a midlife crisis?"

"You're too old for one of those! No, it would be more like a bucket list quest in the waning years of your life. But, I'll tell you what, I spend so much time just trying to put food on the table that if they offered this chance to me, I'd accept it!" Rose said.

"Me too. It would certainly be an improvement over the job I've currently got." Paul said. "When would you start?"

"It kicks off next month."

"Hell, give it a shot. If it doesn't work out, you're welcome to come back and spend winter with us." Paul said.

"You'd do that for me?"

"Please think of us as family," Rose said.

"That's very kind of you."

China Girl
GUANGZHOU, CHINA

Kirk is sitting on his twentieth-floor balcony. Below him, this sprawling port city of twenty million people is in constant motion. Similar apartment buildings rise above older and shorter buildings in all directions. A narrow tower shimmering in dancing colors draws one's attention away from the skyscrapers downtown. Beyond that wall of soaring buildings, rivers encircle the western and southern sides of the city.

The sun is low in the eastern sky, and the car and foot traffic swell and pulse in the streets below. An estimated ten million migrant workers and residents head to work in various factories around the city.

Kirk barely notices all the surrounding activity. He's still dwelling on a recent phone call with his brother. Paul had described an energy-challenged lifestyle in the United States that is beyond his ability to comprehend. Was that call an invitation to assist or a warning to stay away? It was a troubling discussion, and he now feels detached from his vacation plans.

Kirk suffers from regular bouts of apathy that have little to do with his family's quality of life. The apartment is relatively new and well-apportioned. Having slept alone the last four days, he chooses to throw the sheets in the washer rather than expend the energy to make the bed.

He heads out of the apartment with his suitcase.

The elevator ride down is only interrupted twice by neighbors on other floors, and it's a relatively speedy trip to the ground floor. Exiting the lobby, he weaves in and out of other pedestrians and street vendors.

The neighborhood has a modern and protected feel. The streets throughout the city are well-maintained, free of trash, and well-lit. Crime rates are low. Yet, despite all this material well-being, he feels distant.

A familiar vendor on the street sells "stinky tofu" and other breakfast treats. The cook hands him a breakfast burrito-sized pork and leek pancake wrapped in paper. He quickly swipes his watch across a bar code on the stand and then takes the bundle. He takes several bites and then deposits the remainder in a trash can along the way. He enters a public restroom and quickly washes some spilled sauce off the front of his trousers, and it leaves an awkward wet spot for the moment.

Within minutes he's at the subway entrance. He moves down a long escalator, scans his phone screen at an entry gate, and then heads down another level to the track. He waits about three minutes for the next subway. After boarding, there are no open seats, and he grasps a ceiling strap and stands in the aisle. He knows the route and doesn't need to glance at the Pinyin map above the door. Almost all of the other passengers fixate on their phone screens.

He reaches his stop, exits past the incoming passengers, and stands on the right side of the escalator as other travelers walk past him on the left side. After two more turns in a crowded yet well-lit hallway, he finds himself in the railroad depot. He glances at the electronic ticket on his phone to confirm the assigned track. The railroad station is majestic and grand, but the long walk along broad halls with concrete floors and matching walls is an effort.

The train is already waiting to leave when he enters and locates his assigned seat. It fills up and pulls out about ten minutes later.

The landscape rushes by at two hundred kilometers an hour as he watches vacantly out the window. The scenery is a blur. He looks forward in the distance and notes the hilly terrain and numerous villages that quickly pass by at speed. He pulls an instant ramen cup out of his backpack, opens it, and then fills it with hot water from a tap at the back of the car. Returning to his seat, he eats part of this second breakfast with chopsticks and then disposes of the rest in a trash bin near the toilet.

Small children in the opposite row glance at him from time to time, and if they sat closer, they might poke his skin to see if it was real. As a westerner, he's a cultural curiosity in a nation mostly populated with Chinese people. At times like this, he knows he's far from where he grew up.

After managing to complete college with a philosophy degree, he spent a semester in seminary. China beckoned when it became clear that he should not be a priest.

Teaching English conversation to five hundred high school students was challenging, especially since almost none had siblings. Four grandparents and two parents indulged each of these kids. These children were subject to enormous expectations that pushed them to outperform other Chinese students similarly motivated. Every child can't be above average, and engaging so many determined children was emotionally exhausting. He felt sorry for the children destined to perform poorly on their high school exams and miss the career gates their more competitive classmates were targeting.

During a phase when he often consoled many high school also-rans on the merits of mediocrity, he met Windy on an online dating site. She was skilled in English and possessed a western-style business degree. He bought her dinner at a local KFC, a decent restaurant in China, and had an instant connection. Life seemed better with her, and she was sympathetic to his lack of job success or career direction. In her mind, his "B" blood type was the source of his angst, and she set her expectations for his future success at a low peg. That development seemed to justify his existence in a way that nothing else ever had. They tied the knot a year later though he never could figure out what his attraction was to her.

The train stops, and passengers file on and off with their baggage before it starts moving again.

He looks to the front of the compartment, and the train's speed is visible in red LED lights above the sliding door to the next car. They're now back to the same rate, with several similar stops still ahead.

Windy also seemed to swallow the story that cultural barriers in China were the primary cause of his employment challenges. She regularly voiced her expectations of being the breadwinner of their family. Her belief in the potency of her "O" blood type and her unerring business advancement set her up for great jobs and many business trips. That left him at home most of the time; fortunately, her regular absences probably made her life with him more tolerable.

So, when his teaching job ended, she consented to him replacing it with a tutoring role for individual students. As the market for English language skills contracted, he ended up with only a few students - which suited him fine.

Almost three hours and three hundred miles away, the train arrives at his destination in Guilin, China. Several stops and the change in elevation along the route added at least a half hour to his trip.

While walking towards the entrance to the train station, Windy meets him along the way as planned. The temperature is warm inside the station. She wears a sleeveless cheongsam silk dress that is tight-fitting and reveals her trim figure; she looks younger than their three-year age difference. They walk out of the train station pulling their suitcases.

She uses a phone app to summon a ride.

Despite many cars on the road, traffic moves smoothly. The driver drops them off at the entrance of a crowded pedestrian-only street. At their hotel, it's too early for check-in, so they leave their bags in a storage room.

Being with Windy allows him to exert effort that he can't muster without her. Perhaps part of this energy is sexual – especially when he hasn't seen her for several days. More accurately, a fair amount of energy is needed to keep up with her; it's as if he's a trailing cyclist getting pulled by her draft.

She leads them along the middle of the road, looking for a particular foot massage place. Finding it, a pool of small fishes nibble the dead skin off their feet and ankles for the next thirty minutes. Windy is sampling some complimentary rice snacks and offers the bowl to Kirk. He's noticed some sizable cockroaches lurking in the back of the shop and declines her invitation. Mentioning this concern to Windy would only spoil her enjoyment. He says nothing.

Afterward, they enter several clothing stores along the way. Since his earnings are very modest, he won't spend much on himself. He's also made a point to never complain about anything she wants to buy, though she's not one to waste money.

They agree to make dinner light and inexpensive; he's pretty indifferent to whatever she usually wants to order, and he can eat almost anything.

They walk up the sidewalk of a tall bridge that allows them to overlook boat traffic moving below. Tour boats load and unload mostly Chinese tourists from a dock area on the river's far bank.

The boats have rows of seating and angled clear glass windows allowing tourists to get a full view of the river and surroundings.

There are statues in the small park nearby honoring some long-dead officials. A young boy repeatedly kicks a soccer ball against the pedestal of one not far from a street lamp. This child playing alone seems like a kindred spirit.

It's the end of winter here, and delicate and feathery cirrus clouds accent the sky in the fading light.

Leafless trees line the road along the river below, their fallen leaves dutifully removed by efficient street cleaning crews months earlier.

Windy pulls a large pomelo out of her bag and peels it, and they eat it a segment at a time.

Windy is effusive about the beauty of this city.

Curiously she now shares her enthusiasm again for those in charge of her country. Like many in China, Windy refers to her national leaders as a "good dynasty." Given the country's incredible economic success over the past fifty years, the one-party government is not only acceptable but popular.

When she finishes sharing these intense feelings, he smiles politely and does not challenge these particular observations. National praise is one of several topics where his counter input would lead to an argument.

China is a communist country that has long recognized the advantage of allowing market prices to organize daily commerce. He senses there is now a somewhat widespread but mostly unspoken understanding in China. If economic circumstances become difficult, the Chinese people might spend more time exploring the idea of a democracy or press to change the team in charge. It's a simple but apparent reason why the government is less inclined to impose policies that would impose much hardship.

The next day they start the second leg of their trip to Yangshou. That village is an even more-trendy tourist center with numerous restaurants, live music, and upscale shopping nestled in a river valley with mountains.

Windy summons a ride, and they are in a car on the way to the dock, where they will link up with a half-day cruise that will transport them. When her phone rings, she answers and mostly listens. The call ends, and she proceeds directly to her email on her phone. Finding what she is looking for, she reads a message to herself and then shakes her head. Windy's smile has vanished.

"Did you have any trouble getting off from work?" Kirk studies her face looking for hints about the call. Windy works in a marketing role for a clothes retailer and visits manufacturing facilities around the country.

"No trouble at all."

"Everything is okay then?"

"Well, our company is struggling. But we've talked about that."

"Yes, that's why I'm asking."

"Well, that was my boss."

"There's a problem?"

She waits a minute before responding. "They just gave me my termination notice. I knew there was an issue, but this was an inconsiderate way to do it."

"At least he called you himself."

"Herself. My boss is a woman."

"Of course, I knew that. You've done a great job."

"I did! It turns out my entire department got eliminated."

"Sorry! I hate reorganizations. Got a line on another position?"

Again she doesn't answer immediately but closes her eyes. "Yes, I knew this change was possible, but this moved fast."

"You haven't tested the job market?"

"The market must have already known our company was in trouble. I've been getting calls." Windy said.

"Anything solid?"

"Yes, one company made an offer that's good for a while."

"That's a relief."

"You're telling me." Windy pauses and then looks him firmly in the eyes; he dares not look away. She also brushes back her hair from the side of her face. "This might be the right time to meet your family."

"Windy, that's a long way to go."

"Is it safe?"

He takes a little time to consider the question before replying. "Let's call Paul and see what he says." Kirk is not particularly fond of the idea. It seems like many things can go wrong, it would be expensive, and it would take a lot of effort to make this happen. It exhausts him to think about it.

"That would help," Windy said. "I've read some articles about some serious issues there."

"It sounds like you're on top of the situation, as usual. Let's see what my brother and his wife have to say." Traveling to the United States would be a significant commitment for both of them. Would their relationship even survive such a trip? He experiences a sudden dread that she intends to deposit him with his family and return alone. It's a curious and improbable thought, but not one that is easy to dismiss.

***

On the riverboat, the two sit at a table near an open window on the upper deck. They eat cucumber-sized pieces of fried bread, which they dip into a bowl of soy milk as they watch the shoreline pass by.

"Time for the call?" Windy asks.

He checks the time on his phone.

"Sure, let's do it." He makes the call and switches on the speaker; they hear it ringing. He turns the volume down when the people sitting at nearby tables start leaning in their direction.

"Kirk!" Comes a voice from the other side.

"Evening, brother! You guys still awake?" They instinctively move their ears closer to the speaker to hear the discussion better and block the sound from traveling too far.

"Not too late here in Arkansas."

"Glad we caught you before you went to bed."

"Let me find Rose. Just give me a second."

They listen to Paul walking around with the phone.

"Hi, all. Great to hear from you on the other side of the world!" Rose joins the call.

"Hi," Windy said partly in response and perhaps to remind them that she was listening too.

"Hi, Windy," Rose said.

"Windy and I have some time off. Would you guys mind if we swing by?"

"That would be terrific!" Paul said. "When are you thinking of coming?"

"Soon." Kirk looks at Windy, and she's listening intently. "First of all, is it safe to visit?"

"Kirk, that's a subjective question. You're going to find there are a lot of changes." Paul's voice sounds confident but tentative. Kirk notices the uncertainty, but he's not sure that Windy does.

"Paul, we're talking about the United States; how different could it be?" Kirk wants to dwell on the challenges of making this trip.

"Don't underestimate these adjustments. Net Zero has had a serious impact." Paul voices this with more of an accepting than critical tone.

"Paul, let me rephrase my question. If you were in my shoes, would you be afraid to come home now?" Windy nods to affirm that this is what she needs to know.

14

"Well, Kirk, things are different. You got meat?"

"Yes, of course."

"You got reliable electricity?"

"Naturally."

"You've got a car?" Paul said.

"We don't need one. Public transportation meets our needs, and we sometimes rent one for trips."

A waitress stops by their table with a metal cart and offers a choice of Green, Oolong, or Jasmine tea. Windy points at a blue teapot, and the waitress leaves it with some tea cups. The waitress removes the empty dishes from her cart's lower shelf and moves to the following table.

"Well, in that case, you're in for some surprises." Paul's tone is encouraging.

"Paul, can you share some of your concerns with us?"

Maybe Paul's referring to some things Kirk can use to kill this trip without leaving fingerprints.

"Is Windy okay with camping out?"

"We've never really camped out. Lots of affordable hotel options, and why sleep out in the wilderness?" He puts his hand on Wendy's. "We do hike on well-groomed trails in the woods."

Windy nods her head to show Kirk her agreement on this point.

"Hiking? Yes, that gives you a taste of the outdoors. Anyway, what do I know? We'd love to meet your lady finally." Paul's insights are vague and challenging to follow.

"So, personal safety is not a major issue?" Surely Paul can share some worry that will allow Kirk to dismiss this idea.

"Kirk, I didn't say that. We've not traveled much lately, and I'm not familiar with the current situation on the ground in Houston. I'd think it ought to be fine; many people still live there."

Windy is listening to this call and doesn't appear to be following the entire discussion. She looks at her husband inquisitively and with a bit of

15

uncertainty. He shrugs his shoulders to suggest that he's also struggling to follow the call.

"Paul, you're saying things are fine where you live?" Those two are just too elusive! Why are they being so nondescript?

Rose now leads the discussion. "There are some minor inconveniences where we live. For example, we scramble to keep the woodstove going when it's cold."

"Well, that doesn't sound too bad." Kirk said. "So you can't think of anything to justify why we shouldn't make this trip?" This discussion is not going as he had anticipated, and they are deliberately not addressing the real problems.

"You don't know the half of it. If you come, bring some clothes that you don't mind getting dirty." Rose isn't sharing a whole lot of details, either.

"What half are you not telling us?"

He says this in an exasperated tone, then looks at Windy. Her expression is blank.

"You kidder. Hope to see you in Arkansas soon." Paul said.

"Well, we'll talk it over and get back to you once we decide."

"It would be great to see you two," Rose said. "We'll respect whatever you elect to do."

They wrap up the call. Windy looks at him curiously.

"Did you get all that?" He asked.

"Not really. Paul and Rose are both very vague on the situation."

"That was my take. It sounds like there's a lot of hardship where they are. They didn't say anything about any possible dangers that we might face!" Kirk said.

"I know what you mean. It might be a little unpleasant, but doesn't sound threatening."

"Yep, it's what they're not telling us that we should be worried about! There's a lot that could go wrong that we need to consider. Maybe it's not a good

16

time to make this trip?" He pulls her closer while the two of them sit together. Their boat motors steadily forward. They pass smaller boats fishing closer to shore.

The banks of the river appear lined with a forest of stone that rises hundreds of feet. A Shilin Karst landscape gives the shores an eerie feel as if some immortal creature threw mountain-sized rocks at the waterway and missed.

The food arrives. It's a special meal of fried tofu, seafood, and various savory Chinese dishes. The freshwater shrimp are fried and tasty. Kirk reaches for another one with his fingers, and Windy hands him a pair of chopsticks.

She looks toward his eyes and then averts her gaze. "At least we don't have any kids to worry about yet." She looks over to a small child sitting at an adjacent table in a high chair.

"No, you're right about that." He feels childlike, and the idea of having the responsibility for one is terrifying. Through their first five years together, she's been on birth control, and it's not been an issue.

Her face lights up from what she misinterprets as encouragement.

Only two of her grandparents are still alive, but they are impatient to continue their lineage; at least one grandkid is a must. Her parents are more patient but share persistent hints that her fertile years are running out. There will be a lot of joy if they can deliver a child soon and considerable grief if they can't – at least from the vantage point of their closest relatives in China.

"Yes, probably a good time to make this trip," Windy said.

"Really?" This remark comes out in a startled tone that a native English speaker would not have missed. She's already made up her mind, and he immediately recognizes that there is no longer any value in trying to discourage her. Her blood type also makes her stubborn.

He dutifully places a dumpling in her bowl, a Chinese way of showing affection. He then kisses her lightly and notices an older passenger at a nearby table smiling at him. There are thirty million more young men than young women available for marriage due to the One Child Policy. He's heard that no one smiles when a beautiful young Chinese woman ends up with a

17

western guy. That gentleman must not have worn his glasses. Kirk smiles back and gives Windy another light peck for good measure; it induces more grins in their direction.

Windy talks excitedly about the things they need to organize for this trip.

***

After reaching their hotel, they check into their room.

He's not feeling particularly amorous after her announced decision to travel to the United States and have a kid.

They must go through the motions for their fifth-anniversary celebration. They don't have a tub in their home, but there's one here. He opens the faucet.

She hears the water running and enters the bathroom. She smiles when she sees the rising water. She tests the warmth of the water with her hand and pours some hotel shampoo in to create bubbles. They soak together for a while and talk about their years together. Kirk has always called her his little porcelain doll; her hairless arms and legs induce envy in western women.

They quickly dry off before moving to the bed. Windy takes the lead in directing his attention in a playful yet commanding mode - which she knows is a bit of a turn-on for him. This practice hasn't always been his preference. Yet, since becoming a bit of a kept man, perhaps it's an adaptive adjustment. Don't ask him what turns her on. She's never really shared any particular fantasies with him.

Windy seems satisfied with his efforts though nothing is said. He goes to the wall to adjust the thermostat so it won't be too cold under the blanket. When he returns to bed, Windy is already asleep.

The Lost Woods
MARCH, THE LOST WOODS

Eacher sits on his scooter in front of a tall chain-link fence. He presses a buzzer mounted on a panel on the gate and wipes caked dust and sweat from his face with a handkerchief.

A camera inside the fence pivots towards him, and a voice requires him to display his identification. He holds his driver's license just below his chin and the recording equipment swings out of the way. The barrier swings slowly open. He enters the compound. He then follows a two-way traffic road that bends slightly to the right and then curves back towards the left to shield most of the drive from view from the encircling perimeter road.

He enters a concrete parking garage, leaves his bike in one of the many visitor slots on the ground level, and notes the availability of more parking on lower floors. This parking area is surrounded by a waist-high concrete wall with thick glass extending to a high ceiling. The design naturally channels him toward a sliding glass door that opens as he approaches. He then exits this building into a garden area with enormous Southern Live Oak trees with long branches spreading horizontally about ten feet off the ground on all sides.

As he continues along the paved path, he notes several marble and bronze statues of delighted wood nymphs and laughing children in various games.

An elderly man in a light blue robe and tennis shoes notices him on the path and comes forward to meet him. "First time here?"

"Yes. Am I in the right place?"

"I guess that depends on why you're here."

"Well, I don't think I'm here for a religious retreat." Eacher quips.

"Well, that would depend on your religion; it's not a bad place to have one. Are you a scientist of some sort?"

"Actually, I teach geology," Eacher said as they walked together toward what appeared to be the center of the complex. He sees parts of a blue steel roof that adorns some sort of decorative structure. He notes several ponds with

19

large and multi-colored Koi fish amongst large floating lotus plants in bloom; nearby are various benches and wooden platforms ideal for soaking in the aura.

"Ah, that explains a lot. You should enter that building we call 'The Temple' and take the door to the immediate right. It will lead you to your coordinator."

"Thanks. Beautiful place you have here." Eacher said.

"Not mine, I assure you. I just look after the gardens on behalf of the owner."

"Well, it seems like an idyllic setting. It's much nicer than I would have guessed from the industrial-looking checkpoint at the entrance."

"We do need to be careful. Hope you find what you're looking for." With that, he waves goodbye and heads off.

Eacher enters The Temple. It is a simple structure with counter-high intricately carved white marble and windows above, providing a view into the surrounding gardens. Just beyond the entry, the ceiling is about fifteen feet above an oval room with plush powder blue carpet in a slightly sunken area. There is no evidence of any symbols, statues, or artwork suggesting a particular religious affiliation of this structure.

He instinctively removes his shoes and takes a little time to walk around inside an area well-designed for worship. He observes a slightly fragrant odor in a comfortable temperature-controlled room. He spends some time to soak in the ambiance and spiritual essence of this remarkable space. Renewed, he pushes open the door, crosses a short landing, and then descends some stairs to a level just below the outside garden. He then follows a hallway to a classroom capable of holding at least fifty people.

An attractive middle-aged woman is writing at a desk in the center of the room. She looks up when he enters. She rises as he approaches.

"Mr. Eacher, my name is Dora. I'll be your host while you're here. Did you have any trouble getting here?"

"I must have had to stop a dozen times to charge my scooter. It took me a few days to get here." Eacher said. "Please forgive me if I still smell like a campfire."

"Well, the good news is that you made it. Welcome to our program."

"It's my pleasure! What a beautiful place." Eacher glances around the room. It is lined chiefly with individual white chalkboards around the sides. The only light illuminating the room at the moment is limited to several spotlights focusing on her desk. "Are there many others here?"

"No, we used to host a lot of entry-level journalists and environmental advocates; that was years before the boss had second thoughts on where to focus his resources. You and the two others we invited are our only visiting scholars. My job is to support your training and make sure you're comfortable. Please follow me."

He follows her out of the room, and the lights flick off when they cross the threshold. He also believes the airflow into the room they just left ceased at the same time. That would make sense. No one wastes energy needlessly these days. She guides him through a well-lit hallway with high ceilings that lead to a different underground complex. Here the walls are covered with expensive artwork and paneling that give this area the intimate feel of a private library in a country estate.

She stops at the third door on the left and asks him to place his index finger on a biometric reader. He does so, and the door quickly and quietly opens. "Here's your room. You'll find a well-stocked bar and refrigerator. Meals can be delivered to your room, or you can join others in the dining room." She points to a larger room at the end of the hall. "Our group study room is right across from your suite." She steps into that space, and the lights flash on, revealing a much smaller classroom than they had seen earlier. It is well upholstered with built-in projectors, drop-down screens, large mahogany desks, and matching office chairs. Some chairs are standard design, and others are kneeling chairs to protect aged backs.

"You guys thought of everything!" He said.

"Check your email; it will give you a map of the property, the location of the athletic and recreational facilities, and all meeting instructions for your group."

"Thank you!" He said. "This is more accommodating than I had anticipated."

"You climate skeptics are an appreciative group. See you tomorrow at 0800 hours."

***

Eacher looks around the room. Two other women his age are sitting in similar seats to his, and he's never heard of either and doesn't recognize their faces. He's about to introduce himself when a life-sized hologram of Mike suddenly appears in the center of the room in their small classroom.

"Great to have you all here at our retreat." The associated voice comes over the ceiling speakers and does not seem connected to the image moving around the room. "I'm not known for supporting any criticism associated with climate change. If you believe certain parties, I am single-handedly funding a large portion of the world's Net Zero activism."

"You're not?" The lady to his left blurts out in surprise.

"No, of course, I have in the past; I got a lot of excellent press coverage. However, what is less well known is that I've lately been funding a small portion of their opposition. I'm not going to pretend that it makes the overall effort objective, that's a far cry from the truth. You, of all people, know that's not the case."

"So, we're here to enlighten you on any concerns that we might have related to climate science or Net Zero policy?" Eacher asked. He slouched in his chair and now sat up as straight as possible.

"That's a benefit that I get from funding this program. Dora will send me the highlights of any discussions. The real purpose of our effort is to help you work on the things that allow older people to be more effective."

"We're definitely not young anymore." One of the women said. "The exercise component of this program scares me."

"No doubt, Irene, that you'll face some serious physical challenges. If we don't toughen you up a little, you won't last long." Mike said. "Assuming you complete this fellowship, I'll ensure you get a credit card for your travel expenses and some nice gadgets. Thanks for coming, and good luck. Do you have any questions before I return to other business matters?"

"I've executed the release you required us to sign? If we die during this training, your organization has no liability. Should we be worried?" The other woman asked.

"Brenda, I won't deny that there are physical dangers in the activities set up for you. Attempting them at your age is even riskier. Believe me, I want you to succeed and get something useful out of these efforts."

"You're actually open to hearing what skeptics have to say?" Eacher asked in awe. He felt his heart beating strongly just from directing this question to a likeness of a billionaire. Eacher's confident that Mike no longer lives in the United States. He apparently moved most of his assets out of the country before the worst of Net Zero was inflicted. When you pay for the activity that induces certain events, you have a pretty good idea of how to best protect your property from associated consequences.

The image moves slightly towards Eacher and looks at him directly. Once again, he hears the voice from the speakers above. "Politically correct viewpoints are aimed at the public. If we had shared the uncertainty related to the science discussion with them, none of the policy measures would have ever been implemented. Even so, someone should still pay attention to what the science tells us – especially after forty years of being subjected to an information blanket."

"So, you don't need us to pull our punches on our perspectives?" Eacher said.

"Absolutely not! What you share with me will be shared with some of my most important friends. Keeping them adequately informed can help us change the world. I've been advised that each of you has been making some efforts to educate the general public, but I'm doubtful they'll be of much use. This country is in a different economic position than it was ten years ago. It

23

wouldn't matter if the majority realized there were issues with what they've been told. Most people can do nothing to make a difference at this point." The image abruptly disappears.

***

The next day, an alarm goes off in Eacher's room. The Alexa device in his room requests that he put on his athletic gear and meet the team at the track in fifteen minutes. He rolls over and ignores it. However, there must be a motion detector, it only gives him sixty seconds before repeating the instructions.

He quickly gets dressed and heads out. After stepping outside, he realizes it's still chilly and returns to his room to get his wind jacket. As he reemerges in the hallway, he notices Irene exit her door dressed in a gray sweatshirt with black sweatpants. Her gray hair, cut short, suggests a low-maintenance and practical personality. She is slender and about six inches shorter than Eacher. She's not bad looking for her age. He looks forward to learning more about this kindred spirit. He glances surreptitiously at her left hand in search of a ring.

She notices him looking and smiles. "Nope. No longer married."

"Me either, not that you were asking. You look fit. I can't imagine that the physical part of this program is going to be a challenge for you."

"Don't bet on that. It takes a special kind of idiot to take this on at our age! Hurry, it's almost time."

The two rush out the door and head for the meeting place. Dora is already waiting there with a clipboard and is looking impatiently at the time on her phone. Brenda comes rushing out the door a few minutes later. "Sorry, I'm late."

"Not quite, but had you missed the scheduled time, I would have been required to document it. Today is simply a physical fitness test. You'll be required to complete two miles at whatever pace you can, and I'll time it accordingly. I realize that you indicated on your application that you had no major health concerns, but please let me know if there's something that we should be aware of. Mike is a bit of a skeptic himself when it comes to people."

***

As the three advanced in the program, sixty percent of their time was spent on physical activity. There were long hikes, navigation instructions with compasses and stars, rock climbing, and swims in brisk lakes. When the blisters healed, shin splints hobbled him. Even so, he persisted.

In one phase, the three undertook survival and evasion training. The staff interrogated them as if they were prisoners of war, and these exercises did little more than convince each of them that they never wanted to be captured.

In another portion of the instruction, they engaged in hand-to-hand combat drills. Eacher quickly learns Brenda has a black belt in Judo, and Irene practices Tai Kwan Do. They make quick work of him as he primarily focuses on trying to protect himself.

The classroom time is a bit of a welcome respite, as it offers them some relief from their sore muscles and aching joints.

As it turns out, Irene has considerable experience as a climate modeler. She is well versed in the assumptions used in the models used by an organization set up by the United Nations to identify human-induced climate change issues. It's called the Intergovernmental Panel on Climate Change (IPCC). She had stopped working in that capacity about ten years earlier.

Brenda had worked in utility management at the board level. For years she was cheered as a champion of a reliable and affordable electrical grid. Then one day, she was quoted as saying that carbon capture and storage was a needless waste of fossil fuels. It became her moment of fame as the press swarmed to interview her and paint her as a climate skeptic. It was a moot point since all the fossil fuel power generation plants were getting axed anyway. After being shown the door on short notice, she never found another position in the industry. She didn't know enough to criticize any aspect of climate science but came to this program hoping to better understand what she'd been accused of.

They were all sitting in their instruction room just two weeks after the start of their training. Dora opened the session. "When Mike asked me to put together this program, I quickly realized it would be an enormous challenge. In cooperation with the major search engines and social media applications, the government has been blocking any materials written by people identified as climate skeptics. Try as I might, I couldn't locate anything that seemed even remotely controversial. I hope you brought your personal reference material with you. Today, I'd like to allow you to show me some of the materials you would post on the Internet if you could. Let's start with your area of expertise and expand from that point of reference. You will never find a more receptive forum for this type of discussion. Irene, you've got a lot of background in the climate science arena. Would you mind going first?"

"Sure," Irene said. "I'm still trying to organize my presentations. Please bear with me since this is my first time giving this one."

"Well, share what you can," Dora said.

"Let's get to the heart of the matter," Irene said. "When the United Nations chartered the IPCC, they had already decided that manmade greenhouse gases in the atmosphere were responsible for global warming. They were so confident in this conclusion that they immediately set up three different committees. The first would validate the science, the second would confirm the damage, and the third would develop and evaluate solutions."

"Why was the IPCC so fixated on the anthropogenic greenhouse gas theory?" Brenda asked.

"Since fossil fuels provide most of mankind's energy needs, the ability to regulate them would deliver an incredible amount of political power to those in charge," Irene said somberly. "Though climate science was in its infancy at the time, the IPCC was only focused on this theory. There were many benefits for others to go along. From the outset, the smoking gun was an earlier version of this chart." Irene pressed a button on her remote, and the first slide appeared on the classroom projection screen.

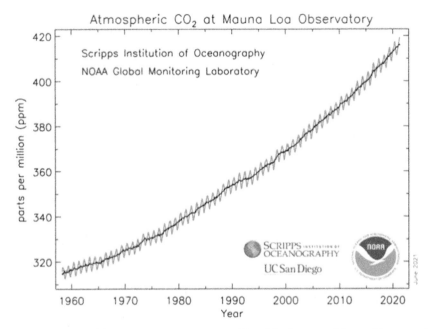

"Yes, how could anyone ever argue with this inescapable evidence of mankind's impact on our atmosphere?" Eacher sarcastically commented.

"Well, that's how it was used to justify the IPCC's charter. Yet even this seemingly compelling evidence that mankind has undeniably impacted nature is oversold. This chart concerns the net atmospheric carbon dioxide increase from all sources, not just manmade emissions." Irene said. "Ninety-six percent of all carbon emissions worldwide come from nature."

"Why would that matter?" Dora asked.

"Well, let's imagine your weight seems stable, and you add a daily cookie to your diet. The next thing you know, your weight increases at a rate consistent with the calories in half a cookie. Did the addition of the cookie solely account for your weight gain?" Irene asked.

"Well, that would depend on what's going on in your life," Eacher said.

27

"Precisely. Let's say you added the cookie when the temperature was warm in the summer, but you know you'll burn many more calories in the winter, which is approaching fast. Do you keep the cookie in your diet?"

"I'd eliminate the cookie," Eacher said while patting his tummy for emphasis.

"Assume that once you drop the cookie, you won't get it back," Irene said.

"I'm not sure I completely follow your story, but from what you've described, there are a lot of other factors in play," Brenda said. "Personally, I like cookies."

"Me too," Irene said. "Fossil fuels are the cookie in this metaphor. The amount of carbon dioxide they emit act like the calories in a diet. The IPCC claims that fossil fuel emissions account for all the carbon dioxide emissions in this chart. That's equivalent to saying that the cookie accounts for your calorie increase. From one vantage point that's true at this moment. Still, in the larger picture, it depends on what your total calorie demand is and what your total calorie intake is. In fact, if you could magically eliminate all manmade emissions, carbon dioxide levels would already be falling."

"Carbon dioxide emissions for all those natural sources don't change. Right?" Dora asked.

"That's not true at all. When there's more carbon dioxide available, plants use more, and the oceans absorb more. In fact, the IPCC believes that the ocean carbon dioxide emissions have increased by a third over the past few hundred years. The increase from that one source alone is more than twice the size of manmade emissions and about four times as large as the growth in net CO_2 emissions. Falling carbon dioxide concentrations are much scarier than rising ones."

"Can you explain that last remark?" Dora asked. "Why would lower CO_2 levels in the atmosphere be a concern?"

"Well, for starters, carbon dioxide is plant food. Greenhouses add extra carbon dioxide to help plants grow faster. If carbon dioxide levels fall, it could lower crop productivity and reduce the world's access to food. In addition, if carbon dioxide levels fall below 150 parts per million, plants stop growing. If that happens, most life on Earth will go extinct. About twenty thousand years ago, carbon dioxide levels reached 180 ppm, its lowest level in the last half billion years." Irene moves to the next slide. "This shows our carbon dioxide levels falling for the past 160 million years."

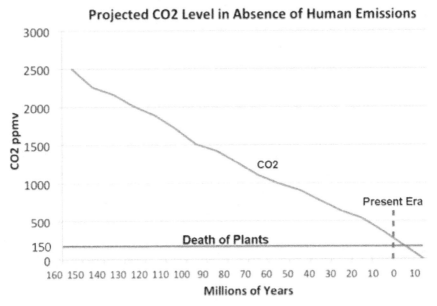

"Wow, I've never heard that we were so close to the end of our days!" Brenda said. "Why did our carbon dioxide levels get so low?"

"The atmospheres of Venus and Mars are almost entirely composed of carbon dioxide. Earth only has four parts per ten thousand. Mother Nature accounts for the difference. When multicellular life began to flourish about six hundred million years ago, creatures that utilized calcium carbonate to build their shells soon evolved. Their remains became sediment on the ocean floor when they died. Over time, the associated carbon dioxide got taken out of circulation. Our current increase in atmospheric CO_2 concentrations might extend the presence of life on our planet for millions of years - though that's simply speculation. The oceans contain two hundred times the amount of carbon dioxide in our atmosphere. They can easily absorb the small amount added to the atmosphere in the last century."

"Can we move on?" Dora encouraged her to get back on track.

"Yes, you're right," Irene said. "Let's recognize that when the IPCC founded their organization in 1988, this was less than ten years after the satellites started collecting temperature data from space. Since then, a considerable amount of money has been spent to examine our atmosphere and oceans with the latest technology."

"If the weather and climate were so easy to understand, we'd be able to accurately predict the weather for longer than three days in advance," Eacher said.

"True. My point is that a vast amount of data is now being collected from satellites, sea probes, and many other sources. Much of this new information does not support the hypothesis that carbon dioxide is our planet's thermostat. The IPCC rushed to their preferred theory forty years ago for their own reasons. Still, it's increasingly clear now that decision was premature," Irene said. "I'm afraid there's currently no agreement on why the climate changes."

"This is why we brought you here," Dora said as she glanced up at a clock on the wall. "Help us understand what you believe is really going on."

"Take a look at this chart." She switches to the next slide. "Note the size of the impact of this extra CO_2 in this chart."

What's happening at the surface?

Dr. John R. Christy

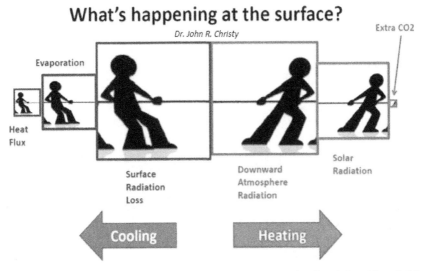

"You mean that little fellow you can barely see on the far right side of this tug of war?" Brenda asked. "He's pretty tiny!"

"Yes, he is, and as a result, he's not likely to cause much warming or cooling by himself," Irene said. "Other forces are the major climate drivers."

'She's right." Eacher said as Irene gave him an annoyed glance. Eacher was trying to support her and not compete with her. He hoped she recognized the difference.

"99.96% of the energy that powers our climate system comes from the sun. Even so, the Earth's orbit around the sun is currently more elliptical than circular. On January 4th, when the Earth is closest to the sun, 6.9% more solar radiation hits our planet than is received on July 4th."

"What?" An annual solar radiation variance of almost 7% a year? That's huge!" Brenda wrote furiously in her notebook.

"Yes! Here's the slide that illustrates what's going on." Irene said.

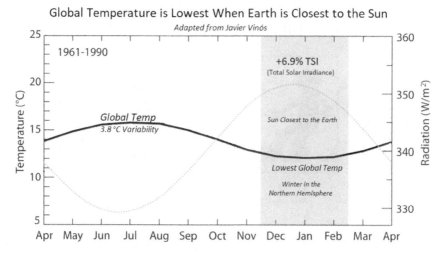

Global Temperature is Lowest When Earth is Closest to the Sun

Adapted from Javier Vinós

"That looks complicated." Brenda looked up briefly and returned her attention to her notes.

"Let me try to simplify it for you. The temperature scale is on the left, and the solar radiation scale is on the right. The months of the year are along the bottom. The thick black line is the average global temperature over the year, and the dotted line is the amount of solar radiation reaching our planet. The shaded area represents winter in the northern hemisphere."

"You're saying that the world is almost four degrees colder when it receives the most solar radiation?" Eacher asked. "What kind of mojo is that?"

"Pretty miraculous if you ask me!" Irene said. "The specifics of how this miracle is performed are beyond the scope of this discussion. A large hint is that January also corresponds with the highest amount of energy radiated into space from the North Pole. The incoming solar rays are reflected by ocean clouds and snow. Throughout the year, Earth remains in an almost constant state of energy imbalance. It gains energy between October and May and loses it the other half of the year."

"That's amazing," Dora said.

"Well, what seems incredible to me is how much heat is sloshing through the atmosphere and oceans to pull this off," Eacher said. "You're right." "Irene said. The scale of what's going on is incredible. I imagine that it works something like a giant vacuum cleaner. The extra heat in the planet gets sucked up from wherever it shouldn't be, moved around, and then sent into space. Why would it matter if a small amount of that heat came from having a little extra CO_2 in the atmosphere?"

"What could possibly be that large?" Dora sounded skeptical.

Irene looked at her slide list and selected one. "Doubling atmospheric CO_2 levels is supposed to induce a forcing of less than four watts/m^2. The North Pole can radiate 157 watts/m^2 by itself in the winter! Would you like me to further explain this particular climate theory?"

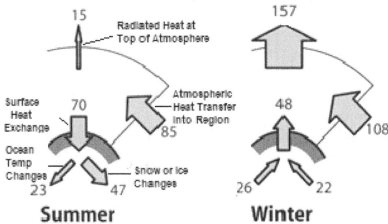

North Polar Cap Heat Flow
70 - 90° Latitude (watts/meter²)

Adapted from Javier Vinos, Climate of the Past, Present and Future

"No, but I don't understand this illustration." Dora said.

"Well, here are the basics. Water vapor is the main greenhouse gas, and the temperature determines the maximum amount of water vapor in the atmosphere."

"So?" Dora asked.

"I'll restrict my discussion to the North Pole, but it works similarly at the South Pole. The water vapor concentration might be thirty times that of carbon dioxide in the summer; those greenhouse gases limit the amount of heat that can radiate to space; the heat transmitted to the area mostly melts snow and ice and warms the ocean. In the winter, there is almost no water vapor in the air. There is practically no resistance to heat radiating out of the atmosphere. Heat is released when the oceans cool and water freezes. That heat, and the incoming heat, is radiated into space."

"I thought you'd keep it simple!" Dora said.

"Okay, let me describe it a different way. Suppose you have a building with a heater and no windows, but you have lots of insulation in the roof and walls; do you think the building would stay warm in the winter?"

"Sure," Dora said.

"Imagine that you left the front door open when it's cold. Do you still think your house is going to stay warm?"

"No, of course not," Dora said.

"The greenhouse gas theory is about adding a little more insulation to the atmosphere; the reality is that a little bit more doesn't help when a portion of the atmosphere has none."

"Interesting, I'll think about it. See you tomorrow." Dora said.

Just Off the Boat
JUNE, HOUSTON

As the boat enters the Houston Ship Channel, Kirk's heart beats faster. While he wasn't keen on making this trip, they're now here, and he's elated. He has been away so long. They both stand on the deck, gripping the guardrail as they await for the city to come into view. An American flag in tatters is fluttering on a listing flagpole along the shore; it almost startles him just to see it after so many years. He's shared some stories with Windy about growing up here, and he still considers the United States his home.

He puts his arm around his wife as their vessel chugs along; she presses closer to his side. He attempts to softly sing her a verse of *America the Beautiful* but doesn't remember all the words. He ends up humming some of it.

Behind them are stacks of cargo containers loaded in China that are transporting various manufactured goods into the United States. Several of them are stenciled in red letters with the words "Solar Panels" and different Chinese characters he's never learned. Next are dense rows of tiny electric cars about the size of a golf cart. In addition, massive fiberglass wind turbine blades are almost as long as the ship. They are secured with straps above the other cargo. China is the manufacturing hub of the planet, and many different vessels are needed to move these goods.

This boat is more of a shipping vessel than a cruise ship, and the passengers only got to access certain parts of the boat. He was satisfied with the Asian dishes served every meal, which was the trip's highlight. They initially spent much time on deck as they crossed the Pacific Ocean.

Then after days of staring at an empty expanse, they lost interest. After that, they spent most of their time together in their windowless cabin on a lower deck. After viewing the limited selection of Chinese and South Korean video offerings with captions, they found themselves going a bit stir-crazy. They are both eager to exit the boat.

The area around the dock is active, with forklifts and cranes ready to move the cargo.

They are in an area that has long been a very industrial part of Houston. It traditionally served as the center of the chemical and refining industry.

Massive domed storage units are visible all along the route. Around them are industrial facilities surrounded by expansive parking lots and fences.

What immediately strikes him as strange is how few trucks and automobiles are in the parking lots at various processing plants. It is a weekday, and his recollection of this area is that it usually is bustling with lots of workers and activity. He remembers Highway 225, a road that serves as an Interstate artery for this part of town. Many pickup trucks, vans, and fast-moving cars raced to and from work at high speeds. From their elevated perch, he notices that the expressway is now filled with hundreds of Vespa-like scooters, a small number of cars, and various trucks of all sizes.

On the plus side, the air has less of an ethylene and diesel smell than he remembers; he is pleasantly surprised that it is no longer noticeable. Even so, smoke hangs hazily in the air over the local houses. The dense accumulation reminds him of a low-hanging fog, which seems out of place for June. In addition, an orange-tinged dust cloud is visibly wafting over the highway; the road itself seems to be the source.

He still mulls over why Windy was so interested in making this trip. From what he's been able to piece together, she seems to be open to the notion of staying in the United States to raise a family. It's a curious and unlikely idea. She respects and listens to her parents and grandparents, and he couldn't imagine them not living close by. Was it something that she thought would somehow be to Kirk's benefit?

The boat stops, and several unintelligible announcements are garbled over the ship's broadcast system. They return to their room briefly and then move out when they hear a long ship horn blast, their cue to exit the boat. There aren't many passengers, so the ship's gangway is not crowded.

They move along the corridor and arrive at the customs and passport inspection lines shortly. The offloading travelers from their ship are mostly Chinese with various English skills. They are now mixed with the tourists of another ship and can overhear Spanish conversations. Kirk doesn't comprehend much of the discussion going on around them.

Windy is dressed casually in jeans, sandals, a designer shirt, and an expensive purse. Her hair is dark, straight, and stylishly cropped at the shoulders. The nails on her hands and toes are trimmed neatly and painted a shade of pink.

He's dressed in straight-legged jeans, a designer tee shirt from his wife, and some black walking shoes. He's wearing tinted polarized sunglasses with a dark brown frame. While his hairline is just starting to recede, his hair is medium brown and cut short.

He joins the United States citizen line, and she enters the visitor line with her Chinese passport.

There is a single inspector in this part of the terminal. She glances at the visitors in front of her, briefly looks at their passports, and waves them past. When Windy reaches the window, the examiner does the same thing.

Kirk is also quickly waved through when it's his turn. How nice that this process does not take much time! This had not been their experience when passing through Chinese customs while entering or exiting China.

They both pass through the processing area so quickly that they must wait a little while for their bags to arrive at the baggage carousels.

As they exit the luggage area pulling their suitcases behind, they enter a long hall with glass walls. He anticipates that a taxi queue will be available to take them to their destination. They look outside and don't spot one.

Most of the other passengers leaving are loading onto several tourist buses. An armed guard stands by while the bags are packed into storage areas along the lower right side of the bus.

Others greet relatives or friends who are picking them up in some fashion.

Untroubled, Kirk brags about the strength of ride sharing in the US and pulls out his cell phone to query the Internet. No cars are available.

They discuss a public transportation option. Kirk and Windy agree that they don't know enough about the security of the public bus or light train systems to trust that their luggage would not be at risk.

They follow a sign to the rental car area. There are no lines and only one booth open. After a brief discussion, they learn that this company wants seven hundred Chinese yuan daily for the rental car and an additional five hundred to prepay a few gallons of gasoline. There apparently is only one single vehicle available - an economy car.

Now Windy springs into action, and she lets the attendant know that these prices are outrageous.

The attendant picks up his cell phone and calls someone, and Windy winks at me expectantly. This worker then shakes his head and hangs up the call. "I apologize, but we're now out of cars."

She stares in disbelief. Kirk tries to console her and reassure her that there are other options.

They again turn to their phones to search for another solution. They each call numerous taxi numbers to no avail.

He has one bar on his phone for the local signal strength, and the battery is almost empty. He moves to a wall socket to charge his phone, and one of the security people rushes to stop him from doing so. He turns his phone off to save the little charge that's left in case of an emergency.

A few scooters are standing-by outside, and the drivers are wearing orange vests stenciled with the words "Taxi" on the back. Kirk almost suggests they talk to these guys but doesn't see how they'd carry their luggage. If they offload their bags onto a different scooter, what would they do if the luggage driver just took off?

Some rough-looking people are loitering around the outside of the terminal. They occupy the available benches, and he notices tarps and various tents strewn along the fence line.

Kirk might be paranoid at this moment but senses that they are showing considerable interest in Windy's expensive-looking suitcases and purses. One or two approach them for spare change and a closer look. Kirk quietly points out his safety concerns to Windy, and they both move back into the terminal.

They move directly to an information booth. A woman sits there, chews gum, and looks at Kirk and Windy indifferently. She listens expressionlessly to their questions.

The booth helper picks up the phone and calls someone. After a short discussion, she asks if they can afford eight hundred yuan a day for the vehicle and six hundred yuan for a few gallons of gasoline. She also indicates that this company can pick up the rental car from their hotel in Houston for an additional two hundred yuan.

"Yes, we want that option," Windy said. "Does it include insurance?"

"No, that's an extra three hundred yuan a day.

"Okay, give us the insurance too."

Kirk and Windy then return to the rental car counter to complete the transaction.

The same clerk who met them before does not seem surprised they're back.

He asks for an international driver's license and a credit card. Kirk hands him his old expired Texas driver's license, and it's acceptable. They quickly review the terms and execute the agreement. The clerk gives him the keys, and Kirk and Windy head to the rental car pickup area, where only one vehicle sits. Kirk clicks the fob to open the trunk, and there is no response. He opens the car door and pulls the trunk latch lever on the inside of the door, but nothing happens. He tries the trunk with the car key, and it opens. They quickly load their bags.

The car is in pathetic condition and Windy jokes that she is happy that the trunk latch works. The car is about ten years old and shows more than two hundred thousand miles on the odometer. The rearview mirror is missing, and there is little tread left on the tires. Much of the paint has been replaced by rust. Kirk dutifully notes everything on the inspection form and takes a picture for his records. He presses the ignition button, and the car starts on the third attempt. He puts it into gear and gives it a little gas. It moves forward. He presses the brake, and it holds. "It seems safe."

"If you say so." Windy shakes her head.

As they drive to the exit booth, an animated cowboy image greets them on a screen and asks about any issues with the car. When Eacher complains, it asks him to drop the inspection sheet in the slot on the stand. He complies.

"Welcome to Houston," a recorded voice cheerily announces in a thick southern accent as the gate arm raises and they are on the way.

***

Windy navigates, and Kirk drives as they travel along the highway. The main roads are mostly in decent shape, but he has to exit periodically because of unfinished construction projects. He points out that the major arteries in Houston always seem to be involved in ongoing upgrade efforts.

The feeder roads for the high-speed highways are in terrible shape. For these, he has to slow down to avoid numerous potholes. The scooters race by on both sides; they must have mostly been locals since they expertly avoid the worst hazards at high rates of speed. One scooter barely misses colliding with their bumper as the driver swerves to avoid a pothole while passing. "Can you believe how these people drive here?" He asked.

"Yep, pretty crazy." She returns her focus back to her phone screen.

Putting his finger on what is different from the areas he is driving through is not easy. His general perception is that everything just seems more run down. Maybe it's because he's grown accustomed to immaculate neighborhoods in China. More likely, there's something off that he can't yet recognize.

His apprehension is making him wary of potential danger in every direction. He sits at a light and continuously pivots his head in all directions in search of potential carjackers. He stops a car's length from the vehicle in front of them at the light just in case some criminal sneaks up, and he has to quickly reverse direction. He catches himself staring at other drivers who seem amused by his awkwardness.

Wood smoke also hangs over a good portion of this part of town. Many of the large trees that used to line the road and shade neighborhoods are gone; short tree stumps mark where they once stood.

There are few billboards advertising anything though several steel billboard frames are still visible along the road and appear available for rent.

Some changes are more subtle. Many doors and window openings have steel bars protecting them from potential intruders. Many people are driving with the windows down despite the heat and the humidity.

He doesn't register his observations with Windy. Glancing over at her in the passenger seat, she still uses an image of a map on her phone screen to navigate. Still, she is also reading text messages and emails. He imagines that she assumes that these rough neighborhoods are typical.

Even in better neighborhoods, tall fences with barbed wire along the top enclose the front yard. There are guards for some of the more expensive-looking houses. Many people sit on their porches or hang out in the street. He might have expected this in April in Houston when the weather is more temperate, but not in the summer.

The engine starts vibrating louder than he expects. He looks at the gas gauge, and it appears broken. Are they even going to make it to their hotel?

Knees in the Breeze
THE LOST WOODS

Eacher, Brenda, and Irene are often back in the classroom. They take turns giving lectures, and today is Eacher's turn.

"I'd like to start with the oldest timeline today and then move forward in time. Here's a high-level picture for the last half billion years." Eacher hits a button, and his first slide appears on the screen.

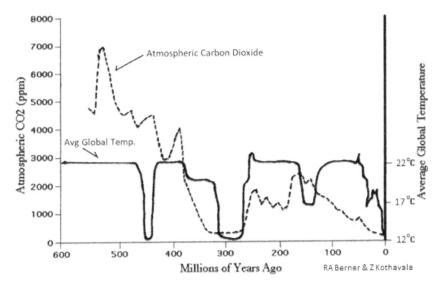

"That's curious," Dora said.

"Well, it does give you a sense of the amount of work that's gone into analyzing ancient rock deposits to create this analysis. Note that the solid line shows average global temperatures, and the dashed line shows atmospheric carbon dioxide levels. There has not been much of a correlation between these two variables. In fact, there was an ice age around four hundred and fifty million years ago when carbon dioxide levels were ten times higher than their current levels."

41

"You're right. Atmospheric carbon dioxide levels and global temperature levels don't seem to move together very often in this slide." Irene said.

"I've got another observation on this graph that intrigues me. Our Solar System orbits around the Milky Way Galaxy about every two hundred and fifty million years. The primary ice ages, as evidenced by significant long-lasting temperature drops on this chart, have shown up about every hundred and fifty million years. A fascinating theory suggests that certain parts of the Solar System's journey make Earth susceptible to Ice Ages that last tens of millions of years."

"That takes a bit of imagination," Dora said. "This is a fascinating discussion, but perhaps we should focus more on the basics?" Dora said.

"No problem." That last comment is another reminder that Dora has not been very open to their insights. Eacher continues.

"So a hothouse Earth is actually normal?" Irene said.

"From a geological perspective, they've been more common than long cooling events. An Ice Age consists of numerous cycles. During our current one, the most recent cold periods last a hundred thousand years and cover the higher latitudes in the northern hemisphere with thick glaciers. Then there will be a warm interglacial cycle, like the one we're in now, that might last for ten to twenty thousand years. Each of these long freezing periods and short warming cycles is called a glaciation. Here's a graph highlighting what a hothouse world might look like compared to what we are currently experiencing." Eacher switched to the next slide.

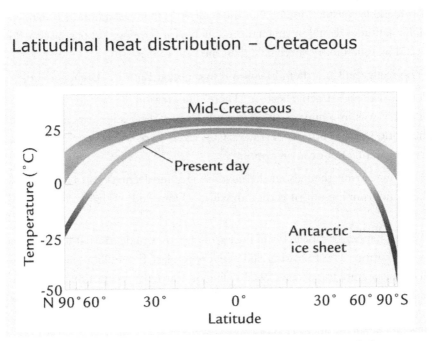

Latitudinal heat distribution – Cretaceous

Brenda looks closely at the two graphs. "When was the Mid-Cretaceous period?"

Eacher smiles. "Assume this chart represents the hothouse conditions on Earth about a hundred million years ago. Most people aren't aware that in such a world, the temperatures near the equator are very similar to today. The difference is that these same tropical temperatures would occur up to forty degrees latitude – about the latitude of Madrid, New York City, or Beijing. Apparently, natural mechanisms associated with tropical climates maintain those constant temperatures."

"Curious," Dora said.

"Our ongoing Ice Age has delivered more than forty-six glaciations in the past two-and-a-half million years. In the very improbable event, it's now finally over, it's plausible that Earth might revert to a hothouse mode again. The polar ice would melt, and the sea levels would be about a hundred and twenty feet higher than they are now. Those changes would drive

43

considerable coastal flooding, but the tradeoff is that vast amounts of land at higher latitudes would be much more suitable for farming. A hothouse world would be much more survivable than the next glaciation."

"You really think another glaciation is in our near future?" Brenda asked.

"I'm afraid so," Eacher said. "There's no reason to believe otherwise. Mankind was in a hunter-gatherer mode twenty thousand years ago before the world warmed up. Atmospheric CO_2 levels were so low, that agriculture was apparently not even an option."

"So, you're concerned about the next ice age, and Irene is concerned about the planet running out of carbon dioxide," Dora said. "That sounds pretty dismal."

"What's happened repeatedly in the past is a strong guide to what will happen in our future. The following slide covers the last five million years. Note that temperature trends have been falling on Earth for most of this time. We only emerged from the last glaciation about twelve thousand years ago. Our current temperature anomaly is at the intersection of the left axis and the dotted line where the little circle is shown."

Five Million Years of Climate Change from Sediment Cores

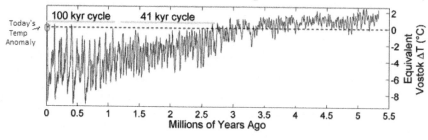

"Almost all the temperatures over the last three million years are colder than they are right now," Irene said. "Why are we obsessed with the idea of global warming?"

"Good question, but let me clarify that this data is from a specific location in Antarctica. Since we believe the tropical temperatures would be similar to what they are now, the global temperature anomalies are almost certainly smaller. Even so, this is the pattern the Earth has followed for millions of years. Why would anyone believe that our planet is at risk of overheating shortly?"

"I'm confused," Dora said. "There has been a lot of climate change in the past?"

"Yes, quite a bit, as my materials show."

"Why am I being told that recent warming is unusual and without precedent?" Dora asked.

"Please judge for yourself based on what I'm showing you. Let's now continue to step through time and take a look at what happened the last half million years." Eacher said. "Take a look at this graph." The next slide flashes up.

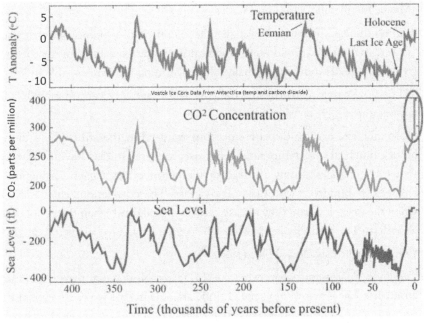

Time (thousands of years before present)

"Ah, the trends that Al Gore featured in his movie," Dora said.

"You've seen this graph with the last four glacial cycles before?" Eacher asked.

"Who hasn't? I remember Al Gore getting on a man lift to emphasize how much warming he thought the manmade carbon dioxide emissions would induce. Look at the correlation between carbon dioxide and temperature! That's another point he really emphasized!" Dora said.

"Well, let's look at those assumptions more closely. If carbon dioxide drove the warming, how much warming did it drive?"

"At least ten degrees!" Dora said.

"And how much has happened since all the recent CO_2 was released into the atmosphere? That's the circled part of the middle graph."

"I can't tell from your chart, but I'd guess about half a degree," Irene said.

"So, if carbon dioxide is such a potent warming gas, why hasn't it already caused more warming?" Eacher said.

"Maybe it still will," Dora said flatly.

"I don't think so. It's already well dispersed in the atmosphere." Eacher said. "Future carbon dioxide additions might drive some warming, but the existing levels are already inducing virtually all the warming they are capable of."

"Then how would you attribute the correlation between carbon dioxide and temperature?" Dora asked.

"Recently, the carbon dioxide emissions released in the atmosphere didn't induce much, if any, temperature increase. Several studies have confirmed that CO_2 changes during the recent glaciation cycles lagged temperature changes by hundreds to thousands of years. The correlations exist because when the oceans warm, they release carbon dioxide and when they cool, they absorb it. The causality is opposite what you were led to believe."

"That's hard to swallow," Dora said.

"Well, one last point before we leave this chart. Notice that the temperature anomalies for recent interglacial periods are a degree or two higher than the present. Climatic tipping points didn't happen in the past when the climate was warmer, and they seem unlikely to happen in the future."

"I still can't believe that such a central part of that movie was so far off the mark," Dora said, shaking her head.

46

"There are other examples of bad science getting featured. Ever heard the Hockey Stick story?"

"You mean when the US beat the Russians in the Olympics?" Dora asked.

"No, but that's a great underdog story." Eacher switched to the next slide.

"This chart shows temperatures over the past ten thousand years from an ice core in Greenland."

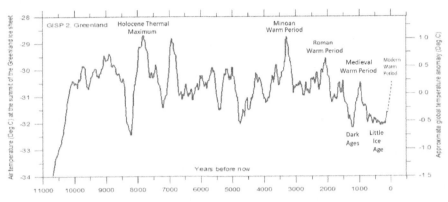

"There seems to be a downward trend," Irene said.

"The last eight thousand years of cooling is called the Neoglacial." Eacher said. "Note that current temperatures are below other temperature peaks in the last ten thousand years."

"That dotted line to the right suggests that recent warming might be completely consistent with past warming patterns?" Irene asked.

"I couldn't agree more. Look how normal that looks." This graph appeared in the IPCC's First Scientific Assessment Report."

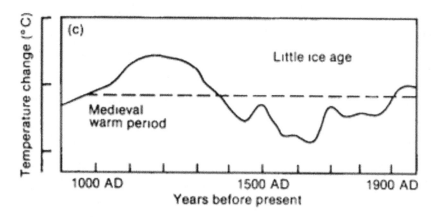

"There's no temperature data, but it shows a similar picture to what was happening in Greenland," Irene said.

"After they posted that sketch of the Holocene temperatures, the IPCC apparently got a lot of pushback on their claims that manmade emissions were driving climate. From that point forward, they wanted to eliminate the evidence for the Medieval Warm Period." Eacher said.

"How do you get rid of the Medieval Warm Period?" Irene asked.

"You really can't eliminate the document trail that supports it. There is plenty of evidence that it happened. For example, the Vikings occupied Greenland during that warm period and fled when the climate became too cold. Grapes were grown in England far to the north of where they can be grown today. Some glaciers in North America have recently receded and revealed the remnants of forests that thrived there a thousand years ago. There is considerable historical evidence confirming it really existed, especially in the northern hemisphere." Eacher said.

"So the IPCC was stuck with it," Brenda said.

"Not at all. During the following assessment report cycle, the Holocene was barely mentioned. In addition, they began to claim that the last ten thousand years were relatively well-behaved. Further, they lamented the availability of historical proxies and dropped all mention of the Neoglacial Period. Then in the next assessment report, this graph showed up."

48

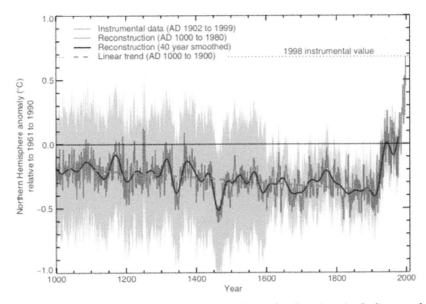

"Oh, I've heard this story. Skeptics challenged why they had distanced themselves from the established Holocene evidence," Irene said.

"True, and this new chart was quickly dubbed 'The Hockey Stick'. The IPCC crowd loved this novel interpretation! They featured it in the Scientific Assessment, the Synthesis Report, and the Summary for Policy Makers in 2001. It was also all over the news! It gave them exactly what they needed for their climate alarm narrative."

"Definitely politicians driving that organization!" Irene said.

"No doubt. Skeptics found severe issues with the data and the methodology for this particular chart and challenged it. While the IPCC quietly retracted it, its supporters defend it to the present day. The IPCC then released similar graphs in their following two Assessment Reports. Given their persistence and willingness to choose obscure tree ring proxy data over more reliable ice core data, historical data, and many other proxies, the most interesting question is 'why'?" Eacher said.

"Because it helps their case?" Irene said.

"More than that. It distracts the public from the real question about Modern Global Warming. Take a look at this picture." Eacher said.

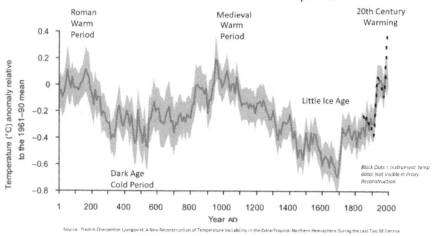

Temperature Reconstruction for Northern Hemisphere Shows Modern Warm Period not Exceptional

"That looks like the last two thousand years of the data from the Greenland Ice Core," Irene said.

"Yes, it's similar and certainly supports that this temperature reconstruction might be in the ballpark. Why would anyone believe that carbon dioxide caused recent warming when the temperature increased on schedule? Cooling trends followed all the previous warming spikes. Why would anyone expect anything different this time?"

"Really?" Dora asked. "What would that mean?"

"The Little Ice Age was not a cakewalk. Dealing with something similar in the future will not be trivial."

"Really? The next Little Ice Age?" Dora obviously didn't believe much of what Irene or Eacher shared with her.

"The Neoglacial will almost certainly continue and edge us ever closer to the next glaciation. With colder weather, the oceans will overwhelm manmade emissions, and atmospheric carbon dioxide levels will start to fall. We're close to a climate emergency, but not for the reasons the IPCC's politicians and followers insist on."

***

Irene seemed to thrive in this environment. Eacher survived it.

Unfortunately, Brenda didn't make it through the course. She returned home during the second month of the training after realizing that she had no interest in challenging climate science. Dora explained to Eacher and Irene that she had expected at least one class member to not complete the instruction.

Earlier in the day, Eacher and Irene each individually and separately navigated the tire house. It is a training structure made of discarded auto and truck tires stacked to form walls that could absorb bullets and shrapnel. They shot live ammunition at moving targets and tossed hand grenades to clear rooms as they negotiated their assigned path through the structure.

They have one last jump. Irene and Eacher will be dropped from 15,000 feet, open their parachute around 2,000 feet and then land on a planted field. They'll then link up and navigate together back to their rendezvous point. It's a less challenging jump than the one where they were required to land among the trees. It's an exercise that's more of an expensive morale builder than anything they would likely use going forward.

The helicopter that will take them to altitude is privately owned and not subject to the same air restrictions that shut down the commercial aviation industry.

They are sitting in their regular classroom in a review session. "Why should we believe that the IPCC is not acting in the best interests of many on the planet?" Dora said.

Irene moves her hand as if to pluck the question out of the air and then continues. "They are unwilling to assist the most impoverished countries in financing fossil fuel power generation. For such countries, fossil fuels would be the most viable approach to emerge from their dire economic circumstances. In addition, without better energy choices, many millions die from the long-term effects of breathing in smoke from wood and animal dung while cooking in enclosed spaces."

"Great point. Eacher, same question, your turn." Dora said.

"Well, the IPCC should champion objective and unbiased science, and that's not happening enough. Policymakers and politicians are willing to spend much of the public's money chasing biased research efforts. That's likely money that would be better spent for other, more pressing problems."

"Okay, next question. The Russians funded western environmentalists in their efforts to discourage fracking. Do you think the Chinese might have hired environmentalists and activists to encourage developed countries to pursue Net Zero policies?" Dora said.

Eacher looks a bit confused since this question was never discussed in any of their prior sessions. He blows air into his closed fist.

"Will that be on the test?" Irene asked.

"Well, I wouldn't be surprised if it comes up on your final exam. What are your thoughts?" Dora said.

Irene looks at Dora first and then Eacher and then responds. "Well, let's look at the results. There's little question that these Net Zero policies and beliefs demolished the economies of developed countries and eviscerated their manufacturing capability. By default, China did become the world's only superpower. It was an inexpensive and brilliant strategy if the Chinese bribed the NGOs and environmentalists to pull this off."

"Okay," Dora said.

Eacher then adds these thoughts. "Look, there was some advantage for Europe to roll the dice on wind turbines. They had to import most of their energy, and the idea of locally generated power must have been seductive for them. But, to guess that the United States would follow their lead is not a chess move that anyone could have anticipated. Who could guess that the United States was willing to abandon its substantial fossil fuel endowment to buy renewable systems from China? Also, who could guess we'd pursue Net Zero when they did not? I don't buy it."

"Net Zero policy has been such a sweet deal for the Chinese. I just had to ask if you thought that they had somehow orchestrated it," Dora said and then changed the subject. "This session is over. You two are free for the rest of the day. Meet me at our rendezvous point at eighteen-thirty this evening." Dora stands up and quickly exits.

Eacher looks at Irene. "You think they'll kill us tonight?"

"Nope, it would have been easier and cheaper to snuff us out at the beginning. Why spend all this money on us if they didn't really want us to do something useful when we finished the program?" For a second, their eyes meet.

"Hope you're right. Looking forward to dropping out of the sky with you later!" Eacher said, attempting to overcome his fear of another terrifying jump from high altitude into the darkness.

Irene's reply is in the same mode. "Don't even think of breaking your leg on the landing and forcing me to hike back by myself!"

"You mean you won't carry me if that happens?" Eacher teased her.

They continued the banter all the way back to their rooms.

***

The following day, after only a few hours of sleep, Eacher and Irene are dosing off at their desks in the room where Mike first greeted them.

Dora walks in with a stocky young woman in her early thirties. Dora coughs loudly to wake her two exhausted skeptics; the visitor has several tattoos on her upper neck and lower arms. Dora sits at one of the desks and directs the young lady towards the remaining desk where Brenda once sat.

Mike's life-sized hologram suddenly flashes on. "Welcome to your final exam. Your successful completion of last night's training and this exam will formally mark the end of this program for both of you. To make it interesting, I invited one of our climate journalist program graduates to administer the final questions. Dora will personally judge the responses. Good luck!" With these remarks, the image disappears.

"Let me introduce Connie. She lives in the local area as a freelance journalist and has previously assisted with some similar discussions. She's been briefed on your background. Good luck."

Connie pulled out her notepad and launched the first question. "Eacher, describe how fossil fuels cause extreme weather."

"Well, thank you for your question. Extreme weather has long been an issue for humanity. Hurricanes, tornados, floods, and droughts are part of the natural weather cycle. The scientific evidence does not support the claim that those events occur more frequently. Take a look at slides 32, 33, 36, and 39 in the notebook on your desk."

Connie opens the binder on her desk and turns the pages. She then looks up at Eacher. "Doesn't pass a fact check. Irene?"

"Well, look at slide 74. The global climate disaster death rate fell by an incredible ninety-eight percent between 1920 and 2020. With enough energy at our disposal, mankind can handle any extreme weather event we encounter."

This time Connie doesn't even open the binder. "Nope. Not true. Next question."

This back-and-forth discussion continued for the next hour. Everything Eacher and Irene argued, Connie deemed wrong and then looked increasingly bored.

Finally, after the last rejection, Connie closed the binder with some finality and looked at Eacher and Irene in contempt. "If you don't appreciate the importance of decarbonization and all the benefits of a clean energy future, why do you think you'd be able to pass this exam?"

Both Eacher and Irene simply sat there quietly without responding to her challenge.

Dora stood up, thanked Connie for her assistance, and helped her to the exit. She came back to her desk. "Well, what did you think?"

Irene answered first. "Well, if she is not remotely interested in anything we have to say, why would you select her to give us our final exam?"

Dora looked at her intently. "Great question. What do you think?"

"I think there is no better example of someone who has no interest in the truth. That reporter treats climate science like a religious zealot might regard some holy book. She simply compares what she hears to what she wants to believe." Eacher said.

"Unbelievable!" Irene said.

"Remember, this facility used to train journalists," Irene said. "That program had more physical fitness and focus on the approved materials. They used the Temple a lot to sing songs and encourage each other. It was essentially a faith-based exercise."

"That explains a lot!" Eacher said.

"Well, she's one of many reporters in the real world," Dora said. Her editors determine what's allowed to be published in newspapers and magazines, and she has to comply. I suggest you don't bother journalists and let them do what they must. They are part of a group of young people who know little about this particular topic, but are convinced they know everything they need to know. Focus your efforts elsewhere."

"I see your point," Irene said. "Essentially, we shouldn't waste our time with reporters."

"It's worse than that. Most people have gotten their news from these same sources. You should lose any false expectations you may have that many people are open to what you want to discuss."

"Point taken. Best if we set our expectations low." Irene said.

"Pretty much. You both pass the course, by the way. You're judged on the quality of your answers and not by how they are received by others."

No Place Like Home
HOUSTON

The car engine continues coughing. It backfires, then jerks, and Kirk slows their pace to reduce the strain. After a few minutes, it starts firing on all cylinders again, and he maintains the slower speed as a safeguard.

The large buildings of downtown Houston are visible from Interstate 10 as they pass by on the north side. Nothing looks particularly different until he notices people camped out along the bayou near what used to be called the Theater District. Trash covers the ground near the tents and plastic bottles and debris float in a filthy mat on the water.

They arrive at the hotel a few miles further in an area called The Heights. Kirk vaguely remembers this area as an upscale and expensive place to live. When he had reserved this room while still in China, it seemed like it ought to be all right.

An armed guard is in the lobby. When they ring the bell for service, she keys in a passcode and heads into the office. She then puts down her sawed-off shotgun and checks them in from behind a thick fiberglass partition. She assigns them a room on the top floor. "I need five hundred yuan for the electricity deposit." She said.

"You mean in cash? Can't we just use a credit card?" Windy asked.

"Sorry, too many credit card disputes. I can use your debit card for the initial deposit."

Windy simply hands her five one-hundred yuan notes and asks for a receipt.

The clerk examines the notes closely and then, once satisfied, hands them a steel ring of metal keys; she asks them to keep them in the office when off the premises. Physical keys seem old-fashioned. Maybe they'd use one to get into a house in China, but not a hotel. Kirk remembers using electronic door and elevator cards in the United States.

They learn to their surprise, that this hotel has no working elevators. They use one of the keys for getting through the fenced-in steel security gate that blocks access to the stairways to the upper floors.

He lugs the heavy suitcases one at a time up each flight of stairs. He sweats profusely from the heat of the day and this exertion. Windy offers to take one of the suitcases, but he's afraid they are too heavy and tries to manage both himself.

He finds himself moving from one shaded area to the next while negotiating the stairs; by the third floor, he is struggling. Further, the building's concrete, brick, and steel absorb heat and then radiate it back into the stairwell so that even the covered areas feel like a sauna. To redirect his attention, he tries to recall the cooling breeze during their month-long boat trip from China.

Two floors later, he is almost exhausted, and his skin is starting to feel clammy. They finally reach their door, and Windy tries the key, but it doesn't work.

He's spent, and his clothes are sopping wet; he slumps against the wall in what little shade is available on the walkway. Windy leaves him sitting next to the suitcases and staring south over a sea of three-story townhouses. To the left, he sees the familiar skyline of downtown Houston. To the right, Memorial park no longer appears to have many trees.

Down at street level, a scooter carrying two passengers appears below and stops next to their rental car. One person dismounts, enters a combination into the door lock, and then races off with their rented vehicle. While Windy had texted the rental company that they no longer intended to use it, its timely retrieval evinces an urgency to extract it from this neighborhood.

Windy is back within fifteen minutes, and the room key works this time. She enters and flicks the light switch on while Kirk follows her inside. The lights and ceiling fan work, but the air conditioner does not. Windy calls the desk and is told that none of the other available rooms have operational cooling systems. They elect not to attempt to change hotels.

They try to rest on the bed with the windows open and the ceiling fan set to its fastest speed but are still uncomfortable. They lock the door, return to

58

ground level and take a short walk around the area. Once again, the numerous tree stumps indicate where the shade trees used to be.

The neighborhood around the hotel is littered with garbage and overflowing trash bags of all sizes left along the road or in empty lots. Graffiti covers most of the walls. Tarps line the streets on both sides, and eyes fix on them from beneath as they walk by. They quickly wrap up their walk and return to their room.

Dinner consists of rice crackers and jerky they brought in their suitcases. They eat it without ceremony and elect to go to bed early.

While she falls asleep almost immediately, he lies awake, wondering how perilous this trip will be.

The next day they wake up early, and the morning air outside is comfortable. After some discussion, they agreed to leave almost all their valuables and one of their phones locked up in the room safe. They then walk together to the light rail stop. Some panhandlers approach them along the way. They hand small coins to the first two beggars, but after the third solicitation, they just start tuning them out.

Based on the urine smell and the occasional piles of feces and associated fly swarms, he wonders why there aren't more restrooms available in the area. He suspects he knows the answer to that question when he later notices some public toilets in a park surrounded by an even more significant number of temporary shelters. Public bathrooms are a homeless magnet.

They take a side trip into a local neighborhood that Kirk remembers as an affluent area. None of the yards are cut, and weeds grow high among the debris in front of most houses. The windows are mostly all boarded up on the first floor. Kirk notices that some of the brick is pocked with what appears to be bullet holes, suggesting an attack of some sort. Steel gates protect the front openings where door screens allow some air to enter these dwellings. Some residents sit on the front porch in rocking chairs or swings with shotguns or other weapons. They sneer at Windy and Kirk as they pass by.

59

Many people with dirty hair and clothes wait at the light train station. Alongside them stand well-groomed people in business attire; Kirk notices several teenagers jump over the entry gates instead of swiping rail passes. A security guard with a rifle watches them do it and does nothing. When the train arrives, it is overcrowded and standing room only.

The seat cushions are cut up and torn, and graffiti is sprayed inside and outside the rail cars. The train is in sad shape, and the window glass is completely missing from several windows. Broken shards on the floor confirm what happened to the windows. Here too, a pungent body waste smell permeates the car.

They exit the train near City Hall in downtown Houston. The well-dressed people are met at the light rail stop by armed security guards that accompany them toward the high-rise buildings. The rest of the passengers quickly disperse in all directions.

The streets downtown are in severe distress. They learn that since many restrictions have been placed on cement and bitumen materials, the potholes and road repairs are now filled with clay and gravel. This is a poor decision, given the volume of dirt clouds in the air. This change gives the city streets the feel of roads they've seen in impoverished third-world countries where colonial infrastructure disintegrated.

Kirk is allergic to dust and now finds it tough to breathe at times. His eyes also water from the irritation.

He remembers back to his first arrival in China. The air pollution was so unhealthy that he didn't see how anyone could live in a city like Beijing. Later he learned to tolerate it better. Eventually, the air quality improved so much that it was no longer an issue. He had never thought much about the air quality in Houston in the past. However, now it is a nasty irritant and worse than anything he's ever seen in China.

Windy seems to be thinking the same thing. She fashions her scarf over her mouth and nose to filter dust particles that would otherwise end up in her throat. They discuss the distress and hardships faced by locals; she questions why people would be okay with this pollution.

Neither of them notes any major building construction anywhere in town. At some locations, small orange cones or large orange barrels warn drivers and pedestrians of various road concerns. However, Kirk noted several unmarked street hazards where the traffic warning devices had probably been stolen. In addition, certain types of plastics are stripped from scooters and anywhere else where they are not thoroughly secured. There are so many plastics that he speculates that people tend to steal first and see if they are worth anything later. The plastic and tires that can't be sold for recycling can probably be burned for warmth in the winter by people too shortsighted to worry about the toxic risks of doing so nearby.

Windy and Kirk eat lunch in the late morning at a sit-down barbecue. They only serve vegetables, but the potatoes are tasty and loaded with lots of cheese and butter. Even so, they discuss how it is still in business. It doesn't seem like a meal to either of them without meat.

Kirk decides to show Windy the underground. He remembers that it extends below much of the downtown area, and pedestrians would use it to stay out of the sun and the traffic. They enter a building on Main Street that he has used before to access this system and are immediately stopped.

"I'm sorry. Do you work in this building?" A uniformed guard challenges them.

"No, it's getting too hot outside; we're just trying to get to the tunnel." He said, expecting to be allowed to pass.

"Then I'm sorry, I can't let you proceed. The tunnel system was closed a few years ago, and the buildings are no longer connected beneath the streets, and all the restaurants and shops down there closed."

"That's too bad. Any reason why the City of Houston closed it?"

"Not for me to say." The guard said. "You guys aren't from around here?"

"No, we're from China," Windy said.

"Well, glad to have you here. Almost everything in our stores comes from China, and Houston is blessed to have a port where everything comes in. I bought a standard lead-acid battery scooter for less than half of what my brother paid for the same Chinese scooter in Oklahoma City!"

"Well, you've got to love those Chinese!" Kirk said. The conversation was a bit tedious, and he was ready to leave.

Windy nods like she is glad to hear such nice things about her country.

They exit and immediately move to a shaded area on the east side of the building. Kirk and Windy continue walking around from one shady spot to another, but it is just too hot. They are tempted to rest below one of the trees where others are lounging, but they elect to keep their distance.

Windy and Kirk decide to go back to the hotel during daylight hours. Downtown Houston doesn't strike them as a place they want to be after dark.

After getting off a crowded bus not far from their hotel, they notice an open supermarket nearby. A laundry mat, barber shop, and a pool supply store on the same block are boarded up and unavailable for business.

Upon entering, they walk past a bunch of shelves covered with various trinkets, dry noodles, bobble-headed animal figures, and imported cans of food. The plastic trinkets and containers are much more expensive than Kirk would have guessed, and he wonders if any of these items came from the boat they arrived on. There are a few loaves of locally made pita bread in the bakery and packages of corn and flour tortillas for sale.

They want to buy some cereal and head for that aisle, and there is only a limited selection. Their search for milk leads to some hermetically sealed containers that don't require refrigeration, and they pass on both.

There are imported crackers and imported bottles of spices and sauces where he doesn't even recognize the language on the bottles.

In the fresh fruit section, a store clerk guards the seasonal vegetables. They are not available to be touched and squeezed and are located on shelves behind him. It looks like food that can be grown locally and would probably not be available in the winter.

There is no frozen food section. Some freezers had once been used for this purpose but now sit empty.

62

Windy finds a box of dried green tea and a small bag of sticky rice from Taiwan. She also runs across a tin of well-sealed but expired moon cakes. These pastries aren't the expensive kind you'd buy for moon festival celebrations in China, but cheap imitations that Windy would typically never purchase. She adds these items to their wobbly shopping cart.

There are fruits, vegetables, and soups in the canned food section, and they choose a few for dinner. The prices are higher than expected.

The conveyer belt next to the cash register is not working at the checkout counter.

"Do you have cash?" The clerk asked. "Our system is down right now." The clerk is dressed in shorts and a distressed tee shirt. He also has a nose ring and a multi-colored tattoo that covers most of his right arm.

"We have a little bit, but can't we simply charge the groceries?" Windy asked.

"Sorry, but that's not an option. Show me the cash you've got, and we can try to work something out that's fair."

"Can I write a check?" Kirk reaches into his backpack for a checkbook but catches himself when he remembers that their funds are in a Chinese bank.

"No, sir, I'm afraid I'm not allowed to accept a check without our system."

Windy pulls the cash from the front pocket of her pants.

The clerk adds up the cost of the items on his pocket phone. "Your total is two hundred and sixty-two yuan."

"Really? For this?" Kirk asked.

"You guys new in Houston?"

"Just got off the boat," Kirk said.

"I'll let you in on a secret. If you want food in this town, you should order it online. The expanded post office will get it to your door weekly. Our food in this outlet is manhandled by everyone who comes in off the street." The clerk looks around while telling them this. Kirk supposes it isn't something that he wants his manager to overhear. "Even so, we're one of the few retail establishments that can compete with online shopping."

"Good to know." Windy hands the clerk three one hundred yuan bills, and he takes them and hands her a ten-dollar and a twenty-dollar bill.

Windy looks at the bills curiously.

This is the first US currency either has seen since arriving. The current exchange rate is slightly more than one US dollar to one Chinese yuan. The dollar's value continues to fall while the yuan is as good as gold. Most people use dollars for occasional transactions and keep all their savings in yuan.

Kirk has read in China that the yuan now enables commerce in the United States for all practical purposes. The federal government could peg its currency to the yuan if they were willing to stop printing money. Still, the government does not have that choice. The resulting inflation is a form of wealth tax on the masses. This explains why all regulatory and accounting requirements require companies to pay their employees in dollars. That way, the dollar remains viable until the employees can quickly convert their funds into yuan.

This clerk seems a little too eager to dump these bills on them. Kirk assumes that he'll somehow profit from doing so. The clerk is definitely getting a better exchange rate from them than he'd get from a bank.

"Can you find something you want that costs about eight dollars? We're short on change today." The clerk gently pushes Windy's arm away, so she doesn't try to return the dollar bills to him.

Windy grabs a small pack of gum from the counter to her right, and the clerk nods his acceptance.

"Sorry for the inconvenience." The clerk said. "When our system works, we don't normally have these problems."

They put the purchases in Kirk's backpack and head out the door. As they walk outside, a child beggar approaches them with an extended hand. He is persistent.

"Sorry, I don't have cash." Kirk shows him his open hands with nothing in them.

"Yeah, I bet." The youngster said.

Windy hands him her pack of gum. The child leaves immediately.

A minute later, a dozen other kids show up in a group. Some of these are elementary-age children with physical handicaps; one has a hair lip, and another has a deformed hand. Kirk cringes that these sorts of health issues have not been addressed.

This new group is much more insistent on pestering Kirk and Windy for food or money. Apparently, the beggar with the gum updated his friends about Windy's gift, and not one of them will take no for an answer. No good deed goes unpunished comes to mind.

Windy asks them to leave, and they start to jostle her and Kirk; little hands touch their pockets. Kirk moves between Windy and the group and puts his arms out to give Windy some distance. She seems really rattled by their persistence. The children race beneath his arms and pull on Windy's shirt.

They don't make the mistake of giving this group anything of value. They continue on in the direction of their hotel with the swarm of kids around them. A block later, all the children suddenly run off in different directions. The two of them are left standing by themselves. While Kirk is relieved that they are no longer being pestered, he is wary that something is seriously wrong. Then he sees why they ran.

About a block in front of them, several armed men are heading across the street. Kirk sees the weapons and grabs Windy's hand to casually spin her in the opposite direction away from the action. With their backs toward the men, they steadily walk away but are careful not to simply run – which Kirk believes would attract attention. They turn at the next intersection, and he places his hand on her side to guide her in his chosen direction.

Once out of view, Kirk quickly rushes back to a rusty chain link fence they've just passed to take a peek. Windy wants to keep going to put more distance between themselves and the people they just walked away from. She tugs on a handful of his shirt to encourage him to leave. He gets a quick look to confirm that they aren't being followed. However, he sees the men moving into the yard of one of the townhouses. He motions for Windy to come to see what's going on. Windy is reluctant to stay but then relents from his insistence. She moves to the fence and watches the action to his right and right next to a tarp.

The unlucky target is in the middle of the block. The attackers take different positions in front of that residence. One of the men can be heard giving instructions and is clearly in charge. Another individual takes a crowbar and removes a well-nailed board from one of the windows.

The nails scream, and then the panel lands with a thump as it's tossed into the yard. The window frame is quickly negotiated and pushed upwards; the window glass in the structure does not seem to be broken. All of the attackers, except one guy outside holding a rifle, enter the house. Within a few minutes, the front door opens, and the thieves start running out with pillowcases full of stuff. After the last one leaves, the door is left ajar. The intruders all quickly leave the area heading back the way they had come.

Kirk and Windy wait longer and then proceed on a different route back to their lodging. Ten minutes later, they enter the office and explain what they've just seen to the clerk. The clerk shows no surprise and bullet marks on the wall where similar invaders had once assaulted them. In their case, the hotel management even had video footage of the intruders. Still, the police claimed they could never locate or capture them amidst all the people without established addresses in the city. She laments that this type of thing happens too often.

Kirk and Windy take their ring of keys, pass through the steel gate to the stairs, and then continue upwards. Almost immediately, they hear a couple of gunshots. They move to the inside of the stairs as they ascend, crouching out of view of the street. As they reach the upper floors, they can see bullet tracers in the distance arcing into view before disappearing. Had it been darker, they would be a lot brighter.

Once in their room, they notice that the lights no longer function. They quickly confirm that the electrical outlets are not operational either. Why the hotel doesn't use programmable door cards now makes sense. They don't work when the electricity is down – which apparently happens often enough to be a real issue.

They open the windows, and a sweltering smoke-infused breeze flows through the space. The faucet pressure is acceptable, but the water is cloudy and reeks of chlorine. They each take a quick unheated shower. After putting on their fresh clothes, they start to sweat through them.

It seemed like cooking something for dinner was a good idea when they were shopping, but without electricity, neither their electric stovetop nor microwave worked. Kirk pries open the moon cake tin and hands Windy a slightly stale lotus and black sesame walnut pastry; she smiles weakly at him and then slowly eats it. He offers to open up one of the other items, but Windy passes. Since he doesn't want to eat a can alone, he contents himself with the remnants of their jerky and crackers.

Using Windy's laptop, Kirk video conferences an old buddy that used to live across town. There is some battery charge left on this computer, and they still have access to an operating Chinese satellite internet connection. Windy sits next to him to listen to the discussion.

"Wayne, this is Kirk. How are you and your family?"

Wayne's face appears on the laptop screen. "Fine. You're in the United States?"

"Actually, we're near the center of Houston right now. We'd come to visit you, but I can't seem to find a bus that would get us there. This is my wife." Windy waves at the screen.

"Nice to meet you! Kirk, we don't live in Houston anymore. It's a good thing that you didn't simply try to stop by and surprise us. Also, coming to see us is not all that important, and it's nice that we can connect like this."

"Yes, it's a treat just to be in the same time zone! How's the job?" Kirk asked.

"That's a painful question!"

"I'm sorry. I didn't mean for it to be!" Kirk said.

"When my company closed and I lost my position, I got that question a lot, and I did my best to explain something I didn't understand at the time."

"But you do now?" Kirk asked.

"In a way. We've all lost a lot of leverage. It's as if we've all been suddenly transported to a world where people are more reliant on what they can only produce themselves. Believe me, we're a lot poorer for it."

"Is there any chance of going back?"

"I don't see it," Wayne said.

"Look, I'm not someone who has any business asking about anyone else's job. I've had my own struggles!"

"I'm sorry to hear that. I was under the impression that things are better in China."

"That they are," Kirk said. "There's just less demand for my particular specialization."

"That sounds like a good problem; it indicates that your manufacturing system is still intact."

"I've never thought of it that way," Kirk said.

"Stay here for a while, and you will think about it regularly. We now have a farm where we can grow our own food. Physically exhausting work, but it just feels like we have more control over where our next meal comes from. It's also cooler out here in the country."

"Makes sense. What do you guys do for fun?"

"Mostly, we farm."

"It must be more pleasant than here. Our electricity is out, and we're sweating our butts off."

"Oh yes, I remember those days before we moved. You'd think there would be advantages to living in a large city, but that's no longer the case. You face the regular loss of power, over-crowded public conveyances, and the daily risk of getting mugged or kidnapped. There are few advantages."

"Yeah, we've kind of noticed that."

"If you live in an apartment, you don't have much room to grow vegetables. Others will steal your food if you try to use a garden plot on the street."

"Definitely disturbing," Kirk said.

"Getting around town is also a challenge. Apartment dwellers have no place to securely plug in an electric car. Try that in a shared garage, and you'll get a crazy electric bill for charging someone else's vehicle. At least you can bring an electric scooter inside to connect it. I also wasn't comfortable with the lack of protection from the weather and the thugs when my family drove around town on motorbikes. Trust me, we're better off out here."

"So, you're not employed at all?"

"I'll do some service stuff online occasionally, and I'll also do telemarketing during the holidays. Not much money."

"Sounds tough," Kirk said.

"I do have a brother that's made a lot of money and pays a lot of taxes. Now that guy lives the good life. His family enjoys a gated community, a modern house, and an electric automobile! What's really amazing is that they actually use all the appliances in their house! He even has a natural gas-fueled electric power generator - though I don't understand how he gets the fuel for that."

"No solar panels or wind turbines?"

"No, he can afford reliable energy," Wayne said. "His kids also get the best online education that money can buy. I've also seen bananas, South American wines, and other imports at his house. You can still have a good lifestyle if you've got the income!"

"He's got it made! We've not even seen those products in the stores in this part of town." Kirk said.

"No, and you won't either. It's all home delivery only. If you don't have enough money or a street address, it's like none of that stuff exists. Suffice it to say that the middle class has all but disappeared in this country."

They chatted a bit longer. Wayne points out that the city, county, and some local charities all run soup kitchens all over town. He suggests that they try one if they get hungry. However, he warned them to be careful there and don't bring any valuables. He's seen people knifed over a tray of food. They end the call.

"Well, that confirms it," Windy said. "This city is no place where we'd want to live. Food is so scarce the government distributes it to the poor a meal at a time. What a place!"

"Yeah, sounds like it. You would think that mass transit would be a big advantage, but everyone is just too exposed. Having your own ride is more important than ever."

That ends the conversation. After that, Kirk and Windy lie around, trying to avoid overheating. It was later explained to them that the electrical outage they are now going through is not uncommon for this time of year. Summer is this area's high-utilization season for electricity, and the wind is quite unpredictable in early summer.

Neither Kirk nor Windy slept well on this night. Kirk lies in bed, mulling through their various options to get to his brother's farm; indeed, there must be some viable solutions.

On the Road
HOUSTON AND THE LOST WOODS

Eacher was admiring the modifications that had been made to his scooter. It looks exactly as it did before, but the battery is now incredibly expensive and this gives this scooter a much larger range and improved acceleration. He tests it on the driveway and is shocked how quickly his bike can ramp up speed.

Dora comes over to him. "Careful there Cowboy. Get careless with this bronco and you'll slam into a tree."

"Some ride! It might really come in handy. Any hidden machine guns or grenade launchers?" He laughed.

"No, it's designed to help you escape, not wipe out any potential threats. There is a biometric key that insures that you're the only person that can start this vehicle. Also a smoke generator." She points to a finger print reader then to a new toggle switch with a flip up cover.

"Can I try the button for the smoke now?" Eacher asked.

"No problem, just use it away from this complex. I don't want to upset everyone else around today."

"You got it, I'll try it out on the way."

"So, you're all set to go?"

"I think so. The first visit you set up for me seems curious." Eacher said.

"Well, that was something that Mike insisted on without my input. I don't know much about who you'll be meeting with there."

"I'm also being kept in the dark on why they even want to meet with me. I've been asked to show up and comply with whatever they want."

"Well, they did explain that there will be a cashier's check on location after you complete that visit." Dora said.

"Yep, I guess you'd call it an offer I can't refuse." Eacher said.

"That visit will be the least of your worries. Is there anything else that concerns you?"

"I'm a little nervous about who I'll be sharing this information with. I've not really done much outreach in the past."

"You'll do fine. Just start with people that you already have a relationship with and then branch out to others as you get more comfortable with the drill."

"I have no qualms about this material, I've taught some portion of it for almost thirty years. Even so, I still don't understand why your boss funded my additional training and support here."

"That's between you and Mike. Perhaps it's some form of penance?"

"You mean for inflicting so much damage to the United States from the Net Zero program he championed?"

"I'm not going to guess his motives. Anyway, do us proud and let us know if we can ever be of further assistance." Dora said as she walks away.

As Eacher begins to move toward the gate, he notices Irene walking towards him. "Hey good looking! I thought you weren't leaving for a few more hours!"

"That's still the plan, I just wanted to say goodbye." Irene responded. "You know, don't take this the wrong way, but you seem more buff than when you first got here."

"We both are! It's a surprise that we didn't end up in the hospital!"

"Maybe we just got lucky! I'll see you at our scheduled meeting." Irene smiled again.

"I look forward to it. In the meantime, if you need any help getting ready for that debate in September, let me assist." Eacher said.

"I told Dora that you would be the better choice to face their climate champion, but she insisted that Mike thought you were too polite." Irene said.

"Neither of us signed up for that kind of exposure, but maybe it will be a rare opportunity to present information in the media that they don't normally cover." Eacher said.

"What are the odds? They've never done so in the past! However, any publicity is good publicity, no?" Irene said.

"I'm not so sure, but there's no one I know who is more capable of representing all the materials we've covered." Eacher said. "See you soon!" With those words, Eacher started moving slowly toward the exit on his scooter. He was already looking forward to the chance to see her again in about a week.

As he exited the gate and negotiated the perimeter road not far from where he guessed the temple compound would be, he touched the smoke generator switch lightly. It sent a small dark cloud rising upwards and outwards and blanketed the road behind him. If Irene was still outside, she'd appreciate this sophomoric gesture.

***

Kirk and Windy had expected to stay several more weeks in Houston, but now don't see any reason to stay longer. Even so, the challenge to get to Paul's farm is not a trivial one. Kirk is actually ready to forgo the trip all together and head back to China. Windy briefly considers that suggestion, but is not interested in such a short trip. They've spent too much money and time just to get here.

While it might seem reasonable that people would migrate more northwards, cold winters are a lot more dangerous than hot summers. So, most escaping Houstonians head to smaller towns within the state and the rest seem to choose adjacent states.

Kirk and Windy do learn a number of things about Houston from talking to other hotel guests.

The Mexicans and Central Americans allege that their living standards are just as good as those in the United States. The migrants leaving the United

States are now more numerous than those entering. With very few visitors crossing the border, who cares how long they stay?

Transfer payments now generally originate from other countries into the United States. The same services are still in business, but now the transfer payments flow in the opposite direction.

Kirk and Windy start working on the challenge of how to get to Paul's house.

They hear a number of rental car war stories. They were lucky not to have had more issues with the one they rented. They quickly rule out that option.

They go to an electric car rental concession, but those cars are generally newer and even more expensive to rent. In addition, they'd witnessed that electricity was scarce and the availability spotty; refueling that car multiple times on a long distance trip without knowing where they could reliably recharge is a risk that they don't want to take.

They research bus routes online. They could get a seat in Houston in a few weeks, but would have to get off the bus in Dallas and wait around with exposed luggage until the next bus connection. Then, they'd have to do the same thing in Shreveport and Little Rock. Once they were close they'd need to find a way to travel the final segment to their house. They also notice that many of the buses on the road are over-filled and standing room only; some of them even have people sitting on the roof in makeshift upper decks. In addition, the tickets aren't cheap. It just seems like they'd be pushing their luck with buses.

Trains aren't an option. There is a train that travels from Houston to New Orleans regularly, but their destination is more north than east.

They even consider buying a cheap car. The cost would not be much different than the rental car over the same time period and perhaps they could carry extra gasoline cans. Even so, they fear the sales tax to buy one, the property tax to own one, their lack of a valid driver's license, and also any mechanical and refueling issues that might bite them on a trip. They decide not to mess with it.

Anyway, Kirk hears of a creative solution on how to get to Arkansas. For some reason, the home moving business has a diesel subsidy from the government that allows them to get fuel to relocate people. It's a support program designed to relocate most of the city dwellers. They find some telephone numbers online for some home moving contacts that might be able to assist them.

They call for quotes to move their suitcases to Arkansas. The price to do this is only a few hundred yuan per piece of luggage.

They have an encouraging conversation with one driver and convince him to allow them to accompany their luggage to its destination. The agreement is that they must serve as his moving staff for the trip. For that he promises to move them and their luggage for nothing. It seems like a fair exchange.

***

The box truck shows up at the appointed time and calls them to come downstairs. Windy takes the door key and then heads down to the office to check out and get her cash deposit back. Kirk grabs the suitcases and slowly and deliberately navigates down the stairs.

Kirk and Windy reach the van at about the same time and the driver looks at them warily. While they are clearly well-fed, Kirk would bet that they just don't look strong enough to help him move anything. However, the driver says that he is impressed by Kirk's work with the luggage on the stairs. He shakes his head and asks them to throw their bags in the back of the truck. Kirk and Windy both think that letting their bags out of their sight seems like a bad idea. After some discussion on this point, the driver offers to let them put the suitcases in the front cab with them. They agree.

"Call me Gus." The driver said.

This solution isn't comfortable, but they elect to simply sit on one suitcase and place the other on the floor of the cab. They try to fasten their seat belts, but the straps aren't long enough.

The truck pulls out and right away the truck starts hitting potholes. The suitcase does not offer much cushion and both of them get jarred every time the truck hits one of the many pot holes. The truck proceeds about thirty minutes in some direction and stops at a house.

"Time to move." Gus said.

Kirk and Windy step down from the cab and look confused. Kirk reckons that Gus wants to test their skill and energy to pack and move a load.

The owner of the house has packed about sixty boxes of various sizes. Gus directs Windy and Kirk's attention to them, rolls opens the rear of the truck and yanks out a long ramp from the back of the truck. He then goes over to a tree nearby, stretches himself out where he can get a good view, and waits for his new moving team to load the boxes.

Thankfully he has a dolly. That helps them move the boxes once loaded; a lot of the boxes are the small type which are easy for them to stack. Some of the larger boxes are just too heavy and tend to slide off the dolly on the way to the truck.

The client looks concerned as he quickly figures out that this particular moving team has little experience. He steps in to assist and even walks next to the ramp to make sure the boxes don't fall off the dolly as Kirk ascends it. By the time they finish, the customer is the one moving them up the ramp and Kirk is walking below acting as if he would try to catch the boxes if they fell in his direction. The owner of the boxes knows better than to test either Kirk's ability or willingness to come to the rescue of a falling box; he takes extra effort to get the boxes into the truck safely and without accident.

Windy holds up her "half of the sky" in this arrangement and takes over the role of supervisor and keeps both of the men from doing serious damage to themselves or the contents.

After several hours all the boxes are loaded up. Gus walks over and takes a glance and then secures the boxes with straps to the inside wall of the truck. They then head out for their next drop off or delivery. This time they do throw their suitcases in the back of the truck.

The driver tells them that this was an easy stop. He promises that the next one will be much more strenuous.

First Impressions
ARKANSAS

W indy watches as the truck pulls up to a chain link fence opening and stops, and notices a woman walking over from the direction of a large garden. That woman kicks her boots on the edge of the porch and knocks off some mud.

The gate is open, and an older man walks toward the truck. The woman follows behind him at a short distance.

"Can I help you?" The man asks while looking at the driver.

Kirk exits the vehicle and steps in front of the truck.

The man on the ground sees him and moves quickly to embrace him. The woman joins the hug. "Kirk, you world traveler! Welcome home!"

"Rose!" Kirk gives her a hug. "Let me introduce my wife!"

Windy steps down from the truck and stands next to her husband. She expected to arrive today and is dressed for the occasion. She is wearing a colorful designer silk shirt, a fashionable skirt, and some high heels that she struggles with on the gravel. Rose and Paul converge on her simultaneously, enveloping her in a joint hug. As Windy limply endures the gesture, Paul and Rose seem to sense her reluctance and quickly step back from her.

At this point, Gus exits the cab and goes to the truck's rear. "Want your suitcases?"

Windy watches as the two brothers walk to the back of the truck. The rear door opens, and two people in the rear compartment hop down and move to the front passenger seats.

One of the other riders in the rear hands down their suitcases to Paul and Kirk without exiting the truck. They take them and return to where Rose, Windy, and Gus are standing.

"You guys are some good workers," Gus said. "Thanks for making this trip with me."

Windy smiles weakly, and Kirk walks over and lightly shakes his hand in a gesture that is more of a courtesy than an expression of appreciation.

Gus looks around. "Nice place. Need to move anything?"

"No, we're good," Paul said. "Thanks for bringing these guys home."

Gus nods and turns to Kirk, "You've got my number if you need to book another trip."

Kirk motions with a casual two-fingered hand salute, suggesting he will consider the idea.

Windy is caught a bit open-mouthed and wide-eyed at the thought of another trip with Gus. A two-finger salute? She thinks she ought to give him a middle-finger salute! The nerve of this guy. She had no idea what they were getting themselves into. This is the way it works in the United States? What a crazy system!

They watch the truck back up and then drive away down the road.

"What a trip!" Windy said just after the truck pulled out of hearing range. She feels anger and a deep sense of violation from the trip; she is doing her best not to allow these and other emotions to surface. A week of sleeping in the woods with no bed, shower, or decent food was hard to get used to. Long hot days in the dim light in the back of the truck with strangers that she mostly didn't trust. Her beautiful suitcase has been ruined, and the zipper will not zip; she'll need to strap it shut when they return to China soon.

"Windy, we got here safely and with our luggage intact."

"Are you sure? When I open my luggage, I tell you whether we got here with everything. The suitcase seems lighter." Windy's English skills occasionally struggle when she gets emotional. She is clearly fired up about all that has happened the past week. Her husband is not a discerning individual. It was good to have him nearby in case any of the other passengers got frisky with her, but what were they doing in the back of a moving truck in the summertime in the first place? How did he allow them to get roped into such a stupid arrangement? Some of the other options might have worked. Why did they rush into this one?

"He let us sit in the front."

"Maybe he did today. We saw our share of the box part of the truck, and he worked us for five solid days before he finally got us here. This is an awful way to travel!"

The more she thought about it, the more she just felt that they were lucky just to be able to complete the trip. They could have ended up in a ditch a long way from here, and then what would they have done? There is a difference between adventure and dumb choices.

"Yes, but we're home!" Kirk said.

A young woman has come out of the house and has moved in their direction. Standing next to Paul, she seems timid and confused and doesn't seem to recognize who has arrived.

"Clare, this is my brother, Kirk, and his wife, Windy. They're going to be here for a while." Paul said.

"Welcome," Clare said. "I heard you were coming."

Kirk looks her up and down. "I can't believe it! You were this tall the last time I saw you." He puts his hand about waist high. "You've grown into a woman!"

Clare smiles weakly. "Glad you made it."

Windy was about to say, "me too," when she changed her mind and said nothing. Windy ought to engage her in further conversation but doesn't. She finds herself moving away from the group as they continue to chatter with each other. She knows she should be more social but is lost in her thoughts. She is struck by the fact that both Clare and Rose are excessively dark-skinned. She also immediately notices that Rose's skin is leathery. Windy could have stayed close to home and been a rice farmer if she wanted to look like that. Rose doesn't have enough long-sleeved shirts or better hats? She thought they ought to have brought some cone-shaped farmer hats from China.

She notices the mixed appearance of everything as she slowly and gingerly continues walking towards the house on the rough ground. The rough-looking cabin fascia with wood logs, a rusting fence, and a listing barn capture her immediate attention. Offsetting those worn structures, she notices a flower garden near the house and the deep, pleasant tones of a wind chime hanging from a tree. These people are poor, but at least they've attempted to maintain it. There is also a home-made looking pine reef nailed to the front door. In the distance, she notices a well-trod path through some weeds that leads to an expansive garden laid out in neat rows.

"We made it!" Kirk reaches to hold her arm. Windy accepts it passively, breaks it off, and continues toward the house.

"Not what she was expecting?" Paul asks as they all follow her careful steps toward the cabin.

"Not sure, but this is nothing like what we're used to. Windy is definitely a city girl." Kirk said.

"It's a pretty hot day. Maybe she'll relax in the shade?" Paul said.

Windy sits by the front door in one of their rocking chairs, and she isn't rocking. She looks warily for places where poisonous insects or snakes could hide; there are spaces between the boards on the porch floor that she is scanning one gap at a time. "They couldn't have a solid floor here? What happens if someone gets bitten by something that lives below this decking? Who designed this place?" She thinks to herself.

"Would you like to go in?" Paul is about two feet away, and his deliberately gentle tone barely registers.

"Are you sure that you don't mind us being here?" Windy is looking for any hint that they aren't welcome. Just the slightest off-word, and she can start working on her plans to find a hotel and then head back to her hometown. She was wrong to think that the United States would exceed her low expectations and that they might willingly move here.

"You're family!" Paul responds brightly but still in a soft voice. "I'm so glad I've finally gotten to meet you in person."

"It's a long way from where I grew up." She said. She's not sure if she intends to suggest that the distance is a long way from the Middle Kingdom or that the standard of living has much to be desired. Both assessments are valid and could be supported by what she's seen. She is aware that she is a bit anxious and takes a long breath hoping it will help her calm down. Their traumatic journey here over the past week is what really has her rattled. The long boat ride is a distant memory.

Paul smiles back without responding to her comment. "Well, we're hoping to catch up with you and let you tell us all about it."

She looks at Paul briefly and then gives her husband a hard stare. Did Kirk deliberately withhold information so that she'd agree to this trip? She next looks at the front door as if it leads to a trap door that will deposit her in the basement. She is afraid to go in but wants to show courage and good manners. "Lead the way."

They enter the main room, and she still feels lost and disoriented. She smells the smoke from what looks like a cast iron heater and the insect repellent. She looks warily at the logs piled next to it for evidence of scorpions or spiders. She notes the warmth of the room and the lack of air conditioning. She remembers the long sweaty nights in Houston; however, she recognizes that it does seem to be a little cooler here than it was there.

Paul carries her luggage to the guest room.

"Here's your room." Rose stands outside the door to the guest room, motioning for Windy to follow.

It isn't clear if she will head back outside or follow everyone into this bedroom. She looks down and notes the worn carpet. She notices a bathroom door down the hall with a mirror and toilet visible and some adjacent vinyl floors.

The artwork consists of various tools and other country memorabilia nailed to the wall. The LED lights are bright, but they just confirm the decrepit condition of everything. Windy slowly makes her way into the bedroom.

Paul and Rose follow her through.

Once inside, she makes a point to remain on her feet and tries to avoid touching anything.

Kirk comes in and motions for Rose and Paul to leave them alone.

They quickly exit and close the door behind them.

Kirk tries to hug her again, and she just shrinks away from him. He reaches again to hold her, and she pushes back to distance herself from him. "How can I help?" He asks.

"I'm sorry, I'm just rattled by how we got here."

"Well, it was an exhausting trip! Also, this place is more primitive and less modern than anticipated." Kirk said.

"That was a bad way to travel. I thought you knew what you were doing when you nudged us in that direction."

"I'm sorry, you're right."

"Let's go home. We've seen enough that we'd rather be back in China."

"Windy, we just came halfway around the world because you wanted to meet my brother and his family. Let's recover from the trip before we seriously consider heading back. Think of this as a destination resort?"

"Is that where the term 'resort to desperate measures' comes from? Who lives like this?"

"Look. Put on some shorts, something short-sleeved and some comfortable shoes; let's go for a walk. I think you'll warm up to this place once we decompress." Kirk is sweating profusely and wipes the sweat off his face with a hand towel.

She doesn't respond to his suggestion. She shakes her head to show her grave doubts about what they've done by coming here.

He sits on one of the twin beds and looks up at her hopefully.

She dusts off a chair next to the twin bed on the other side of the room and carefully and cautiously sits on it. "You think we're okay here?"

"Yes, the tough part is behind us, and we're just not used to living in the country."

She swats at the bedspread to ensure there isn't something on it. She places her suitcase on the coarse wood floor and opens it. She takes out a silk blanket and lays it on the twin bed, and then has a seat on top of the blanket.

"Okay, we can stay for a while, but I think we made a serious mistake coming here."

"You're probably right."

"Glad you think so. When I say it's time to go, we leave. Okay?"

He nods his head in agreement.

She slides out of her clothes to his appreciative gaze. She is grateful for his delight in seeing her naked. He may be a depressing guy to live with at times, but he really is physically enthralled with her.

She is not regarded as a pretty woman by Chinese yardsticks; she's not ugly but just plain in the looks department. None of their extended family members have ever won a beauty contest.

When she reached 26 without being married, her family deemed her a "leftover woman". That moniker is generally laid on women too picky about their marital prospects. In general, such women simply wait too long to pull the trigger and end up never getting married or having kids. She did indeed have the education and income standard for these ladies.

Her family got involved and posted her biographical data and pictures at a matchmaking fair in a nearby park. They started to better understand the situation when little interest was shown in her as a bride. Then, when Kirk materialized from sources outside of their communication efforts, they were immediately ready to encourage him. The whole family was ecstatic when he married her before she turned 28.

What drew her to America on this trip was the notion that it is a country not particularly up to speed on Chinese beauty standards. She would endure hardship to avoid the routine scrutiny she's been accustomed to at home.

The point is that the American men, or women for that matter, can't seem to tell if she's pretty or not. It's as if she's now being assessed on a different metric than the one she faced in China. Here, she gets a pass for simply being somewhat exotic. Suspecting this was the case before she left home, she brought clothes that would impress.

She throws on an outfit that is a little too stylish for the woods but won't make her overheat. She also puts on some brand named walking shoes that she brought. They don't provide much cushion for walking or running, but they look sharp.

He throws on some cut-offs, a tee-shirt, and some flip-flops and gently touches her shoulder.

Her attempt to zip up the suitcase is unsuccessful and she simply closes it, tucks it in the corner, and places a beach towel over it. She continues to inspect the bedsheet for evidence of bed bugs. Satisfied that there are no red streaks on the sheets, she follows Kirk out of the room.

By the time she reaches the front entry, she is already sweating. "What's wrong with the Air Conditioning?" She asked.

Paul overhears the question and volunteers an answer. "I'm sorry, but electricity prices are too high right now."

A slight breeze blows through the house, but it's as warm as a hair dryer. She doesn't understand why life has to be so uncomfortable here. She had always heard that Americans were materialistic, but this seems masochistic. This is not what she was expecting.

Kirk takes her arm and gently maneuvers her out the door.

There is a can of bug spray on the table, and he sprays her neck and exposed skin. He grabs a wide-brimmed hat on the wall and places it on her head. He then walks her toward the woods at the back of the property.

The heat is more bearable under the shade of the trees along a trail next to the creek. Wind turbines line the top of two ridges high above them. They are loud, though the blade flicker from the blades is not particularly bothersome given their distance from those machines.

She is surprised to notice many different types of feathers on the ground. She relaxes a bit. "What happened to your family that they have to live like this?"

"Net Zero happened." Kirk said.

"Did you and your brother grow up like this?" She realizes he is probably getting a little tired of her biting questions, but how do you fix something if you can't recognize the problem.

"No, we didn't grow up here. We grew up in Houston."

"You had air conditioning?"

"Yes, of course, we had air conditioning. We used it a lot."

"Okay, why doesn't your family have air conditioning now?"

"They own the equipment. However, can't apparently afford to pay for the electricity when the weather is hot." He said.

"What? Isn't that when you need it? Why not?"

"Well, global warming, of course. Rose and Paul are working to save the planet." He said.

"Saving the planet? From whom? From what?" This is not a subject they've ever gotten into before. The global warming discussions they've had together in the past focused on the merits of various renewable products the Chinese manufacture and sell to other countries. Of course, the Chinese could not use these same products to run their own electrical grid; they wouldn't be competitive if they did so.

"But wouldn't their use reduce their carbon dioxide emissions?" Kirk said.

"What? Carbon dioxide is plant food, and why would you do that?" Then she rattles off something in Chinese that she knows he will never understand.

He has a somewhat blank look on his face. "Well, plants require carbon dioxide, but it also generates a greenhouse effect that makes the whole planet warmer. The United States chose to reduce their carbon dioxide emissions to lower levels."

"Your family lives without air conditioning because they're convinced that the planet is getting too warm? How is this possible?" This is the kind of logic that confounds her. She's thankful that China didn't actually implement the similar global warming timelines that most developed countries agreed to. She hopes they are never dumb enough to follow the United States' example, and she's pretty sure they're not.

"No, the United States has shown considerable leadership! We reduced a significant chunk of our fossil fuels, cement, and farm gases that generate greenhouse gas emissions."

"Is the planet cooler now?" This ought to be an obvious question for him. "If what the United States is doing is not working, why did they do it in the first place? Why are they still doing it?"

"Well, there hasn't been much warming for quite a while."

"Lowering your country's emissions led to this result?" Windy asked.

"Well, personally, I doubt it. The world's carbon dioxide emissions have still been increasing every year. The amount the United States cut was offset by developing countries that increased theirs."

"And now that you've done *this* to yourself, you're sure this was the right thing to do?" They must get some benefit out of the educational system in this country. She's thrown the question out not to trap him in an answer but to firmly move him to a better understanding of how she sees what's happening here.

"Now that you put it that way, it doesn't seem like what the United States did was very useful." The wind turbine noise is quite loud at this location, and he almost walks into a tree, and she catches him in time and tugs him back onto the trail.

"I'd agree with that," she said. Point made. She thinks maybe she's pulled him along far enough today exploring the problems she's noticed.

"Well, China is going to be doing the same thing soon. They'll stop increasing their carbon dioxide emissions by 2040."

Nope. Kirk is just not getting it. "You think so?" She laughs for the first time this trip. "Carbon dioxide is not bad for the environment. I know because I grew up with a lot of air pollution. Now, that is a real problem! China has worked hard to improve our air quality by removing contaminants from the air, and CO_2 is not a pollutant."

"Oh, come on." He said. "You can't really argue that! Even China has a carbon trading system."

"Believe it. That carbon trading system is a token system that doesn't cause much damage. I've actually seen some discussions in Chinese on this. Your country and Europe want to chase science fiction and political nonsense. Why is China supposed to talk you out of your delusion? Didn't you notice that neither China nor India followed your lead?"

"We exempted you from the requirements to reduce your carbon emissions because you were a developing country, and many of your people were still in poverty."

"That used to be true. Right now, we're a much more stable country than yours." She hesitated a moment to let this sink in. "We've recently landed the first person on Mars and are now working toward a manned observation station there in the future. You really think we're still a developing country?"

"That developing country exception was one of the original provisions of the Paris Agreement. Well, it's hard to force China to do anything."

"Especially when it makes no sense!" She said.

These are harsh words for him to hear, but true. "I could also point out that we catapulted our country out of poverty. We're in no hurry to go back based on suspect science or inadequate energy replacements."

"Well, I'm glad this walk has cheered you up. Why didn't you ever mention this before?"

"It just never came up. Ready to go back to China?"

"Windy, listen to me. It was hard to get here; let's stay a while longer."

They arrive at the water hole, and no one else is in sight. It's essentially a tiny oxbow lake fed and drained by a creek. The water looks clean but not clear enough to see the bottom. He runs down to a pebble beach, removes his clothes, and jumps into the water. Leery of bugs, she leaves her clothes on the shore near his and gradually follows him into the lake.

The cool water changes her mood and further pulls her out of the funk she has been in since they first arrived.

"At least stay for a few days?" He asked.

"Okay."

The bottom of the pool is mostly sand. Kirk and Windy stop and hold each other as they move to deeper depths. The water is about neck-high for him, and she wraps her legs around his waist, so their heads are at the same level. He feels himself responding to her touch, and she reaches down to confirm his response.

She gently lowers herself. Once coupled, they move together. Her arms drape around Kirk's neck as she studies his face.

"Maybe it's not so bad here?" He closes his eyes and breathes slowly while undulating beneath her.

86

She also closes her eyes and purrs "love you" as she arches her back in rhythm to his movements which presses her chest into his. Only their heads are visible above the water.

A few moments later, Rose, Clare, and Paul arrive in their swimsuits with Cappy behind them.

Rose pokes Paul and gestures towards the clothes on the sand.

Windy and Kirk quickly disconnect and establish separation as they tread water.

"Did you know they were coming?" Windy whispers to Kirk while they both swim near each other.

"No, they never mentioned it."

Clare jumps in the water, and Cappy quickly follows. He immediately tries to swim out towards the deep water where Kirk and Windy are treading water. He quickly gives up on that idea and paddles to Clare.

Rose and Paul walk down to the water and ease in until it is about chest high on Rose.

A few minutes later, Rose and Paul get out of the water. Clare joins them on the sand, and Cappy shakes himself off vigorously, getting water all over Rose, who doesn't seem to care.

They yell goodbye to Windy and Kirk. The four of them take off together back down the trail.

She and Kirk holler back and tread water a little longer. When they are sure they are alone, they quickly return to their clothes and put them on without drying off.

Windy feels refreshed.

"Want to finish what we started?" He reaches to touch her backside.

"You hold that thought." She darts ahead down the trail in front of him.

He follows immediately and soon catches up with her. They walk hand in hand back to the cabin.

The Casino

The Casino
LOUISIANA

Eacher arrives at a large casino hotel on the Red River in Shreveport for his mandatory meeting. He is covered in a crust of road dirt and sweat.

He still does not know who he's to meet with or what will be discussed. He was simply given the address and the time.

He parks his bike in the garage amongst many others and informs the front desk of his arrival as instructed; they hand him an elevator card. They then direct him to a private locker room where he can shower and change into some fresh clothes he brought. Cleaned up, he makes his way to a particular ballroom on one of the upper floors. He taps lightly and hears the "Come In" command.

He twists the knob, opens the door, and enters.

The room has twenty to thirty chairs set up in the shape of a U and all oriented towards a drop-down projection screen in the front. The tablecloths on the table are white and the chairs blue.

Roughly ten people are randomly spread out around the room in various seats. The attendees are all dressed casually, and all seem to have a similar notebook on the table. There's a cigar smoke odor in the room and various glasses suggesting that alcohol is being served.

The attendee who had directed Eacher to enter the room continues to give him instructions over an amplified microphone that continues to fill the space with its volume. The speaker welcomes Eacher without getting out of his chair, and he does not introduce himself. Eacher is guided to the left column of seats, where he takes a seat.

The dim lights in the room and the emergency lights provide a low lighting level. The temperature is comfortable though the air reeks of cigar smoke.

A film presentation lights up the screen, and the narrator's voice features a British accent. The film shows the IPCC's usual contentions. It shows projections of the ice melting in the Arctic Ocean, Greenland, and Antarctica.

It shows corals bleached white and smog so dense that some small Indian town residents are limited to about five feet of visibility. Floods inundate neighborhoods, droughts dry out vast regions, and hurricanes and tornados create havoc amidst swirling emergency efforts. An animation shows some disturbing projections of sea level rise for the next seventy years. Everything sounds ominous and terrifying.

Remarkably, there is no need to actually point out the film's blatant assumption that all climate change is now caused by human influence. Geologists schooled on past climates aren't fooled, but political correctness is not constrained by such technical reservations. The film wraps up, and the room lights return to full brightness.

"Do you have anything to say about what you've just seen in this film?" The speaker asked.

Needless to say, Eacher is confused. Renting this venue and paying for the air conditioning would have been unimaginably expensive. He knows nothing about the scientific preferences or opinions of the others present in the room. Do they have a view in one direction or another? He feels like a whore that isn't sure if she is supposed to be taking her clothes off or praying for penance. "Well, I'd say it's a commercial for IPCC claims."

"A commercial?" The voice sounded amused.

"It follows their normal assertions and hits all the highlights."

"You're obviously a skeptic. We in this room try not to favor one side or the other on this topic." With this last comment, he punched something on his phone, and a cart with a lie detector was rolled into the room.

"Are you serious?" Eacher asked.

"Yes, we want to better understand the sincerity of your beliefs."

"And, what if I refuse to cooperate?"

"Then we'll just assume that you're lying." There was a discernable southern twang when the voice pronounced the last word like a large cat in Africa.

While the speaker was talking, Eacher did his best to estimate the age, ethnicity, and sex of the other occupants of the room. Even so, they all wore some sort of head cover that made that simple observation unavailable.

"Shall we begin?" The polygraph was moved next to Eacher, and he was strapped with various cords. "Are you ready for our questions?" The voice continued.

"Sure, why not?" Eacher said.

"First, how much have you been paid by the oil and gas companies to tell your version of climate science?"

"While I am a geologist, my specialty is on ancient climates and the rocks associated with them." The speaker looks at the technician who nods. "So far, it looks like you are telling us the truth."

"I've never received any money from oil and gas companies," Eacher said.

The polygraph operator started shaking his head.

"Our operator tells me you're not telling the truth."

"Okay, you're right, I did receive a $250 stipend for a presentation that I gave in 2010, and they also paid about $1,000 for my plane ticket and hotel room."

The worker nodded toward the speaker, indicating that he now believed me.

"Do you believe that manmade carbon dioxide emissions are harmful?"

"No. CO_2 is plant food and good for the environment. A little more will do us good. While it's theoretically a warming influence, it's not likely to make much of a difference." Eacher said.

"I don't need a dissertation."

"Got it." Eacher said.

"Do you believe the global surface temperature record has been reliable over the last seventy years?"

"No."

"Do you believe that the IPCC's climate models are credible?"

"No."

"Are you concerned about global sea level rise?"

"No."

"Do you think the increased carbon dioxide in the atmosphere is causing extreme weather issues?"

"No."

"Our polygraph expert doesn't see any issues with any of your answers. Have you ever been given training or instruction on how to beat a polygraph test?"

"No."

The questions continued for another fifteen minutes. They mostly questioned Eacher on the presentation they had shown him earlier.

With few exceptions, all of his answers either cast doubt or rejected the scientific basis of the material shown to him. It was reassuring that none of the other answers he gave were considered lies.

The voice then asks that Eacher step out in the hallway for a few minutes while they compare notes. They remove all the straps. A waiter comes out in the hallway with him, closes the door behind them, and remains with Eacher.

Eacher walks over near a window in the hallway, and the waiter follows.

In the distance, there's a bridge over the river. The roads are mostly filled with electric scooters and a small number of larger vehicles.

A few slow-moving barges pass each other in opposite directions along the river.

"Who are these guys?" Eacher looks around to confirm no one observes them.

"Some are guys that like to bet big and tip well when they win. I don't recognize the others."

"Did they give you instructions on how to keep an eye on me?" Eacher asked.

"Yes, they asked that I make sure you didn't try to eavesdrop outside their room to allow them their privacy," the waiter said.

They stand watching the river for another ten minutes, and then the door to the meeting room opens, and they're invited back. Eacher is reconnected to the lie detector.

"We have one further question for you," the voice said.

"Fair enough," Eacher said.

"Who's your favorite presidential candidate in our upcoming national elections?"

"I'm sorry, I haven't paid any attention to them. Given our country's current challenges, what difference could any of those candidates make?" Eacher asked.

"Another honest answer." The voice said. "I don't know if what you are claiming is scientifically correct or not, but I will say it appears that you thoroughly believe it."

"I'd agree with that observation," Eacher said.

This seems to satisfy them. Eacher is disconnected from their apparatus, and they hand Eacher an envelope containing his promised check. He waves goodbye and heads for the exit. When he opens the door to the room, he is startled to note that an old nemesis now stands in the hallway. Professor Baker was the man who had been head of his academic department when his tenure was denied. He has not seen him in more than twenty years.

"Professor Baker surprised to see you here," Eacher greets him as politely as he can and even attempts to smile. He barely suppresses the instinct to say something impolite.

"The pleasure is mine. Hope you have a nice trip wherever you're going." Professor Baker said.

With those words, Professor Baker enters the meeting room, and the waiter escorts Eacher back down the elevator to the lobby. He requests Eacher's elevator card and then walks into the elevator with it.

Meal

Meal
ARKANSAS

They spend the next day outside. The day is slightly overcast, and the clouds periodically shield them from the sun's direct heat. The weather is sticky and hot here in the summer, and there are few opportunities to avoid discomfort. Kirk and Windy have learned to spend a lot of time under the shade of the trees to escape the humid afternoon air in the house.

They watch Paul remove a tiny and bloated tick behind Cappy's ear. He pulls it off carefully with a pair of tweezers, so he doesn't leave the head buried under the skin. He sets it on the table to show it to Windy and then points out the dangers of Lyme disease and other tick-borne infections. Ticks are a problem in this area, especially this time of year. She immediately decides to keep her distance from this dog. She wants to buy some more suitable clothes to protect her outdoors.

When they enter the house in the early evening, they learn that Rose has allowed Clare to spend the night at a friend's house.

The smell of roasted meat and apple permeate the house. While this seems like another meal to Windy and Kirk, Rose is excited about the items on this evening's menu. She indicates that she and Paul only eat chicken once or twice a year; eating their egg layers takes too much of a bite out of their egg production. Even so, she does point out that since most hens only lay eggs for two or three years, the older birds are more likely to join them for dinner.

Paul and Kirk wait in the living room for the meal like expectant fathers. Paul brags that Rose killed the hen and plucked the feathers herself. Windy offers to assist, but Rose has everything in hand. She heads into the kitchen and tells Rose she's there to get some cooking pointers.

Windy is an accomplished cook, so Kirk knows she just wants to socialize.

Windy enters the room first to announce the completion of the meal. Rose then brings out their infrequent meat indulgence on her best china platter. She sets it in the center of the dining room table; it looks like a miniature Thanksgiving Turkey. The place settings are set up with cloth napkins and mostly matching silverware.

Rose and Paul had already decided to turn on the electric stove to bake their dinner.

They also agreed to turn on the air conditioner for this meal. Paul discretely assures me that the electricity cost projections for the next few hours seem fine, and if he's wrong, there's no telling what this meal will cost. He closes all the windows, and we wait for the cool air to flow.

As the air conditioning cranks on, Windy's entire demeanor changes. She suddenly relaxes and looks comfortable sitting at the dining room table.

"Can we say a blessing?" Rose asked.

"Of course." Kirk was about to say something, then bowed his head as Rose took the lead.

Rose is thankful for the food, the chance to meet Windy, and her family's safe journey to their home. She also asks for protection from tornados, droughts, and forest fires during the rest of the summer.

Before she finishes, Kirk opens his eyes and notes Windy staring at Rose and Paul, who both have their eyes closed. He winks at her, and she smiles back.

Rose wraps it up and then starts passing around the food.

"So, how was the swim?" Paul asked.

Windy's eyes grow wider. In China, sex wasn't something one talked about at the family dinner table. It is a popular activity, as evidenced by over a billion and a half people in Mainland China. Still, it isn't usually the subject of a family dinner conversation.

"Not bad," Kirk said. "It was nice to get wet."

"I'll bet," Paul snickers initially. He then attempts to keep a poker face.

Rose adds to Paul's observation. "I thought the two of you might get a little nippy by the end of the swim."

"Yes, that part of the lake seems a bit deeper," Kirk said, hoping the conversation would move on to another topic.

"Yes, I remember the swims Rose and I used to take in there; those are some of my best memories in Arkansas."

"Mine too," Rose said. "Paul was a little younger and better looking, and the water hole was my favorite place to be. It was a regular routine for us. I thought we might be able to give Clare a younger sibling from our swims there."

"It wasn't for lack of trying!" Paul said.

"I think that's a little bit too much information," Kirk said, looking towards Windy, who is now staring at the ceiling.

Rose gestures at the food on the table and asks them to eat before it gets cold.

The vegetables are fine, but there isn't a lot that is in season in the area yet; they serve some tomatoes, beans, and bread to go along with the chicken. Some leaves must be salad leaves, but they don't look familiar.

They eat quietly for a while, just savoring the food. Frogs are croaking, and a chorus of crickets is audible over the noise of the air conditioner.

"What a great meal!" Kirk said.

"Yes, the best we've had in your country." Windy accurately points out. They both know this is a modest spread by Chinese standards; this is the only decent meal they've had since arriving, and windy does not elaborate further.

"I agree," Paul said.

Rose smiles. "It's the least I could do for our visiting family! We haven't had much chance to create memories with you guys."

"Is everyone comfortable?" Paul asked.

"Yes, it's quite nice," Kirk said. "Windy, you're okay?"

"Yes, it's delightful right now." Windy's face is sweet and sincere when making this statement. Perhaps a little air conditioning might be the missing ingredient to meet her expectations in this part of the country.

Paul gets up and immediately heads over to the thermostat and turns the air conditioning off; he exhales a breath of relief and sits back down with a smile. "Any plans for the weekend?"

"We're open to ideas," Kirk said.

"Well, Saturday is usually a working day for us, and the next day is Sunday. We could have a service here if you want." Rose said. "Kirk, perhaps you could lead us?"

"Rose, I'm sorry. I'm a bit out of practice." Kirk looks toward his wife.

"Kirk, feel free to participate if you like, but don't worry about including me." Windy is sending strong signals that she's not interested and not really religious. She will take time to honor her ancestors. Still, he's never actually attended any service with her other than their wedding.

97

"Okay." Rose quickly agrees. "Maybe next weekend we can organize something?"

Paul changes the subject. "Well, I've got to work in the garden tomorrow to help Rose. These fresh vegetables take a lot of time."

Rose nods in agreement.

"I noticed that." Kirk states flatly and intones. "Need any help?"

"No, we'll be fine," Paul said. "Why don't you and Mindy take the scooters out for a ride this weekend?"

"That would be nice! *Windy*, do you agree?" Kirk corrected.

"Yes, I spent much time on scooters when I was younger. That would be a nice way to get some breeze." Windy said.

Paul and Rose finish their meal quickly, and Windy and Kirk follow their lead and eat faster than they usually do. Rose insists that they eat all of the chicken. The few remaining pieces of meat are given to Cappy. The bones are set aside to make soup, taken into the kitchen, and placed in a pot overnight in the oven to utilize the residual heat.

When Rose serves some berries for dessert, the room is already starting to heat up. "Why don't we take this dessert on the porch?" Paul asked.

Kirk notices flying insects circling outside the window. When he looks at Windy, she looks distrustfully outside toward the porch.

"I'm sorry, but it's been a long day, and I'm quite full already," Windy said. "Would you mind if we simply help you with the dishes and go to bed?"

"No, we've got the dishes. Go ahead, see you tomorrow." Rose said.

Kirk returns to the bedroom for a second and brings back a carton from his suitcase that he hands to Windy.

Windy smiles and presents the box to Rose. "This traditional Chinese drink should help keep you and Paul warm in the winter. It's a type of alcoholic beverage that we drink on special occasions. It is so wonderful to be here with family."

Rose accepts the package carefully and with a smile. "Thank you!" Rose said. "Should I open it now?"

"Sure." Kirk opens the box quickly and pulls out a bottle and several little shot glasses. He twists the cap off and fills the small cups with the clear fluid.

They each down a shot while toasting Paul and another while toasting Rose. The liquid is strong and burns in their throats, but the taste is not unpleasant.

Kirk looks at Windy and notes that her cheeks and face are both flushed red. She's missing an enzyme that doesn't allow her to drink much alcohol.

"Sorry, enough for me. Good night!" Windy said.

"No problem." Paul looks at Windy curiously as if he's noticed her color change. "We need to make this last a few more outings anyway. It's quite special. Thank you, and sleep well!"

Kirk escorts her into the bedroom, and they quickly go through their nighttime routines and take turns in the bathroom. They lie down on their separate beds, and she instantly falls asleep. He stands up, returns to the dining room, and rejoins Rose and his brother sitting at the table.

"Back for more drink?" Paul points to the bottle.

"Not anymore, or I'd be asleep too. This 'Mao Tai' is strong and actually quite expensive in China. Windy wanted to give you something memorable."

"It was kind of her to do so," Rose said. "It tastes a bit like moonshine."

"Yes, it's got some similarities; there's a reason they call it white liquor."

"It's terrific to have you back home," Paul said.

"Yes, your wife seems like an impressive lady," Rose said. "I don't think you could have found a more intelligent and capable woman."

"I'm lucky to have her."

"You guys will be here for a while?" Paul asks while glancing at Rose. This seems to be something they've discussed together.

"Not sure. That's really up to Windy."

"Well, if China is like it was here ten years ago, then I can understand the culture shock. Probably best if you simply accept her viewpoint."

Rose said. "Having said that, you know you are both welcome to live here with us. It would be tight, but I think we could all get used to it, and there is strength in numbers."

Kirk anticipated that Paul and Rose would make this offer. He's surprised that it happened so quickly, and he has no doubt it's a serious proposal.

"Better not to suggest that to Windy at the moment. She really needs to warm up to this lifestyle before she considers it. We're accustomed to a higher quality of life."

"You'll need to tell us all about it," Rose said.

"Well, simply imagine the way things used to be here. Throw in some fast trains and lots more people, and you get the idea. Why have things changed so much?"

"Are you sure you want to discuss this now?" Paul looks at Rose and then looks back at Kirk.

Kirk notes the persistent reluctance to address the specifics. If they had only been more direct on the phone, he and Windy wouldn't even be here now. Now that they've made the trip, it's time to dig into what happened. "Afraid so; I'd like to be able to give Windy some insights on what happened."

Rose clears the few dishes on the table and goes into the kitchen to finish cleaning up.

"Well, in that case, there's nothing I'd enjoy more," Paul said.

"Thanks. Looking forward to your thoughts on this." Kirk pulls his chair away from the table, leans back, and crosses his legs. He laces his hands behind his head. He listens closely and hears the sound of wind turbine blades turning in the distance.

"Well, the simple answer is that the United States implemented a Net Zero policy unilaterally."

"So, it was a political decision?"

"Yes, the public believed what was shared with us by the government, the media, and various other entities. The messaging was both constant and consistent."

"What messages?" Kirk clawed a little deeper.

"Well, the first priority was to scale back our use of fossil fuels and implement as much wind and solar energy as possible."

"Why?"

"Oh, come on. Don't play coy with me. We've got to stop releasing carbon dioxide into the atmosphere or face the horrible consequences of runaway global warming."

"And you believe this because...."

"Because the amount of carbon dioxide in the atmosphere has soared."

"You really think so?"

"Kirk, if you persist with these naïve interruptions, I will not cover much material."

It was clear to Kirk that Paul saw this discussion as a pedantic lecture between teacher and pupil. In the past, Kirk, the younger brother, was mainly on the receiving end of his wiser and more experienced sibling. At the time, he trusted most of what he was told. However, Kirk now considers himself more discerning because of his considerable experience and perspectives outside the United States. If there really is a chance that he and Windy would stay here, it would need to be based on a clear and truthful picture of what they would be getting themselves into and why.

"So, a lot of people were sold on those ideas. How did they determine how to implement them?" Kirk asked.

"The government took the lead from their most insistent Net Zero constituents and implemented various policies. Our President particularly wanted to get credit for her actions to cut manmade carbon dioxide emissions."

"That must have been a severe transition period."

"The United States had a straightforward plan. Reduce our CO_2 emissions in half by 2030 and the rest by 2050." Paul said. "Europe had attempted to do the same thing over the previous ten years with wind and solar power. Even so, the only CO_2 emissions they curtailed came from moving their heavy industries to other countries."

"How do you explain that?"

"Europe used natural gas and coal as the backup generator for all their wind and solar power. Both the amount of fossil fuel used and carbon dioxide generated remained the same.

"So the problem was the backup power plants?"

"Now you're thinking like a politician! Our bureaucrats reasoned that Europe's mistake was to insist on a fossil fuel backup system. The President insisted that we didn't need it, and our electrical grid was modified accordingly." The room light dims slightly as if on cue while he says this but then returns to full brightness.

"So, what happened to all the fossil fuel electricity generation?"

"In a tight electricity market, spot prices would turn negative. Only the subsidized wind and solar companies could afford to sell electricity at those times. This preferential treatment destroyed the economics of other electricity generators; the government simply let those generators go out of business. This also applied to the peaking plants that had previously offset much of the intermittent wind and solar energy generated. The reality was that the President didn't even have to pull the plug on fossil fuel electricity generation since the cord had already been severed."

"Just like that, the fossil fuel electricity generators were gone?" Kirk said.

"Kirk, I'm just telling you what happened. The groundwork for real-time decarbonization was widespread, and an active minority played a central role." Paul says this while looking confident that everything done was inevitable.

"What about the airports?"

"Domestic jet fuel prices soared, and ticket prices followed," Paul said. "With only a few people still able to afford to fly, the airports were shut down to reduce operating costs."

"I still can't believe we had to take a boat to get here! There's no chance you'll open the airports again? I assure you they are all still open in China!"

"I've heard that certain private and government planes are still operating." Paul said.

"Cement and asphalt?"

"That was an Executive Order that required government permits to use these materials for anything other than wind and solar power installations."

"Meat?"

Cappy has been lying next to the table and looks up at Kirk when he says this.

"Another initiative. The government implemented that ban over several years to allow people to consume their existing animal stocks."

"Really? The public accepted all these changes?" Kirk isn't buying the story.

"Oh, come on. Most of us were convinced that this path was the only viable alternative." Paul said while he picked up his napkin and wiped the perspiration now beading on his face.

"I can't believe that the average American went along with all this. It's one thing to speculate on a hypothetical transition and another to actually have to live with the resulting consequences. I mean, if I'd have lived here, I can't

102

imagine how much you would have had to pay me to be willing to live without a car." Kirk said.

"Not as much as you might think if you can't afford the fuel to run it. Rather than bore you with the specifics, suffice it to say that the public's access to gasoline and diesel experienced death by a thousand cuts. Then there was a public shaming process aimed at anyone who still owned a non-electric vehicle. Most people took the hint and elected to ditch their internal combustion engine vehicles - even before the state bans on buying new ones kicked in."

"People accepted that change?" Kirk asked.

"Partly. The federal government led the international sales program. The first to sell got the best prices for their used vehicles. A few hundred million cars and trucks were transported to the ports and shipped abroad."

"So everyone got electric cars?" Kirk persisted in his questioning. Kirk hears a coyote howl in the background at some distance from the house. Cappy sits up and looks alert.

"Nope, that would have been way too expensive for most people, and the vehicles weren't really available. Almost everyone I knew bought Vespa-type battery-operated scooters."

"Made in China."

"Yes, mostly," Paul said. "We don't make much here anymore."

"That's unfortunate! Was there much civil unrest?" Kirk asked.

"The major metropolitan areas and the suburbs were the hardest hit. That rioting, looting, and arson served to drive a lot of people out of the cities. Anyway, that's not all that important. We use much less fossil fuel these days, and our CO_2 emissions have decreased accordingly. We showed the rest of the world we were serious about our Net Zero program!"

"Pass the liquor," Kirk said.

Rose fills a small cup and hands it to Kirk.

He grips the cup and empties it into his mouth in a single motion. He feels the firewater smack his throat and hit his brain a few seconds later. "Paul, you're an economist! The United States disrupted a complex economic system subject to a massive government debt by letting the dogs loose. You also eviscerated the fossil fuel industry before you had a suitable replacement. Where was the adult supervision? Think of all the businesses that went bust, the jobs lost, and the obliteration of your health care and Social Security safety nets. How could this possibly have been worth it – especially when neither India nor China undertook similar actions?"

"Kirk, despite the malcontents, there were a lot of people that supported these changes. It was a popular thing to do."

"You know the Chinese now worry that they won't be able to sell many manufacturing goods in the United States going forward. The total private and public wealth in the United States is a small fraction of what it used to be."

"Kirk, we're trying to do something to address a serious problem!"

Paul's certainty and loyal support for these programs started to make Kirk nauseous, and his stomach churned with anxiety. "You should have picked a different path!" Kirk blurted with some volume.

"Excuse me," Paul said. "What do you mean by that remark?" Now Paul is almost shouting.

Ah, the hell with it. Kirk responds at the same decibel level that Paul used; he is definitely inebriated at this juncture. "There had to be a better way to deal with your concerns. You've got little to show for all your sacrifices!"

"That remains to be seen," Paul said.

"You think? Your fossil fuel usage is a fraction of what it used to be."

"And soon, we'll eliminate the rest of it!" Paul said.

"Can you share some of the Kool-Aid you're drinking? I need a glass."

"Kirk, I really resent your pessimism. Rose, what's your take on this?"

"Paul, you have to see it from Kirk's standpoint. He's just come from a place that is still as comfortable as we were ten years ago. I can remember how confused I was when these ideas were first proposed. While it's important to protect the planet, I struggled to understand why that meant we had to almost immediately give up our Subaru. The government had timelines they wanted to meet, but the whole program seemed too disruptive."

"Rose is right. I should be more open to your perspective."

"Your exchange rate with China is now one-seventh of what it used to be just ten years ago. Any idea how that happened?" Kirk looks at Paul, expecting him to respond.

"Kirk, we hit a few financial tipping points." Paul's voice quivers a little bit.

"Such as?" Kirk asked.

"Inflation jacked up our interest rates on our federal debt," Paul said.

"Wouldn't inflation shrink the real size of the national debt?"

"You bet. Which led to the second challenge. Anyone that owned any portion of that debt or dollar assets of any type took a beating. Our currency exchange rate tanked."

"Wouldn't a lower exchange rate make the US economy more competitive?"

"Only in theory. The Chinese have much lower energy costs and infrastructure that enable a very competitive manufacturing sector." Paul looks tired and diminished in the low light of the dining room.

"Paul, enough for one night. Sorry to put you through all this." Kirk looks at Paul more closely. His receding hairline, grey hair, and bald spot on the back of his head show his age. His face is etched with wrinkles carved by the sun but also from hardship. This transition has not been easy for him and his family.

"Hope it was useful," Paul said.

Kirk feels sorry for Paul and Rose, who had to endure these disruptions. "You know the easiest way to make small fortune?"

"What's that?" Paul said.

"Start with a large one." Kirk looks at Paul who's not laughing.

Rose makes no effort to laugh and fills the silence, "I know it sounds weird, but this is just how things are. You could get used to them."

"Kirk, you must agree that our family is much better off than most people." Paul said.

"Rose, this is just hard to understand how a democracy headed this direction." Kirk watches her as she looks back and forth between the two brothers.

"The United States has always delivered when we've been at war. We're all just doing what we think is best for the world." Rose said.

"I guess I'll have to process all this more fully," Kirk said.

"I'll send you some online links," Paul said.

"I'll take a look." Kirk's voice sounds doubtful.

"Really?" Rose asked.

"I'll let you know when I see them. By the way, it really was Windy's idea to come back, but now that she's here, she seems ready to return. Please don't ask her to work outside until I'm sure she's ready. She's very protective of her good looks."

"No, we won't," Paul said. "It would be great to have you close for as long as we can convince you to stay."

The Ranchers
TEXAS

Eacher had arranged with Irene to conduct their first public information sharing together.

Mike had some friends that he wanted them to brief, and neither of them attempted to press him for any details.

The location for the discussion is in northeast Texas at a private ranch. They were told that the owners had long hosted guided hunting programs and recently added a small farming operation.

When they arrive together, Irene carries a small bottle of whiskey on behalf of Mike, which she hands to the host. He looks at the label and compliments Mike on his expensive taste. He's an older guy, average height and somewhat muscular looking. He wears a pair of custom shorts and an expensive looking shirt. He introduces himself as Wally. He introduces a young, nice-looking and well-endowed blond as his wife, Gloria.

Irene and Eacher are ushered into a giant game room where the guests are routinely kept busy between hunts. There is a pool table, duck and deer hunting video games, and a long bar with high seats. The walls are lined with a collection of stuffed wild animals – including several deer with large antler racks, some wildcats, and a wild boar. Wildebeest heads and a complete zebra are also on display, keepsakes from previous trips to Africa.

Wally jokes that Irene and Eacher are baiting their guests and then elaborates. Ranchers in this area frequently have productive oil and gas wells on their properties. Giving a climate skeptic-type lecture to people accustomed to receiving such "mailbox money" would be like attracting deer with a corn feeder or a saltlick during hunting season. Saltlicks condition the deer to return regularly to an area in front of a deer stand where hunters conceal themselves on the first day of hunting season. Attracting these animals in such a manner gives the hunter an unfair advantage. It is limited by various state rules on where and how it can be done. Suffice it to say that this particular crowd ought to be an ideal audience for their materials.

To give Eacher and Irene a little challenge, Wally invites their high school-aged kids, Bucky and Buddy, to sit in on the presentation and suggests that they've been brainwashed in school.

About a dozen chairs in the room are scattered randomly in front of a brick wall. There is also an overhead projector that Irene and Eacher can use to show materials on a drop-down screen.

When the hosts indicate that the invited guests have arrived, Eacher surveys the room. There are five retiree-aged people, three thirty-something-looking adults, and the two boys.

Irene stands and introduces herself. They are both under specific instructions from the Lost Woods program, not to mention their training or association with the program they have just graduated from. Even so, they are apparently associates of Mike and are probably already aware of that detail. Irene points out that she and Eacher simply provide good-faith lectures as part of their outreach program.

The lecture starts off warmly enough. Irene introduced her background and her excitement about getting the chance to give this presentation. She switches to the first slide.

Figure 1: NASA GISS Global Land-Ocean Temperature Index plotted as annual average temperatures on an absolute scale similar to a liquid in glass alcohol thermometer

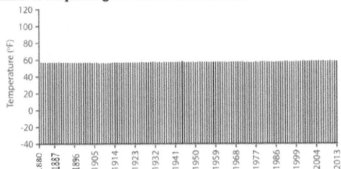

Source: Plot of NASA GISS global average surface temperature from 1880-2013, with thanks to James Sexton for conversion assistance. Data derived from "GLOBAL Land-Ocean Temperature Index in 0.01 degrees Celsius base period: 1951-1980," National Aeronautics and Space Administration, accessed July 10, 2014,

"What are we looking at missy?" A blue jean-clad senior citizen with a massive belly and a string cowboy tie chimed in. His nametag indicated his name in big letters as Tex.

"Tex, this is what average global warming looks like when you get out of the weeds; this chart shows how a calculated average world temperatures would change when you adjust them with the anomaly data. When you examine the small size of those temperature changes from the vantage point of a standard thermometer, they don't look all that scary." Irene said.

'Not much of a change." His petite wife, Daisy, added.

"Just for the sake of clarity, let's take a closer look at how these numbers are actually created. Temperature anomalies are the average of changes that occur relative to a thirty-year mean at each measuring station." Irene clicks to the next slide. "This graph shows the annual temperature anomalies of 3,000 measuring stations with at least 100 years of observation. Each black circle is the annual temperature for a single station and also the temperature difference from normal that a local resident near that station would have experienced that year. The squares in the middle are the calculated global temperature anomalies that were added to the first chart."

109

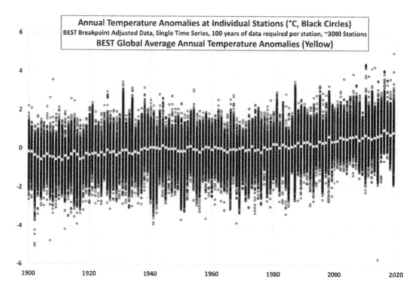

Annual Temperature Anomalies at Individual Stations (°C, Black Circles)
BEST Breakpoint Adjusted Data, Single Time Series, 100 years of data required per station, ~3000 Stations
BEST Global Average Annual Temperature Anomalies (Yellow)

"I don't understand it." Gloria said.

"I'm just trying to explain where the numbers come from. They are averaging a lot of data to show you some very small changes."

"These little numbers are what the climate emergency is about? You introduced yourself as a climate modeler. What did you spend your time on?" Gloria asked as she petted a large Doberman that sat next to her.

"Well, the climate is pretty good right now. We needed the climate models to show that it might be more challenging in the future or we were all out of business. Our competitors came up with some pretty scary projections and we followed suit."

"Were your projections any good dearie?" Gloria asked.

"Not really, but someone else found a way to adjust the temperature data." Irene said.

"Really? That was done? Mike said he thought you guys were honest." Wally said. "Why should we trust you if you worked on a team that pulled a stunt like that?"

"Look, even when I worked on IPCC projects, I would *never* modify actual temperature data." She paused a second to let that message sink in and then continued casually. "*Other* people had that assignment. Here are some of the adjustments for the US database." Irene turned to the next slide.

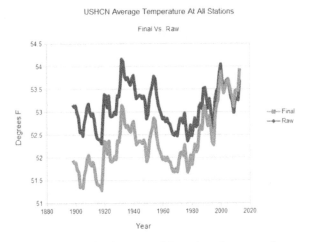

"Well, that's reassuring." Wally seemed less than impressed.

"Oh, that's nothing!" Irene said. "Ninety percent of the global temperature measuring stations used for the surface temperature database are now located in either large cities or major airports. While many of those airports are now closed, there is still lots of concrete and asphalt that attract heat. Those are places where the actual temperature readings can be as high as 5 degrees Celsius above those taken in nearby rural areas."

"That's like nine degrees Fahrenheit!" Tex said. "Sounds like someone's peeing on our leg and calling it rain."

"Yep, it's called the Urban Heat Island effect. If they moved those temperature measuring stations to adjacent rural areas, they'd have a one-time adjustment to make, but they wouldn't need to make any more edits to the data. However, they seem to rarely do that. Their use of the data contaminated by the warmth of the city and the airports requires significant adjustments. In fact, if they don't adjust them enough, they end up with temperatures that are higher than they should be. With all the necessary and

111

subjective edits, they can match any scary projections they want for the foreseeable future."

"Everything you've just told me is hard to believe," Wally said. "Are you sure you're not just making all this up?"

"No, I'm not. I'm just trying to get the word out." Irene then points out that sea levels have been rising for the past twenty thousand years and were higher earlier in the Holocene. She touches on a few more minor points and then wraps it up.

The older members of the audience seem a little irritated from this discussion. The high schoolers seem too distracted by their phones to suggest anything relevant. Irene invites Eacher to take his place in front of the group and she quickly sits down in the front row.

Eacher's task is to talk about how Net Zero has left the country in serious trouble.

He starts by touching on all the individual efforts that blocked fossil fuel investment and the government's efforts to restrict fossil fuel production and consumption.

"Who are those sons of a bitches to keep gasoline prices so high?" Said Tex.

Daisy added, "The same SOBs that shut down our cattle operation!"

"I know what you mean." Said another oldster leaning on a rollator. "I'm getting damn tired of horse meat and long horse rides. If it weren't for our natural gas generators, we couldn't even assure ourselves of air conditioning during the summer."

"Horse meat, hell. I still have wild turkey and all the deer meat we can stand." Said his younger wife in a low-cut blouse. "Net Zero doesn't seem that much of a problem for me, and we can buy most anything we want online."

The discussion continues in this vein for the next ten minutes, and Eacher barely gets a word in edge-wise. As it turns out, the high schoolers aren't really given a chance to say anything nor do they seem to have any interest in doing so.

112

Eacher wraps up the discussion and then asks if there are any questions. When none surface, Eacher asks a few. "So you guys are okay with the fossil fuel industry getting hammered in this country?"

Daisy raises her hand and starts speaking. "Most of us were able to lease our acreage and earn royalty during the hay day of oil and gas operations. These days, we've all got wind turbines and solar farms on our acreage that also bring in some attractive royalty. We haven't noticed many of those lifestyle changes you're talking about. Don't get me wrong, most of us don't like paying crazy prices for gasoline to run our trucks or four-wheelers, but we've got the funds to do it or to buy electric versions. We also have arrangements with local farmers to sell us enough produce and farm our acreage so that we don't have to do any farming ourselves. I don't question that people are seriously hurting in this country. It's just that we're not among the casualties."

Wally adds. "Bucky has an electric truck, and he has to remember to charge it regularly. Still, he's got as much mobility as I ever had when I was a teenager."

"Seriously, who cares about Net Zero?" said the old guy with the walker.

Irene and Eacher are both stunned by the reaction of this group. Mike has apparently picked an affluent group that is getting by just fine. They have the resources where they don't even notice the impacts of climate change or Net Zero on their personal situation. Irene and Eacher could not have chosen a less receptive audience for what they thought they needed to say.

After the presentation, the event hosts serve the most enormous steaks Eacher and Irene have ever seen. They are accompanied by an open bar and an experienced bartender.

Eacher and Irene sit in the room where they have given their presentation. They rest together on a sofa. Away from the rest of the attendees,

Eacher puts his arm around her shoulder.

"Eacher, I've got something to share with you that I haven't mentioned before."

"What's that?"

"I met with some strange people in a hotel in Shreveport."

"Maybe not so odd; I met with the same people."

"Eacher, you met with them too? Why didn't you mention it?"

"While wearing that polygraph gear, they asked me if I planned on telling anyone about their discussion. I understood I wasn't allowed to and promised not to."

"And yet, now you're telling me!"

"Yes, but I hadn't planned to. Those yahoos never mentioned to me that they had met with you." He said.

"So, what did you think of that ridiculous machine they hooked us up to?"

"You mean the polygraph machine?"

"That was no polygraph machine," she said. "I'm not sure what the hell it was, but it certainly couldn't tell if you were lying. Must have gotten it from a Halloween supply store."

"Well, you're more discerning than me. I thought it was real."

"Oh, that's a good one. In your case, it sounds like it accomplished the desired result."

"Did you lie to them once you recognized that the machine was useless?" He asked.

"You know it! I don't know what those fools were searching for, but I wasn't going to help them find it."

"I bet it had something to do with your upcoming debate. I kept waiting for those inquisitors to open my mouth so they could inspect my teeth." He said.

"Too bad we couldn't do it together." She said. "I think we make a good team."

"Nah, they were right to select you! When and where do you want me to show up to assist you with your preparation?"

"I'd guess you should show up to the Lost Woods a few days before. I don't want to waste much time on preparation; we've had enough." She said.

114

"Nothing would give me greater pleasure than to assist you with whatever little assistance you need!"

"Nothing?" She asked coyly.

"Not that I'm aware of yet...." He looked at her fondly.

They laugh and continue to revisit a number of their training moments together.

Eacher didn't need to be strapped to a lie detector to admit he was falling in love with her. He wondered if she thought about him in the same way. He looks forward to spending time with her again in a few months.

Adjustments

Adjustments
ARKANSAS

Kirk wakes up when the toilet lid noisily closes in the bathroom and notices that the other twin bed is empty. He slips out of bed, throws on his shorts, and then walks into the hall to lightly tap on the bathroom door. "Windy, you okay?"

She opens the door and is holding her hair dryer in her hand. "The electrical outlets aren't working!" Her face is fierce.

"What seems to be the problem?" He notices she's holding the cord like she's going to whip it in his direction. He takes a step backward.

"When I plug it in, it doesn't work. The overhead light is on, so I know the power lines are working. Also, the hot shower water only lasts a minute. What am I doing wrong?" She said.

"Let me find Paul and see if he can explain it. Are you almost done with the bathroom?"

"Yeah, it's all yours."

"Thanks." They pass each other in the doorway, and he emerges a couple of minutes later with a shaved face.

He finds Paul heading to the garden with a wheel barrel full of compost.

"Hey Paul, Windy tells me the electrical outlets aren't working in the bathroom."

"What's the problem?"

"It's her hair dryer."

"Well, that explains it. Can you join me on the porch near the kitchen? I want to explain a few things about the electrical panel."

"If there's a problem, shouldn't we call an electrician?"

"Kirk, relax. We're not going to change anything; I just want you to better understand our system."

117

They head to the circuit breaker panel on the back porch outside the kitchen door. Paul opens it up to reveal a strange-looking electronic gizmo.

"First of all, please understand that we have installed a device approved by the power company. It allows us to regulate our electricity usage. It wasn't a trivial project, and the entire panel had to be swapped out with an electronic one allowing individual circuit adjustments. That cost us a lot but would have cost us considerably more if we hadn't." Paul said.

"So, I'm guessing it works like a yard sprinkler system? You've got different zones?" Kirk steps back a bit from where Paul is waving his arms near the electrical box. He knows electricity can be dangerous and is wary of getting closer to Paul's demonstration.

"Yes, that's the basic idea. The key to this system is allowing each circuit to operate below a certain price level that we manually set for each circuit. The system instantaneously tracks local spot prices and limits each circuit accordingly. Think of it this way, if we set a certain price below the electricity spot price, this system acts as if the switch is off. Make sense?"

"Okay.

I think I see."

Paul continues with the explanation. "If electricity prices are low enough, all circuits are open. As prices increase, different lines are shut off based on their priority.

Finally, when spot prices are higher than the highest price set, the software shuts everything off completely except a small trickle charge to keep the software operating. The main circuit breaker can be manually turned off if prices are so high that even a small trickle charge will be expensive."

"That's useful?" Kirk seems less than impressed.

"It'd help if you understood some detail. Is it okay if I use the variable "X" for the fixed price of electricity that we enjoyed ten years ago?"

"Sounds like an economics lecture, but I think I've got it." Paul is now using algebraic expressions to talk about electricity prices. Why does this have to be so complicated?

"Just to put things in perspective, I once saw an electricity price of 900X, but this device protected us from it."

"Incredible! This software is a life-saver!" Kirk meant this sarcastically, but Paul didn't pick up on that, or his lecture would be over."

"Yes, it's never good to get shocked by electricity!" Paul chuckles and then points to a small display at the panel's top. The current spot price for electricity is on display in large numbers.

To the right is another small display that shows the estimated amount of electricity used and cost since the end of the last billing period.

"So, that's what we're trying to manage," Kirk observes.

Paul nods, then points out a fuse breaker in the center of the panel with the label 'pump' written on it. "Our most important circuit is our water well pump which we use to top off our house water storage tank about once a day. This is managed by some tricky software that estimates when the minimum daily price occurs."

"You've got some flexibility on that requirement," Kirk said.

"Yes. Irrigation is trickier because we prefer to water our plants only as necessary. It's such a critical expense that we set this circuit to a 1X price and then manually raise it when we have to water our crops."

"That sounds complicated," Kirk said.

"It is, but it's one of our largest business expenses, so we pay considerable attention to it." Paul then starts pointing at various circuit breakers while he speaks. Each is labeled with its purpose, then a display shows the price set, the amount of electricity used, and the estimated total cost of that circuit since the last bill. We set the limits at 80X for LED lights. 40X for office equipment, ceiling fans, and recharging batteries. 20X for electrical outlets, the microwave, and the clothes washer. 10X for the refrigerator, water heater, air conditioner, dishwasher, electric range, ceiling fans, and clothes dryer. We rarely see electricity prices as low as 10X."

"What are you average electricity prices now?" Kirk asked.

"70X in the summer or winter. Maybe 30X in the spring or fall." Paul said.

"I think I just got my answer. The outlet that Windy is complaining about is in the second group; electricity prices are too high."

"Yes. There are some finer points that I should also mention. Our primary hot water heater is a solar thermal system, so that system warms a portion of the water naturally when the weather allows. We generally take short showers where the water is warm. There's not much hot water, so we hope you and Windy follow our lead."

"Okay, I'll talk to her about her shower time. We had a very efficient tankless water heater in China."

"Not here. We were wisely advised not to install one. While in your part of the world, it saves money by not heating water to be stored, in our part of the world, we'd end up with a lot of really chilly showers when that circuit is off."

"Okay." Electricity conservation rules are different in the United States.

"Our clothes washer is our second most important appliance. We only do large, short loads, in cold water. Put your clothes in the dirty basket near the washer, and we'll manage this for you."

"Yes, I can see how it would be pretty miserable without a clothes washer. Images of women walking back and forth to the creek to beat their clothes against a rock come to mind."

"Women? No, Rose and Clare are busy. I'd be the one heading to the creek. Just let me manage those washer loads. Also, we rarely use the clothes dryer, so just hang your clothes on the line outside or on the wooden drying rack near the window to dry."

"Roger," Kirk said. "Why do you even keep all these appliances around?"

"You know, it's that 'hope springs eternal' thing. We couldn't sell any of these appliances for much, and we keep them, hoping that someday things will be different."

"Was it hard to learn to live without a refrigerator?"

"Only at first. Food preservation is a much more significant challenge without it, but we've learned some tricks. In some ways, we haven't missed it as much because the supermarkets no longer carry frozen food. They'll refrigerate soft drinks occasionally but won't touch anything perishable."

"Any other rules?" The curious thing about this discussion isn't the functioning of the device. Given the electricity pricing challenges Paul and Rose face, it makes perfect sense. The strange thing is how this country reached a point where this type of system is necessary. Why is reliable electricity now a thing of the past? The electricity flows when the wind blows or the sun is visible, and prices determine what circuits get energized; all the balancing is getting done on the demand side. Who needs large-scale battery storage or fossil fuel backup systems when you can simply manipulate electricity through real-time price adjustments?

Paul notices Kirk ruminating about something. "By the way, we have an outhouse near the back porch if you can't wait for the toilet."

"That's good to know. One bathroom for five people is pretty inconvenient!" Kirk said. "I'll update Windy on the rules and her toilet options. By the way, I've been wondering, how do you get your crops to market?"

"In short, we don't have a vehicle to transport them. We can move a box of produce on the back of a scooter, but that's about it. The same applies to moving our food from the fields to the house or barn. We use a wheelbarrow, and it's a lot of work."

"That kind of limits your farming revenue."

"Yes, most farmers in this area have the same challenge. Also, few still own tractors and they couldn't afford to run them if they did. It's one thing to get the food delivered to us from the mail service, but quite another thing trying to put our food in the mail to deliver to others. We grow for ourselves or exchange food with our immediate neighbors."

"Are you still able to get manufactured goods from other states around the country?"

"Shipping is a challenge. We have a home delivery system, but anything you order from more than one state away requires a long-distance surcharge for the extra cost. That charge is calculated based on the road or rail distance and is noted when these items are ordered."

"So, if you were to order a crosscut saw that came from Michigan...."

"You'd pay an extra surcharge. But you could also get that same saw without the toll if you order it from an adjoining state, including the ports in Texas and Louisiana. Most of those goods are made in other countries, shipped to local ports, and provided in this area at the basic shipping rate."

"Any there issues getting mobile devices?"

"Those are all imported. The main challenge is price; most people get by with a simple device without all the bells and whistles. There are also cheap government phone plans and subsidies for users who qualify; most of us would have difficulty functioning without these services. Even so, the coverage is pretty spotty. Our Internet service is getting worse over time, and we're now down to one bar in this area."

"Anything else?" Kirk is ready to wrap it up so he can assist Windy with whatever she's working on.

"Not now. Thanks." Paul said.

He watches Paul head back towards the garden with his load. Paul walks with a pronounced limp. This is a back-breaking and punishing lifestyle for a man his age.

Trip to Town
JULY

Windy and Kirk decide to go out later in the day. They wear helmets and head toward a small local town on a scooter. This bike is like the one Windy's mother used to drive in China, and Windy has handled a similar one a few times. She has no intentions of sitting behind Kirk while he learns to drive. She seems to be getting the hang of it, and he apparently doesn't seem to realize how little experience she has. There are few other vehicles on the farm roads but a fair amount of scooters on the major roads.

The roads are in terrible shape with numerous potholes; repairs were attempted on some and the clay they used either compacted or washed away. She drives slowly and deliberately to avoid them.

The road bends to the left, and she looks up to see wind turbines. Those tall, massive wind turbines are spaced along the crest of the hill while the trees below get cut back. She can see a new road along the summit with several small buildings.

Farther up the road, there are many evergreen trees, and she can make out cabins a few hundred feet away. The trees around many houses have been cleared on the structure's south side. She guessed the solar panels required some room, and the wood stoves took a toll. The pine trees are tall and closely packed; the owners generally have to clear a lot of them to allow the winter sun to reach the panels.

Some discarded solar panels are lying along the side of the road. Old solar panels are classified as hazardous waste, and many people that buy them don't realize that the landfills won't accept them. Even developers have the same disposal issue at the end of a commercial solar project. Lead, chromate, and chromium are a few of the heavy metals that can leach into the ground from an abandoned solar panel and, left alone, can poison the groundwater. The local solution is apparently to discard them on someone else's property and let others deal with them. The panel glass is shattered on most of them, and some were apparently used for target practice. So much for clean energy.

123

They enter the city limits and stop at Renfro's to get coffee. A police officer is standing next to a tiny car not much larger than a golf cart. The word "Police" is stenciled on the side. Little roof-mounted lights about the size of a soup bowl are mounted on the roof. He does his best to look rugged, but that tiny police car doesn't fit the image of a tough guy.

"We don't get a lot of strangers in town." The policeman said. "You're new around here?"

"Well, we're visiting my brother, Paul Stewart. You know him?" Kirk asked.

"Ah, that explains why you're riding his scooter. Yes, I know, Paul. He's a teacher's aide at the college, right?"

"Yes, he's got an economics degree. How's your ride? Is that gasoline driven?"

"No, it's electric. But, I assure you that it's fully charged today and I don't get wet when it rains. It's better than a scooter and a luxury these days, and I even get to take it to my house when I get off work."

"Wow. Great vehicle!" Kirk looks impressed.

"Any problem keeping up with the bad guys?" Windy asked.

"Honestly, I don't even try; I'd never catch those speeders. Those guys mostly run on natural gas in large trucks that formerly used gasoline. They've been modified with illegal conversion kits."

"Go figure," Kirk said.

"When I run across one of those vehicles, I take a picture of it rushing off into the distance and then enlarge the image to see if I can get a license plate number. Generally, those guys aren't stupid enough to leave their license plates on the vehicle."

"Well, stay charged! Thanks for looking out for all of us!" Kirk said.

They wave goodbye to the Police officer and walk into the cafe. It's a vintage-looking restaurant with only a small number of tables and a few booths.

An older waitress leads them to a seat by the window and points out the hand-written menu on the chalkboard. The waitress adjusts some moveable fans to blow directly on them. Egg salad sandwiches, garden salads, and cheese grits are the main items on the menu.

There is a slight coffee smell in the air, but it smells odd. Windy and Kirk don't know if it is real coffee or an imitation product. They pass.

They order lunch, and the waitress heads to the kitchen in the back; it's not clear if she's the only one in the facility or if there might actually be a cook. Windy peers around the restaurant and out the windows scanning Main Street while they wait for their food, and she finds the town less than impressive.

The weather is warm. Windy can see balcony doors open on apartments. The front doors of a small store and a pharmacy are also propped open. There is a sign for the Goodwill Store that Kirk had mentioned; it occupies a space that might have once been a small supermarket of some type. Screened windows appear open, and it seems available for business from this distance.

Except for the little police car they saw, there were few other cars or vehicles on the street. It is Sunday, but she doubts if it looks busier on a weekday. There are a few scooters parking on the road and some souped-up golf cart-looking cars.

The city's streets need considerable maintenance, and the potholes should slow down anyone trying to simply drive through town.

At this moment, a large pickup truck comes racing through town well above the posted speed limit. The policeman glances in its direction but does not attempt to pull out a camera. In fact, at that moment, he decides to walk into the restaurant.

That large truck never slows down; it might hit a few potholes, but the tires are so large it just bridges over them. Windy is relieved that they aren't on the road on their scooter when this lady speeds by.

Windy looks toward the policeman sitting at a booth; instead of racing off to take a picture of that speeder, he just buries his head in some document he's reading.

When they finish their meal, they pay their check; the cash register is near the door, so they close their bill on the way out.

The policeman follows them outside and points out a cracked taillight on their scooter.

Windy doesn't recall it being cracked.

He asks them for their Proof of Insurance form, and neither can find one in the scooter's storage compartment.

He hands two tickets to Kirk. He also advises Kirk that if he can later produce the insurance form, the judge will automatically waive the second ticket. He asks Kirk for his driver's license.

Kirk hands it to him.

Windy is curious why he is ticketing them while he made no effort to take a picture of that reckless offender that just went flying by.

When he notices Kirk's Texas driver's license is expired, he gives him a third ticket.

Kirk stuffs this ticket into his pocket along with the others.

The policeman also insists that they write Paul's address on his copy of the tickets.

Windy doesn't bother pointing out that she was driving; she has no driver's license. That might result in another ticket.

They walk around town. The shelves in the pharmacy are mostly empty, and Homeopathic drugs grown locally are not of interest. They have boxed noodles, dried mushrooms, and bottled vegetables for sale. Windy looks them over carefully and does not buy any.

They leave and walk into the Goodwill Store. It features a collection of used furniture, kitchenware, and all sorts of things that people would have once bought new at a superstore. Some items are on consignment.

Windy is a bit put off when she learns that everything is used. Kirk teases her a bit about her resistance to wearing discarded clothes and steers her toward the lady's clothes area. Windy is petit and moves to a section of the store where the long row of clothes racks are aimed at teenage girls and young women.

"How about these shorts?" Kirk asks while holding up a pair of low-cut short shorts.

"You would like those!" Windy said. "Perhaps they have one in your size." She briefly looks around to locate something equally ridiculous that Kirk could wear.

"I'll have to look!"

"Here are some jeans that might work for me. Do they have a changing room?" Windy looks around.

"Right over there." Kirk points to a curtain along the wall. "Why don't you try them on?"

Windy grabs four pairs of jeans off the rack and carries them to the changing area. She notes a woman who works in the store coming over in their direction. She presumes that this lady just doesn't want anything to walk out of the store. "Got any field boots?" Windy asks her.

"What size?" She asked.

"Well, something in size seven for me. Maybe something in size eleven for my husband?"

"Your husband is out of luck, but he might find some well-used tennis shoes over on that wall. Here are some tiny Army boots we've had for a long time; might they work for you?"

"I don't know. I'll take a look." She said.

She enters the changing room with all the items she's carrying. A few minutes later, Windy walks out of the changing booth in both the boots and jeans.

"Now you're ready for the snakes and the mosquitoes," Kirk said.

"You're forgetting the spiders, ants, ticks, poison ivy, and many other nasty things," Windy said. "The natural world is a dangerous place! Any long-sleeved shirts?" She thumbs the teen racks and finds a few that look like they might have been surplus from some industrial marketing program. She holds them up to her chest to guess the size. Looks like she's finally found a store that matches Kirk's suspect taste in clothes. The prices are modest, and the clothes are random. If it weren't for all the stylish clothes she's bought him over the years, this is precisely what his closet would look like.

"Should we see if they have any lingerie?" Kirk asks.

"Nope, but perhaps if I put on some of those shorts, it would turn you on?" Windy smiles and thinks, "Yes, he's in clothes heaven here!" She's surprised he's not trying on more of these clothes for himself.

"Yes, little girl, let your rich uncle buy you some candy," Kirk said too loudly.

"Oh, uncle, we don't want candy. Got any meat?" She pulled the shirt collar down slightly to reveal her shoulder and batted her eyes. This guy might not be able to make much money, but he can still make her laugh.

Kirk cracks up.

Windy looks at the store worker, who seems a bit rattled. "Okay. I'm done - you need anything?" She visualizes Kirk with a mullet haircut modeling these items for the public. He'll need to learn to dress if he ever gets a real job.

"Well, I browsed around to see what they had. I think I'm fine with the clothes I've brought."

Windy is a little surprised by this admission. However, looking around, she confirms that the store's selection is limited; it's obviously been well picked over. In this area, people don't make many clothing donations unless a relative dies. Even old clothes can always be used for rags on a farm.

Windy pays with her credit card, and they leave the store. She places her purchases under the seat and then returns to the scooter; she drives a short distance to the end of town. She confirms that there are no auto part stores in town where they can buy a replacement part for the cracked tail light. Kirk taps her on the shoulder as they pass a junkyard with a high fence and an open gate. She pulls over to the parking lot and parks.

Kirk takes a picture of their cracked taillight, and then they walk in through the open gate."

128

The junkyard is laid out in rows of old cars that are mostly stripped and more recent vintage cars that are mostly intact. Those vehicles are lined up along the ground in a row, and weeds grow in the spaces between.

A long row of many makes and models of scooters sits next to the autos. Many of these scooters have been cannibalized for parts, and some are badly bent from accidents.

There are also several rows of appliances. A row of clothes washers appears to have gotten much attention, and many lay disassembled in place. Other machines seem to have simply been discarded with little evidence of parts being stripped – this is particularly true with refrigerators, stoves, and dishwashers.

They don't see anyone on the grounds or in the office but hear activity in a building.

They walk around the open bay and see a vehicle on a lift elevated off the ground a few feet. One mechanic works on a creeper below a pickup truck, while another observes from above.

"Anyone home?" Kirk asked.

"Sorry, we didn't see you come in." The standing mechanic said. "We're closed now."

"Sorry to bother you today, any chance you might have a spare taillight for a scooter?" Kirk said.

"Don't tell me that policeman got you too!" He laughed. "Poor guy, he's got to generate enough revenue to pay his and the judge's salary; I'm surprised he's lasted this long. Call me Dusty." He slaps his overalls and generates a small cloud of dust.

"He also tapped us for driving on expired insurance and with an expired driver's license," Windy said. She doesn't know much about car repair or garage operations but notes that this garage is messy. Replaced parts are lying on the ground, and several puddles of oil have not been cleaned up. The unmistakable smell of gasoline is in the air. She quickly surmises that these people are not very professional.

"Miss, people around here don't normally carry insurance for scooters. It's too much like a bicycle. If you hit something, you'll likely do more damage to yourself or the scooter than anything else. If you wreck your scooter, you still won't meet your deductible. Regarding the driver's license, good luck getting a new one. Tell you what, I've got a box of scooter taillights in my office. It's not exactly the right match, but it should work fine."

"How much?" Windy is almost too afraid to ask. Since she earns virtually all the money in their household, any expenses like this come directly from her earnings.

"A hundred and eighty dollars ought to cover it, and I'll install it at no charge."

"That sounds fair," Kirk said.

Windy is not so sure this is a good deal. Kirk lacks much of a business sense. Even so, she doesn't want to return the scooter with a broken part. That would be rude to Paul and Rose. She nods approval to Kirk.

"More than fair. I've still got to give a portion to the policeman." He laughed.

Windy doesn't appreciate this humor and is surprised that everyone is so open about this type of corruption; it's not a good sign. Kirk isn't smiling, either.

"So, what are you working on?" Kirk asked.

"We're converting a gasoline engine to run on natural gas. The best part is that you don't need a refinery to get usable fuel; that allows people to avoid dealing with government gas stations.

"That's interesting," Windy said.

"Well, the EPA makes these engine conversions so expensive that it's seldom economical to do it legally. So, a lot of these types of conversions come our way. The hard part is finding the scuba tanks or welding tanks to allow us to store the compressed natural gas for fuel. There's a small bootleg industry that produces them."

"I think we just saw one of your customers fly by on Main Street," Windy said.

130

"That would be Sue-Ann; she left here this morning. She just loves to drive, and her family has money. Wish I could get that lady to marry me!"

"So, the policeman probably knows her?" Windy said.

"Knows her? She's the judge's niece."

"Let me get the scooter." Kirk walks out the open garage door.

Windy remained there watching them work.

"Where you from?" Dusty asked.

"China."

"You're a long way from home. What brings you to these parts?"

"Kirk is visiting his brother's family, and I came along for the trip."

"Long way to come. How do you like it?"

"This is nothing like where I'm from."

"Yeah, but I heard your air is bad in China," Dusty said.

"Yes, that used to be true. We're replacing old power plants with more efficient ones; our air is getting cleaner over time. The poor air quality in Houston is the worst I've seen."

"We all have our tradeoffs." He continues working on the conversion. "The things that bother me here are a lot different. It's getting dangerous and lawless. Careful where you go."

"Here's the scooter," Kirk said as he walked it to the front of the garage.

Dusty goes to the office and brings back a taillight, and he quickly installs it and takes Windy's cash.

"You mind if Martin and I get back to this engine conversion?"

"No, please do. Thank you." Windy is ready to leave. This junkyard is foul-smelling and grimy, and she can't wait to go home and wash all the grit off her skin.

"By the way, here's my telephone number if you ever need to reach us for any reason."

Dusty reaches out to offer it to Windy.

Kirk quickly removes it from Dusty's hand and places it in his wallet. "Thank you." He said.

Windy looks up and notes some dark clouds on the horizon.

"Let's get going." She said.

They mount the bike with Windy driving again; she then strokes the accelerator, and the cycle smoothly speeds forward.

A few minutes later, Windy is glancing at her mirror when she notices a truck enter the road and then stay about twenty-five meters behind them.

Visitors

Kirk notices a pickup truck following them about a half block behind. The sky is also starting to darken, the wind picks up, and rain seems imminent. He keeps looking over his shoulder at the truck and the dark clouds. Windy focuses her attention on the road in front.

"See that truck?" He shouts.

"Yes, they should have passed us by now." Windy turns her head, and he can hear her better.

"I'm not sure what to make of it. Can you go any faster?"

At this suggestion, Windy turns the accelerator on the handlebar, and the scooter picks up speed. She has done a pretty competent job of avoiding potholes so far, but at this higher speed, they hit a large one that jars them both. Windy maintains her balance after a terrifying moment where it feels like she has lost control; they keep going.

Kirk holds on tightly as their vehicle bounces around on the road.

The truck closes the distance with them and then keeps pace about fifteen yards behind.

I don't like this," Kirk said.

"Me either. Do you have a weapon with you?"

"No. See that wall of rain in front of us? We're about to head straight into it." Kirk shouted.

Windy says something in Cantonese that is clearly profanity. They hit the wall of rain, and their clothes are drenched.

The scooter feels less steady as water covers the roadway and masks the potholes, and Windy has no choice but to slow back down again.

The rain is so heavy they can't see the truck behind them. Most likely, it's still there since the shower ought to be less of an issue for that driver.

They continue as the rain lessens, and he confirms that the truck is no longer visible behind them. They reach the house shortly later, and Paul comes out to open the gate for them, and he closes and locks it behind them.

"I think we were being followed. What's going on?" Kirk asked.

"Get out of those wet clothes. I'll see you inside." Paul said.

They know that Paul is outside, and they see Rose and Clare walking back to the house from the garden. So, Windy and Kirk take off their wet clothes just inside the front door in order not to drip water in the house.

They start moving towards their bedroom and then stop abruptly as a somewhat elderly black man sits at the dining table looking in their direction. He appears startled to see them naked but smiles in a way that shows both a sense of humor and his recognition of the awkwardness of the situation. He quickly averts his eyes.

"Oops," Kirk said. The two of them quickly dart into their bedroom.

They each take a quick shower, dry off quickly and put some clothes on. Kirk then returns to the living room and allows Windy additional time.

The stranger and Paul sit at the table, and Paul motions for Kirk to have a seat.

"I'm sorry for not mentioning someone was here," Paul said.

"Yes, definitely a surprise," Kirk said. "Mister, sorry to embarrass you like that!"

"No problem." The stranger said. "Sorry to catch you off guard."

"Kirk, let me introduce you to Eacher. He's an old friend that used to teach at our community college, and he's surprised us with a visit."

"Nice to meet you, Mr. Eacher." The room is getting hot without the air conditioner, and Kirk reflexively goes to open the front window to let some air in."

"Please don't open that window. Try the one away from the road." Eacher said.

Kirk crosses the room and opens the other window. The rain has cooled off the air, and a fresh breeze flows into the room.

"So, why can't I open that window?" Kirk asked looking directly at it.

"Those people following you are probably looking for Eacher," Paul said.

"Really? Those guys in the truck are with law enforcement?"

"Maybe federal agents," Paul said.

This sounds ominous. "So, why the interest in Mr. Eacher?"

"Please just call me Eacher. I don't know who they are, but I was told they were in this area and that I might encounter them."

"Why?" Kirk asked.

"I'm not sure, but I'd guess they don't like the materials I share. I've been led to believe that if they catch me here, it might cause problems for you."

Rose emerges from the bathroom with her hair still wet. She is dressed in an oversized tee shirt so stretched that the image on the front is as unrecognizable as an ancient tattoo on an old sailor. She sits next to Paul. Kirk guesses that Clare is in her bedroom.

Almost on cue, Windy comes out of the guestroom dressed in stylish, brand-name clothes that seductively frame her form. Kirk lights up as soon as he sees her, and she sits beside him.

Paul studies Windy for a second and then introduces her. There is no mention of Eacher seeing Kirk and Windy walk by naked.

Eacher looks again at the front window. "Can we close those blinds?"

Rose gets up and adjusts them, which slightly reduces the light in the room.

Paul gives Rose a curious look as if he doesn't understand the concern. "Well, I think we're safe. I've never seen any Feds on this property before. If they show up, I've got a well-built hiding place in a back bedroom. That would keep you out of sight until they leave. Our dog will bark if he hears any visitors."

"Well, I hope you're right. It doesn't sound like we can even be sure it's the Feds. Now, where were we? As a courtesy, are you guys comfortable about me speaking openly about some of my concerns?"

"What do you want to talk about?" Kirk asked apprehensively.

"Some concepts that are inconsistent with the government's justification for its Net Zero policy."

"Look, I was the one that suggested that Eacher swing by and give us an overview," Paul said.

"That's true. I can come back later if now is not a good time." Eacher said.

"No, I think now would be fine. I'm betting these two would be open to what you have to say." Paul said.

"Is that the case?" Eacher asked Kirk.

"Yes, we've been trying to understand what happened here," Kirk said.

Eacher took one more concerned glance toward the window and then looked directly at Kirk and then Windy. "One of the challenges of teaching is determining what your students know and what they don't. Perhaps one of you could tell us what you think happened?"

When Windy said nothing, Kirk took the lead. "Well, the country implemented a Net Zero program based on climate concerns. That Net Zero policy seems to have been the cause of most of the issues we're seeing."

"Like what?" Eacher asked.

"It's challenging to get around, the air is contaminated with lots of smoke and dust, and electricity is in short supply," Kirk said.

"Would you consider these changes useful?" Eacher said.

"No, of course not. Windy and I normally live in China, and we don't have these problems." Kirk said.

"Paul and Rose, would you agree with this assessment?" Eacher said.

"Well, I agree with what you're describing. Right now, the country is using considerably less carbon dioxide. In addition, electric scooters are a lot more efficient than cars used to be. We can live without air conditioning and refrigeration. Personally, I don't see the problem."

"Ah, it looks like some of you have very different opinions on where we are," Eacher said.

"Why would Windy and I ever volunteer to endure all the hardships we've witnessed?" Kirk glances at Rose while raising this issue.

Eacher looked at Kirk and then Paul. "You guys are really living in two different worlds."

Paul crosses his arms. "Everything Kirk described is undeniable, but we had to do something to address our climate emergency."

Rose comes to his assistance. "Yes, I guess Paul is saying that we accepted all the costs associated with Net Zero, and all of this was done to save the planet."

"So the country's transformation was a necessary evil," Eacher said.

Rose looks like she's hesitant to respond to this question.

"Yes!" Paul answers for her.

"Well, in that case, let's skip the review of how Net Zero policy brought us to our present situation. Would you mind if I focused more on the climate science that rationalized it?" Eacher said.

"We offered to let you give us an update when you returned. Our visitors seem interested. Go ahead." Rose did not end the discussion, but Kirk could tell she was uneasy with this conversation.

Paul looked at her like she had just let a skunk in the front door but regained his composure. "No, please go ahead, my friend."

"Please stop me if I say something that makes you uncomfortable," Eacher said. "Paul, would you or Rose like to explain the greenhouse theory to us?"

"I guess so." Getting the chance to participate seemed to defuse some of Rose's reluctance. "Well, the climate was more or less well-behaved until humanity figured out how to burn fossil fuels; those generated a lot of carbon dioxide emissions. That additional gas slows the heat's ability to escape and warms the planet. All that additional warming melts ice near the north and south poles, raising sea levels. Does that cover it?"

Cappy starts barking, and everyone at the table stiffens up in anticipation. He scrambles to the back door and starts scratching the door to get out and Rose follows him. She looks out the kitchen window and spies a small animal rushing into the woods. "False alarm," she says when she returns to the dining room. "Just a raccoon."

Eacher and Paul were standing at the edge of the hallway, prepared to hide in the back bedroom. With the uncertainty resolved, both return to the dining room.

Eacher passes by the front window and peaks from the corner of the blinds toward the front gate. Apparently satisfied, he returns to his seat.

Paul also takes a seat and invites him to continue.

"Well, give me a second to refocus my attention." Eacher sits for a second and tries to catch his breath. About a minute later, he proceeds. "Rose, thank you for that overview. Let me show you a chart that I've found interesting." Eacher pulls a yellowed sheet of paper in a plastic protector out of his bag and lays it on the table.

Geomagnetic AA Index - 1868 to 2018
David Archibald

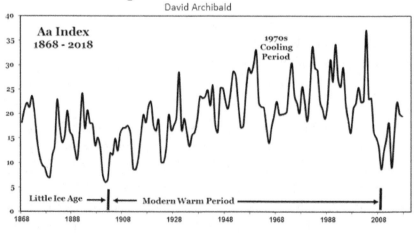

"What does this show?" Paul asked.

"It's a chart of something called the AA Index. It's a geomagnetic signal collected every three hours since 1868. An observatory in the United Kingdom and another in Australia take the measurements. It's designed to detect disturbances from major magnetic storms, and in general, it tends to correspond with sunspots."

"What? Where are you getting this stuff?" Paul asked.

"You're right; it's hard to find. This data corresponds with recent global temperatures as this next graph shows." Eacher pulls another piece of paper out of his notebook.

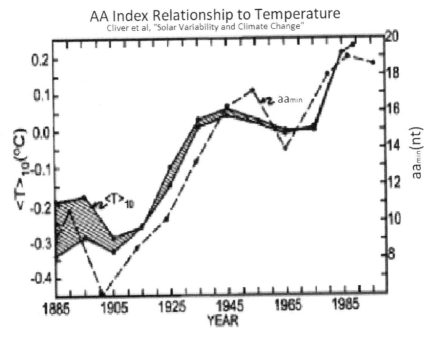

"Now, this one does look complicated!" Kirk said.

"Yes, I'd rather not get too deep into the specifics. Honestly, I don't fully understand what's driving this correlation."

"So, what's your point here, Eacher?" Paul asked.

"These scientists claim that geomagnetic conditions can account for at least 50% of the global temperature increase since the second half of the 17th century," Eacher said. "If that's true, the possible influence of additional CO_2 into the atmosphere is much smaller than the IPCC has been claiming."

"They claim?" Paul persisted.

"I guess my point is that there is historical evidence that certain climate variations have aligned with solar activity. This chart shows changes in solar irradiance and the temperature anomaly over the past two and a half centuries."

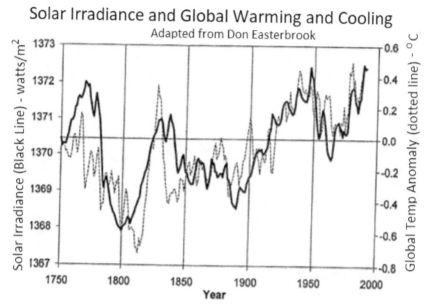

Solar Irradiance and Global Warming and Cooling
Adapted from Don Easterbrook

"What are we looking at?" Paul asked.

"This graph suggests there is a correlation between these two variables."

"If you say so," Paul said.

"Well, the IPCC supporters tends to dismiss a number of influences in their climate models. Let's take a quick look at how well their own manmade greenhouse gas theory explains recent warming." Eacher places another sheet of paper on the table.

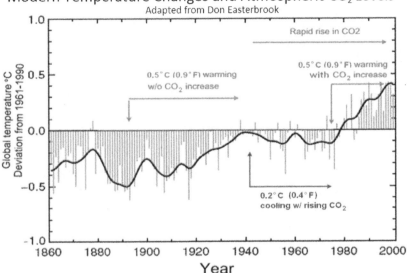

Modern Temperature Changes and Atmospheric CO₂ Levels
Adapted from Don Easterbrook

"What am I looking at?" Rose asked.

"It's a chart of global temperatures since 1850," Eacher said.

"You going to elaborate?" Rose asked.

"Yes. Two long temperature pauses follow the warming trends shown." Eacher said. "This is an example of what I'd consider a poor correlation."

"How so," Rose asked.

"The first warming happened when carbon dioxide levels were low. They increased quickly around 1950 during a cooling period. After 1998, two temperature pauses also occurred while CO_2 levels were increasing. The only warming period that seems to correspond with rising CO_2 levels was the second one, which could just be a coincidence."

"Does seem less than impressive." Kirk tried to restrain a smile.

"It gets better. Here's how well the climate model temperature projections have fared." Eacher places his document on the table.

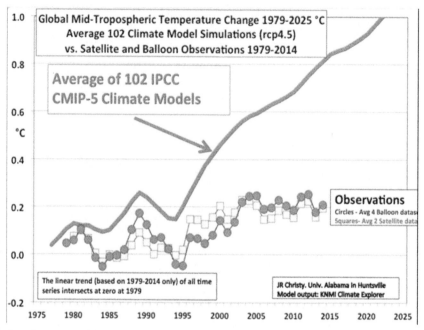

"Looks to me like their projections are a bit over-amped," Kirk said in a matter-of-fact tone. He was thoroughly enjoying Eacher's insights.

"Authorities regularly disseminate compelling evidence that just happens to be fabricated. 'The Holocene never existed', 'climate models are reliable', 'the science is settled', 'there's a scientific consensus that global warming is manmade and dangerous', are just some of the doozies that are inflicted on an unwary public."

"I'm really not comfortable with the direction you've taken this talk," Paul stood up and walked around the table as he arched his back from side to side.

"I'm just a guy that loves rocks. What do I know?" Eacher asked.

"You've got some ideas about what you think is likely to happen?" Kirk asked.

"Yes," Eacher said. "I think we're about to see some global cooling." He explains his reasoning.

"Look, I'm not sure I'm interested in more details about what you think is really happening," Paul said. "Manmade greenhouse gases are a threat to our planet, and we've taken action to address that."

"Yes, I agree with Paul. It's useless to question why we took the Net Zero path." Rose said.

"Well, I respect the sacrifices your family made as part of this country's chosen transition," Eacher said. "It took a lot of faith."

Cappy starts barking furiously. He's focused near the entrance. Rose quickly goes to the front window. "People at the front gate!" she crosses her arm to form an 'x' and points toward the entrance.

"Hiding place?" Eacher asked.

"Yes, follow me," Paul said in a low voice. "Kirk, go see what they want."

Eacher stuffs his papers and notebook back into his backpack. He and Paul head to the back bedroom.

Kirk walks out the door just in time to see the padlock and the chain to the gate falling to the ground. A large stranger dressed in jeans and a short-sleeved tee shirt stands with a bolt cutter. He tosses it behind him and then pushes the gate open. The truck that Windy and Kirk had seen before is blocking the exit from the property.

Kirk doesn't believe he's any good in any type of confrontation, and his stomach starts churning. He's afraid that he's going to throw up.

Cappy barks even more furiously.

"What do you guys want?" Kirk challenges them while his stomach twists in knots; the volume of his voice is deliberately casual, but comes out a little too rushed.

The gate is pushed open further, and two men and a woman enter the compound. The woman seems either very tan or perhaps of Mediterranean origins. She is about five feet, muscular, maybe in her early forties, and there is no makeup on her face. She looks at ease in a command role. She might have served in the military or the police. The two men with her carry baseball bats, and she has a pistol in a holster.

143

"Cappy, shut up!" Kirk said.

Cappy stops barking immediately but continues to growl at the group walking towards the house.

"We're looking for a terrorist." The bolt cutter guy said. "You ever hear of someone named Eacher?"

"Is that even a name?" Kirk asked. "Why were you following us?"

"We thought you might be the terrorist – though you were letting your Chinese lady drive the scooter. We don't reckon the guy we're trying to locate is accompanied."

"Yep, it's not me and definitely not my wife, Windy, or my brother's wife. If we thought there was a terrorist on this property, we'd be helping you look for him."

"Well, we got a report that he has been sighted in this area. Would you mind if we look inside?" The woman is asking, but Kirk doesn't get the feeling she is really looking for permission.

"There's no reason for you to look inside, and he's not here." Kirk feels his heart pounding vigorously in his chest. He's taking chances, something he rarely does, for someone he barely knows. He's never even seen the hiding spot where Paul took Eacher. He finds this whole situation very unsettling.

"Just to be clear, we're going to have a look inside." She sounds both determined and decisive.

"You got a warrant?" Kirk responds without thinking.

After hearing this challenge from him, she immediately directs the two men to enter the house, and they quicken their pace to the front door.

That was definitely the wrong thing for him to say. The woman in charge now seems convinced that this family is hiding something or someone.

"Just get out of the way if you don't want to be hurt." She commands authority, and Kirk finds himself involuntarily fantasizing about her.

All three of them reach the porch, and the two men go in first. Boss lady and Kirk follow them inside. Windy and Rose still sit at the dining room table, ignoring them as they search the house. The men search room to room and do not alert their leader that they have found anything of interest.

They then leave the house and head to the barn. They have no luck there either, but one of the two men insists on taking one of the chickens from the hen house which sits close by.

Kirk suddenly finds his voice and loudly insists that they leave the bird.

They ignore him and head back to their truck with the hen putting up a fight.

"If you see this Eacher guy, give me a call." The woman said as she handed Kirk an official-looking business card showing her name, Layla Knox, and her title as an agent.

The card shows the address of a federal office in Little Rock, Arkansas. "If your tip leads to his capture, we'll have a reward for you. However, I swear if we discover that you've been harboring this fugitive, the law will not go easy on you, and that's after my boys get done with you."

"Give me back our egg layer," Kirk demanded.

Cappy growls again when he hears Kirk raise his voice. He doesn't know what's happening but seems to recognize that something unfamiliar is underway. Kirk grabs him by the collar to keep him from biting one of the visitors.

"Not going to happen." The woman said.

The three of them get back in their truck and leave immediately.

Windy and Rose are peering out of a window. Kirk walks into the house to give them an update. "Those bastards took a chicken. Did they hurt you?" Kirk examines Windy closely for any visible evidence of a bruise or scrape.

Windy seems shaken. "Federal agents can just walk into your house at any time?"

"No, that was very abnormal. I've never seen that happen before." Rose said.

Paul comes walking out of the back bedroom and into the dining room. He motions for everyone to be quiet. Eacher has written these words on a pad of paper: "Have you seen any drones flying around the house? Did you see them plant hearing or visual monitoring devices anywhere on the property?"

"Not me," Kirk said in a low voice while still looking at Windy.

Windy shakes her head and starts to say something but doesn't.

"Stay here," Paul whispers. He goes to check on Rose and asks Kirk to check on Eacher.

Kirk walks to the back bedroom.

Eacher is just now emerging from the hiding place and is still in the same room. He is holding a small device that he's plugged into his phone. This room is clear, and he's still scanning other rooms. He watches a map slowly zoom out on Eacher's phone screen. Lights start blinking on the screen, and he carefully notes where the problem is. There is clearly a small video and audio transmitting device broadcasting from the bedroom where Kirk and Windy are staying. Eacher's phone further shows the location in the room's northeast corner. All other rooms are clear.

Kirk leaves the room for a second and closes the door to the guest bedroom as Eacher requests. He returns to update Eacher.

Eacher leaves the back bedroom and walks down the hallway to the living room, where he talks to Paul in a whisper. Eacher continues to look at the map on his phone as Kirk glances at it. Kirk notices that the map continues to zoom out and shows no other devices in the area. Eacher motions for him to go outside and confirm that he can't see or hear any drones.

He does so and then returns to give Eacher the OK hand sign. Eacher and Kirk walk together to the barn, and Windy, Rose, and Paul follow.

"I've got to get on the road," Eacher said. "My presence here puts you all at risk."

"I'm sorry that's the case," Paul said. "Hope you can stay a few days next trip."

"Thanks for the offer. I might take you up on that. I've stashed my scooter back in the woods there. It's better if I get off your property immediately and then hide until it's safe to get back on the roads. Did you want a thumb drive set of my presentations?"

"Yes, I would," Paul said.

Eacher hands him a flash drive and heads toward the back of the property.

Paul puts it in his pocket.

Kirk walks a scooter outside the barn, drives it out the gate, to the left, and then waits. A few minutes later, Eacher pushes his scooter out the gate and turns right; he pulls off the road several blocks later and walks his cycle into the woods.

Kirk then drives about a mile and pulls over to work on the scooter. Several minutes later, the fed truck passes him by. They slow down briefly, look at him, pick up speed, and race away. Kirk continues to work on his scooter for another ten minutes and then makes his way back home. He worries about how to deal with the audio video sensor that was installed in their bedroom.

Now What?

Now What?

Windy sits on the porch drinking tea the following morning after the visit from the Feds. The temperatures are tolerable now, but it appears it will be another hot sunny day.

She remembers Eacher pointing out that these Feds are dangerous, and their visit confirmed that assessment. These are aggressive people dealing in a world with many other rough people, and this isn't something Windy or Kirk needs to get mixed up with.

Windy enjoyed the discussion with Eacher. While he covered some material that she was already aware of, he did it compellingly and very simply. Paul and Rose seemed better prepared for the discussion than she had anticipated. Eacher's visit was the most exciting thing since they've been here.

Paul joins Windy on the porch. He tells her they've set up a meeting with their neighborhood defense group this evening and invites her and Kirk to join them. She agrees, and he hands her Eacher's flash drive before he heads off to the chicken coop.

Windy goes back inside and brings her computer out to the porch. She opens the flash drive and parses through a summary document describing the various materials available.

The first podcast examined various climate change theories. The first three focused on why the temperature in the tropics is stable at sea level.

- The Iris Effect is explained by changes in high-level clouds.

- The Thermostat Hypothesis suggests that clear skies are daily replaced by clouds and rain in a manner that regulates temperatures.

- Another theory contends that if ocean surface temperatures reach thirty-two degrees, evaporation rates accelerate and constrain further warming.

- The next part covered cosmic rays that bombard the Earth and induce more clouds when the Earth's magnetic defenses are the weakest.

- The last part dealt with the Winter Gatekeeper hypothesis, which outlined how various atmospheric processes transmit heat to the North Pole or the South Pole subject to a solar magnetic influence.

The second piece discussed how El Niño's push heat from the oceans into the atmosphere. Eacher identified those events with a small "x" above the years where they occurred. Here was the graph that Eacher included in the discussion.

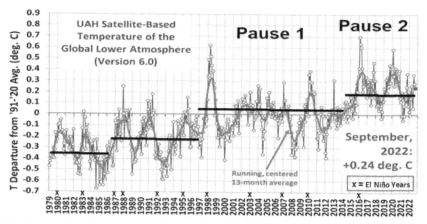

Windy enjoys these various perspectives, which accord with her intuition, though she quickly tires from the effort. She quickly scans the rest of the summaries, copies the files to her computer's hard drive, and turns her computer off. She removes the flash drive and sets it on the table.

Why would federal agents pursue a retired professor? The United States is not the country that she always imagined it to be. She wonders how long it's been like this.

Kirk steps out on the porch and looks at the computer and the memory stick on the table.

"You've got some opinions on what was discussed?" He sits down next to Windy and takes her hand in his.

"Look, I know you've always believed that I've given the Chinese government too much support on their policy choices, but look at the level of trust Americans gave their government." She said.

"Yes, I'd agree," Kirk said. "All this is very disturbing. What good is a democracy when so many people got fed a scientifically suspect story?"

"I don't know. It's your country. If this is what freedom looks like, it doesn't look much different from our brainwashing operations in China. I'm glad our government didn't get suckered into the same Net Zero path." Windy studies Kirk's expression to better understand what he's thinking. "Can you explain why your country would be chasing Eacher?"

"It makes no sense. Ten years ago he might have made a difference, but everyone is all so isolated now I can't imagine he could even be a nuisance." Kirk said. "My father died when I was just a baby. When I was old enough to go to school, Paul started sharing some of my father's oil scarcity concerns with me. I grew up expecting some energy adjustment, but nothing like the one that occurred. Why shut down skepticism if this country is afraid of carbon dioxide emissions? Why force so many companies out of business? Why abandon a reliable and secure energy system?"

"Yes, why do Paul and Rose have to worry about whether they can use the air conditioner during the summer in Arkansas? Why aren't grocery stores still filled with food? Why are so many of the roads disintegrating? Why was it so hard for us to simply travel from Houston to get here? It's tough to describe a worse transition." Windy said.

"Yes, I see your point," Kirk said.

"Would you like to listen to some of these podcasts?" Windy offers the computer to him.

"I don't know. It's way too technical for me. Who am I to judge which scientist is telling the truth?"

"You're right about that. It's all so complicated, especially when you have to disentangle the misinformation from the real science." She said. "I sure wouldn't want to live in this country. Americans have made it really hard on themselves and things are only going to get worse. Are you ready to go home?"

"No, I need more time. This might be my last chance to see my brother and his family."

"Let's not wait too long. If things deteriorate too quickly, we may not be able to get back."

The Candidate

Eacher starts paying more attention to the candidates for President. Curiously, there is almost no online information about the political challenger who won the opposition party's nomination.

He locates a schedule of events on the campaign website and learns that this Presidential Candidate will appear in Little Rock, Arkansas, at a particular place and on a specific day. Eacher makes plans to attend her event.

***

He locates the venue, a high school gymnasium. There are roughly fifteen people spread out in the bleachers on one side of the basketball court. He sits a few rows back in a pulled out section and listens intently. It's difficult to clearly understand her, since there is no sound system available to amplify her voice.

Eacher is the third and last person in line to speak with her afterward. When it's his turn, he notices that everyone else is gone. He is surprised that there are neither reporters nor campaign officials waiting to speak with her.

"Can I buy you a beer?" Eacher asked.

"Well, that's the best question I've had all day!" Jenny Almond said. "Where?"

"I noticed an Icehouse across the street." Eacher is shocked that she's available.

"Yes, that'd be terrific – as long as you're buying!"

They left the venue together and had no problem getting a table in the open air bar. The place was mostly empty, and they chose two seats not far from the swamp cooler.

Eacher bought the first two beers, and they sat back in their chairs and relaxed. He takes a quick selfie of the two of them sitting together.

"You got a particular issue that lights your boat?" Jenny asked.

"Yeah, this Net Zero policy has been a disaster! Eacher said.

"Well, you're talking to the right party." She said. "The other party is the one that implemented it and has kept their hands on the steering wheel ever since."

"Funny how that works," Eacher said. "You'd think climate science would be open to scientific scrutiny. Instead, it seems to pivot on which political party you belong to."

"Yeah, that about sizes it up," Jenny said. "Any reasons *why* you feel strongly about these issues?"

"Yes, I've got some background in the science. I still haven't figured out why our country's leaders believed it was legitimate. It's the biggest load of crap I've ever encountered, yet, it's considered taboo to argue otherwise."

"Yes, no argument there. It's definitely been a feeding trough for a lot of players. Congressmen, bureaucrats, regulators– the list goes on and on." Jenny said. "Even oil and gas companies didn't fight much when it allowed them to attack coal interests."

"You're telling me!" Eacher said. "To have gone 'all in' on Net Zero was about the least advisable thing I ever could have imagined. We abandoned fossil fuels before there were viable replacements. Those sources provided eighty-five percent of the world's energy, while wind and solar provided less than five percent. It's little wonder that we cratered our economy! Despite the absurd transition we allowed, global carbon dioxide emission levels are still increasing at the same rate worldwide. The fastest increases are from Asian countries that didn't sign up for this beat down."

"Man, if I was a rock band, I'd pick you to be my leadoff act. You're saying the same things that I've been saying all tour, yet virtually nothing that I say ever makes it into print, video, or the news."

"Well, I did find one of your campaign speeches on YouTube," Eacher said.

"Only until one of the high-tech companies learns that it's there and removes it for some spurious reason. Our government and their confederates ought to account for the damage they've done with their Net Zero policy, yet, that's never going to happen. If people had the right information and the confidence to believe it, I'd be our next President!"

"Jenny, you're definitely a woman that I can relate to. So, how much of the climate science do you really understand?"

"Only what I've read. What's your background?" Jenny said.

"Well, I'm a geologist focused on reconstructing our climate history based on rock interpretations. I'm as capable a climate scientist specialist as anyone else in the business." Eacher said.

"Well, that's good to know. Tell you what, let me share my contact information with you, and please forward me anything that I ought to be paying more attention to." Jenny said.

"Well, here's a flash drive for starters," Eacher said. "Also, I'll reply to your text message with my contact information. I'll do my best to be as responsive as possible."

"I really need to get going. I've got to meet a Girl Scout troop at a local middle school." She said. "It's a ridiculously long shot I'd ever get elected. My opponent has all the rich people on her side and the soup kitchen vote. I promise you, though, if I were President, we'd dump Net Zero in a hurry."

"Hell, I thought climate skeptics were underdogs, but you're really a long shot for this election!"

She smiled a wry sort of smile, then stood up and tapped him twice on the shoulder before walking out the bar and onto the sidewalk. That gesture also had the additional benefit of assuring the bartender that someone else was picking up the cost of her drink.

Eacher remained seated and watched her mount her scooter and head off down the road. While her candor was refreshing, he recognized that she had no chance of winning a national election."

The Meeting

Rose insists that Paul turn the air conditioner on for their community meeting. They both know the financial risk but want their neighbors to focus on the discussion, not the temperature.

Rose opens up an app on her phone that shows the local electricity spot price. She can glance at it during the meeting to reassure herself that they aren't getting hammered on electricity charges at that moment.

There are about twenty-five people in the room, and Rose recognizes almost everyone. Few new people have moved into the area in recent years. Some of the neighbors look seriously underfed, and she suspects that current events might have been harder on them than others.

Some walked, but the rest rode scooters that now sit in the driveway next to Bart's pickup truck. He's a living legend in the area, and his land holdings are the largest in the county. Stories about the size and scope of his farming business have been whispered among the neighbors for years. He once ran for state office and came close to winning. His farming operations ended when his wife died a few years earlier, and it's rumored that he now lives off mail order food that he buys with his savings.

Rose asks for everyone to sit down, some find room on the furniture, and the rest sit on the floor. She reads the names on the group list and checks off each attendee's name with a pen.

She then proceeds to talk about the recent search of their property. She omits that Eacher was at their house at the time. She describes the search without a warrant, the audio-video device, and the loss of the chicken.

The group is in shock. An outside intrusion, especially by agents operating at the national level, is hard to rationalize. If they really wanted to search, why didn't they get a warrant?

Rose then points out her belief that these are federal agents looking for some terrorist. She passes around the business card as evidence of the claimed credentials.

The group becomes very unsettled. The idea that there is a dangerous subversive in the area is disturbing. Still, it would explain the interest of federal agents.

A massive farmer named Spike is the first to speak. "These people also came to my house and searched. We didn't know about the monitoring device, but we'll look for one when we get home. What does it look like?"

Rose describes the listening video device as a little black box with a small piece of glass on one side that can be stuck to the wall. "In our case, it's planted in that room where our guests are staying." She points to the guestroom. "Let me introduce my brother-in-law, Kirk, and his wife, Windy."

Windy and Kirk stand up and wave at the rest of the crowd. Kirk remains standing and explains that they once saw a similar spy device in a museum in China. He also notes that they found this device right after the Feds left, so he's confident they left it and firmly believes they are monitoring it.

Others confirm that they have been searched too. Someone mentions that they've seen the same truck and people driving around on a local road.

"Should we be concerned about this person they are looking for? Why or how could he harm us?" Someone asked.

"That's something I can't address because I've never met him," Rose said.

"I'd recommend that we all keep an eye out for him but also keep track of these federal agents," Bart said. "Given their apparent willingness to operate without warrants, I don't trust them at all."

Rose gets the room's attention again. "We're all a lot more independent these days. Almost all of us grow our own food. In our case, we hardly buy anything from the outside world, and I know that we are much more unplugged than we used to be. However, this situation reminds me that freedom is a team sport. It's not about us standing alone or isolating ourselves from other locals or the rest of the world. That's suicide. It's about shared respect and our relationships with our families and friends. It's about being there when one of our neighbors needs us."

"Listen to this lady. She's making a lot of sense." Bart said.

"We need a plan and volunteers," Rose said.

"Agreed," Bart said. "Let's continue to utilize our group text messages to send out warnings when we each need help. Can someone put together an updated map that shows where everyone lives?"

Rose steps forward again. "Yes, I'll take care of it. Just list your current email and telephone numbers on the sign-in sheet. I've placed an old quad map of our area on the table; draw in your house and property boundaries and reference them with the number on the sign-in sheet. I'll assemble this information, scan it, and share it with the group."

"Do we need a horn too?" Someone asked.

"The horn approach is too complicated. If you've got one and have a threat, feel free to blow it; the problem is that it won't really confirm where you are or what's going on. More importantly, send an emergency text message and email to the group showing where we need to go and what you're up against." Rose said.

"Should we elect a sheriff or commander?" Someone asked.

"Probably not. I'd recommend we simply keep this neighborhood group available for mutual assistance. You can use the group distribution list for emergencies and anything else the group needs to know. We need to start behaving a lot more like an active militia." Rose said.

"I agree," Paul said. "Who here has a gun or other useful weapon?"

"We've all got guns," Bart said. "The question is, who still here has ammo? As we are all aware, getting bullets these days is not easy. You know the post office has instructions not to deliver ammunition without specific government approval."

"That sounds right," Paul said. "I've got just a few rounds left myself, and if I had more, I'd go deer hunting."

"What are you packing?" Bart asked.

"I've got a 12 gauge shotgun and a few birdshot rounds."

159

"Then you're in luck. I can give you a half box of buckshot, and that should do the trick." Bart said. "The best thing about shotguns is that their shot group is scattered; you still have a chance of hitting your target - even if that weapon is poorly zeroed or badly aimed."

"Thanks!" Paul said. "Does anyone else have any issues?"

Several others requested assistance with ammunition. Bart took notes and promised to deliver their requirements by the next day.

"Anything else?" Paul asked.

"One God-damned wind turbine is driving me crazy." Spike said. Half the year, the blade flicker is right on my house. I still can't understand why they located that damn machine where it would do this to my family; we were here first! Bart, can I borrow your buckshot too?"

"You know buckshot is not really effective on wind turbine blades." Bart hesitated for a while, thinking carefully about what he would say next. "Have you considered dynamite? Lucky for you, I've got a box of that too."

"Someone tell the Feds we found their terrorist!" A woman's voice in the back joked.

Everyone laughed, but Spike was very interested in the explosives and wanted to know when he could pick some up.

"Spike, you know I was kidding. Right?" Bart said.

"Of course. But, if you've got an extra stick or two of dynamite, I'd be happy to buy those off of you." Spike said. "You never know what you might be able to use something like that for."

"Spike, I was just teasing you," Bart said. He coughs and moves as if he is in considerable pain. Years in the sun have been hard on his health, and he looks a lot older since his wife died. "By the way, I've got a birthday party at my house on Saturday, August tenth, in the evening," Bart said. "You're all invited."

This last comment ends the meeting, and everyone hangs around talking. Rose asks Paul to turn off the air conditioning and he rushes to turn it off.

Rose tries to rid her mind of the image of Spike using dynamite to destroy a wind turbine. That could never happen, right?

***

Windy and Kirk form a plan to deal with the electronic bug planted in their bedroom.

That night, they make a point to take off their clothes and occupy the twin bed farthest from the sensor. They quickly turn off the lights and get active. They previously rehearsed making obscene noises out in the woods, which now makes the room sound like a pornographic movie.

Once their sex is in progress, the fact that others might be listening stimulates Windy more than she had anticipated. Suffice it to say she really enjoys the sex.

They don't know what is recorded but want to be sure that the people that planted the device do not suspect that Windy and Kirk know about its existence.

Windy accompanies Kirk the next day, who casually locates that suspicious object in the exact location mapped on Eacher's screen. He places a tall dining room chair in front of it and then throws a coat over the back of the chair to obstruct the view of the monitoring device. During this adjustment, he gets a good look at it. It has been put in place at a height where it has a full view of the bed. This is encouraging in a perverted kind of way. The placement suggests that these agents are more interested in seeing bedroom action than trying to find evidence related to Eacher. They are careful not to say anything they shouldn't in that bedroom and try to keep the bedroom door closed as much as possible.

They had agreed to mention that Windy was on her period each night and avoid sex.

However, that's not the way it worked out. Windy found the energy for some of the most passionate sex that she could remember every night that week. They did their best to keep the noise to a low level that could not be heard in the adjacent bedrooms, but that monitoring device got an earful. Suffice it to say, Windy learned something about the way she's wired.

The video transmitter has been in place for a week when Windy sees Kirk remove it and take it outside. She hears him smashing it with a hammer on a rock outdoors. She's actually sad to see it go for some strange reason. Kirk suggests that they can pretend it's still there.

She brightens up when she hears this suggestion.

A Party
AUGUST

Windy and Kirk help out around the house more, but without air conditioning, they lack the enthusiasm to do much work inside. The bugs seem to be constantly biting, and she spends a lot of time washing her nicer clothes by hand in the sink and hanging them out on the clothesline. The water has a yellow tint, so clothes that were previously white are now more of an almond color.

Paul knows he is scheduled to start his class assistance in early September. Windy notices Paul working on his lesson reviews.

Bart's house isn't far, and they walk over together rather than try to fit on the scooters. There are still several hours before the party is scheduled to start, and they want to show up early and assist Bart with anything he needs. They lock the gate and walk along the side of the road.

When they are still a few blocks away, they smell the meat cooking on the grills; it smells delicious. Windy has wanted to try authentic southern barbecue since the vegetarian barbecue experience in Houston.

Clare looks confused. She doesn't recognize the smell and wonders out loud if something is on fire. The other four in her group are already salivating and reassure her that this is not the case.

When they reach the picnic area behind Bart's house, he is already in the back, sitting under a large tree. Some of his neighbors are in charge of the cooking and are busily working.

"Bart, thanks for having us!" Paul said. "You remember Kirk and Windy?"

"Sure, I remember your brother and his wife. I'm hard of hearing, not senile." He said.

"How'd you get the meat?" Paul asked.

"Let's just say that I've got my connections." He coughs gently. "That's an entire bull you're looking at."

"It smells wonderful!" Rose said. "Do you need any help?"

"No, but you go on over there and give them feedback on how it tastes."

They quickly move to the folding tables set up for the occasion at this invitation. Paul and Rose start making themselves plates of food.

There is also a beer keg on tap with two other barrels sitting in reserve next to it. No one knows where Bart has been able to get either the booze or the ice it sits in. This is going to be an expensive event for Bart.

Clare looks puzzled by what her family is doing. When she sees the meat on their plates, she recoils. "That's gross!"

"I'm sorry, honey," Paul said. "Perhaps you're right." He then quickly stuffs a quarter of a hamburger into his mouth and barely chews it before he reaches for the next piece.

"Yes, dear, I see your point," Rose said. The last part of this sentence is almost unintelligible as she takes a large bite of brisket, which has been slowly roasted on a different grill.

Windy and Kirk are less thrilled with the food and feel no compulsion to gorge themselves since they often eat meat.

Clare distances herself from the grill area and sits under a tree to wait for one of her friends to show up. She takes a plate of grilled vegetables and potato salad with her.

Windy walks over and sits down next to Clare. She hands Clare a half glass of beer. Clare takes a sip and makes a face, but she doesn't pour it out. "What do you think of the party?"

"I can't believe they're eating meat!" Clare said.

"Smells okay?" Windy asked. "Please understand that I respect your decision not to eat meat. There is something very spiritually enlightening to avoid doing things that result in the deaths of innocent animals."

"Yes, but how could my parents enjoy eating it so much? This is uncivilized!"

"How so?" Windy said.

"Do you know that raising cattle generates a lot of pollution?"

"I've heard those claims."

"It pollutes the water, releases methane, and leads to global warming."

"Yes, I've heard those opinions too."

"It's better for the planet if we are all vegetarians," Clare said.

"Clare, we have our share of vegetarians in China. Sometimes they have religious reasons, and sometimes it's just a lifestyle choice. Our government does not dictate our diet unless you're a prisoner. At the same time, I can respect the decisions of those who choose to consume meat, something most of my ancestors enjoyed."

"Windy, it's inhumane to kill animals for food," Clare said.

"Did your parents teach you that?"

"Not so much. You see how Mom and Dad are behaving."

Windy looks over to Paul and Rose, standing in line at the grills. "When did they teach you the importance of vegetarianism in school?"

"Well, it's been part of our school lessons since elementary school. Our high school cafeteria also doesn't serve meat."

"All the kids went along with that?"

"No, a number of them brought their own lunches, which included meat sandwiches. The teachers rarely disciplined us when we teased those students by calling them 'carnivores' and other names."

"I see. What do your teachers teach you in school about China?"

"China is a country that uses a lot of energy and releases a lot of carbon dioxide pollution."

"Anything else?" She recognizes that this is definitely a one-dimensional view of her country.

"China makes a lot of stuff that gets sold in the US."

"True." This discussion brings to mind some of the opinions now circulating in China. There is a cultural perception in the United States that communists brainwash their kids. To some extent, it's an accurate observation. Windy understands the level of patriotism and communist party support that is

165

messaged in the schools in China, along with certain opinions on Hong Kong, Taiwan, Tibet, and the South China Sea. The students in China are also given cultural values from their media and movie developers about the importance of education, marriage, children, and honoring their elders. What's remarkable, however, is that the same Americans who recognize this phenomenon in other countries are oblivious to it here. They overlook the reality that American kids are also deliberately programmed on many issues. These values seem more suspect from her vantage point. There is no need to marry, children are a burden, and mankind is a blight on the planet and the climate. These values are very different from those shared in past generations. "Are you worried about the future?"

"No. Once every country follows a Net Zero path, the climate will never change again." Clare looks confident with this viewpoint.

"They teach you that at school?" Windy notes that this is the type of rubbish that the children in the west are fed. There is little validity to these types of assertions, yet they are made persistently by teachers in positions of trust.

"Yes."

"Maybe you can't just accept everything you're taught?" Windy suspects Clare understands none of the finer points she is trying to make. Children should not be waking up during the night with nightmares of Earth overheating, at least not until there is more compelling scientific evidence than there is now.

"I'll try to keep that in mind,"

"Is there any question you want to ask me?"

"Is China going to stop eating meat?"

"Let me see, how can I answer that? Ever have a bite of beef?" Windy feels terrible about going down this path with Clare. Not eating meat has been drilled into these kids. Were they left alone to make these personal decisions without such pressure, the emergence of a vegetarian diet could be interpreted as both sincere and spiritual.

"Nope."

"How do you think it would taste?"

"My God, it must taste horrible!" Clare appears very concerned.

Windy gets up, walks over to the grill, grabs a slice of brisket and a petite sirloin from the serving area, and places it on a paper plate. She walks back over to where Clare is sitting.

"Any interest?" Windy moves the plate back and forth in front of Clare.

"No, of course not!"

"My mistake. Just throw this plate away for me." Windy hands the plate to her and then walks back to the party.

Clare just holds the plate as if it contains a dead sparrow; she seems somewhat worried that one of her classmates might see her with it. She watches Windy walk in the opposite direction. Then Clare stands up, turns her back to the party, and takes a few steps towards the woods. A few minutes later, she returned to where she was sitting with the empty plate.

Windy has been watching her from a distance. She grabs a cheeseburger and a sausage and carries both in a napkin to Clare. It's not that Windy gets any pleasure showing Clare that at least part of the programming at school is incorrect. Still, it's something Clare needs to understand for her own mental health going forward. Most likely, she'll continue to be exposed to a lot of scaremongering.

This time Clare says nothing, accepts the gift, and gives Windy an appreciative nod.

"Clare, there is nothing wrong with being a vegetarian, but there is also nothing wrong with being a carnivore. We should find a way to have respect for both and compassion for the animals involved." Point made. Windy returns to look for Kirk. She looks back towards Clare and watches her bite into the sausage.

The crowd has increased in size. Most of the newcomers have the same reaction to the food that Rose and Paul did. They would politely say hello to Bart and then rush to the grill. Country music is blasting over the loudspeakers.

167

"Happy Birthday Bart!" Someone shouts, and others echo it around the yard.

Bart just sits in his chair and enjoys the party. He is the center of discussion and enjoys his share of the refreshments. The party is truly a unique respite from their regular farming duties.

When it comes time for Bart to speak, he stands up and walks toward a small raised platform with the assistance of a cane and the arm of one of the other guests. Some people wander over to the area in front of the stage. A spontaneous Happy Birthday song is launched after the music is turned off. When the singing dies out, Bart flicks on a microphone and a switch that activates several light sets that brightly light up the stage and the grill area.

"Friends, many thanks for joining me at this party. I hope you're enjoying the food and drink!" The crowd gives him a long round of applause. "When you've lived as long as I have, you've had a lot of parties, and I want this one to be extraordinary. I've got an invited guest here that I want you to listen to for a second. It was actually harder to get him here than it was to get the beef and beverage. Let me introduce my good friend, Eacher." Bart steps off the stage with some assistance and motions for Eacher to take his place.

Eacher walks up to the microphone and taps it once to confirm it's on. He then introduces himself. He mentions that he is trying to set the country straight about various climate-related issues. As he starts speaking, a few more people move to the area in front of the pedestal. Windy notices that the lines to the beer and the food aren't getting shorter.

"How many of you think our climate is too hot?" Eacher said.

"It'd be fine with air conditioning!" Windy shouts. Several people look at her curiously.

"That's the right answer. There might have been a little warming over the last two centuries, but it hasn't been much. None of us can honestly claim that we've noticed a difference."

A buzz of noise starts in the crowd as people start whispering.

"The slight warming that has occurred has likely been from natural causes and beneficial for us. If you still have fertilizer and seeds, your plants are doing great. How can anyone argue that our present climate is dangerous?"

The audience is quiet.

"Who cares about average global temperature anyway? It's our local temperatures that matter, and those are fine!"

The crowd near the platform remains hushed for some reason. Some noisy side discussions are going on closer to the food and drink.

"We've now got about eight and a half billion people worldwide, great food production, and a rising standard of living outside the United States and Europe. Does this seem like a good time to play Russian roulette with mankind's access to energy?"

The crowd is starting to get antsy. The attendees haven't come to the party to get a lecture. A few people begin to move away from the stage.

"Taking away most of our access to gasoline and reliable electricity was a colossal mistake. The fossil fuels we aren't allowed to use are being consumed by others; OPEC is still in business and doing quite well. Our chosen carbon dioxide reduction efforts have weakened us with little benefit!" Eacher is clearly on a roll.

"I miss my truck." Someone shouts.

"Then maybe you should send it a postcard. It's probably still on the road in Asia somewhere!" Eacher said. "It's time to stop this Net Zero program. Our climate is not a concern or a problem; if it ever becomes one, we should worry about any specific problems that occur whenever or wherever they arise. It's time to say, 'enough is enough.' The climate policy and the politicians implementing it are our primary danger!" Eacher's voice has reached a crescendo at these last remarks.

The crowd is still strangely quiet, and nothing is said for fifteen seconds.

"Look, I'm done. Bart just wanted me to say a few words at this birthday party. Happy Birthday, Bart! I hope you have many more. By the way, Bart bought fifty thumb drives with my latest set of podcasts. It's a take-home gift for each and every one of you. Feel free to copy it and feel free to share it. We need to get the word out. Just understand that the government apparently considers these materials threatening. Be careful who you share them with."

At this point, some of the relatively sober people in the crowd start to look worried. They look left and right to see who else might have seen them listening to these remarks. This is not something you'd expect to hear at a celebration.

Bart moves back onto the stage and grabs the mic. He waves at Eacher as if he's a magician. "Listen to this guy. You won't hear these insights from anywhere else. Get the word out, and don't forget your flash drive!" Bart said. After these final remarks, the music starts playing again. A few folks linger, but everyone else moves away from the platform and back towards the refreshments.

Eacher hands a small cardboard box to Bart and then gestures goodbye to the group. He then rides off on his scooter.

The party continues until all the food and alcohol run out. Then the crowd just kind of fades away. Some are so drunk that they just pass out; they now lie where they fell.

Their entire family, including Clare, gets a flash drive from Bart, who looks pleased by their interest in these materials.

At the end of the evening, they say their goodbyes to Bart and profusely thank him for the invitation and hospitality. He is touched by their appreciation and tells them how much it means to him for them to be there. He seems very tired but content.

They then carefully step around those unconscious in the yard and make their way out the front gate. They head back home together along the side of the road in a festive mood. There are few clouds, and the almost full moon lights their way.

Windy wonders what might have happened had the feds crashed their party and hopes no one in this area ever runs into them again.

Aftermath

Paul sees the Feds drive by his farm several times over the next few days. It is the same truck with two different guys and the same woman.

Paul has received the ammo that Bart promised and keeps his gun fully loaded and at the ready. He does not want to shoot at law enforcement or government agents, but he's got a bad feeling about them. Paul will not sit by doing nothing if the Feds threaten his property or family.

Paul and Rose both get a text message and an email that Bart's farmhouse is on fire.

Paul and Kirk jump on a scooter, and Windy and Rose follow them on the other one. They race to Bart's house and arrive quickly.

His gate is open, and the gate chain is lying in the driveway with a severed lock. His main house is on fire, and flames have already ignited his roof. Paul quickly locates Bart on the ground in the backyard wheezing a small distance from his home. "What happened?" Paul asked.

"Those damn Feds." He said. "They broke into my house in pursuit of the remaining flash drives that Eacher gave me."

"Did they get them?" Paul asked.

"Only a few that I had left. Lit my drapes on fire and took off."

"Unbelievable!" Kirk said. "Where's your hose?"

"Forget about the house," Bart said. "It's too late to save it, and I don't want anyone else getting hurt. I'm screwed, but let it go."

"You sent out the alarm."

"They took my regular phone. Luckily, I had a spare stashed in the barn. Not sure what you can really do."

Bart's leg is bleeding. "What happened?" Paul asked.

"Those bastards shot me. Don't think they thought I'd be able to make it out of the house."

"Let me help you," Windy said.

The blaze is still expanding, and the ground is warm where they are sitting. Paul and Kirk move him farther from the fire.

"Did you call 911?" Paul asked.

"Yes."

"What about your water well?" Kirk asked.

"You can't use it. The electrical lines are fried. Stay away from the fire." Bart said.

It takes several hours for most of the blaze to go out. It has rained recently, so there is less risk that the flames will set the rest of the property on fire.

"We need to get you to the hospital," Rose said. "Do you have fuel in your truck?"

"Yeah, but the keys were in the house," Bart said.

They are all sitting around with Bart cradled between them. It's an eerie feeling watching a lifetime of memories roasted. Rose calls 911 too and requests an ambulance for a gunshot wound. No emergency vehicles have shown up yet, and it has been hours since Bart's call to them.

Paul continues to apply pressure to Bart's wound, hoping to stop the bleeding.

They discuss the situation and agree they should not attempt to transport him on a scooter. Rose looks up a medical advice website and connects to a technician that insists that they apply a tourniquet to stop the bleeding. Windy removes the old bandage and uses a strip of her silk shirt and a stick to apply one to Bart's thigh.

Bart passes out. He's tough, but old and not in good health.

The ambulance shows up in the morning, and they can't revive him. Once the emergency technicians confirm that he's dead, they simply leave his body where they found it.

Windy and Rose return home.

Paul and Kirk find a shovel in the barn, and they get help from others who respond to the emergency. They dig a hole about six feet deep near some other tombstones in the backyard. They gently place the body in the ground without a casket and cover the grave back up. Kirk takes a piece of wood from the charred remains of the house and drives it in the dirt as a temporary grave marker. Paul paces off the distance from a nearby tree and records the details in his phone for future reference.

When Paul and Kirk arrive home, they find Windy and Rose asleep.

Paul and Kirk are exhausted. They each take a cool shower to remove the filth from their skin and go to bed.

***

Later in the day, Paul sits on the porch, thinking about the previous day's events.

"That house could have been ours," Rose said as she walked out onto the porch. "They could have burned *our* place down."

"Yes, but why would they?" Paul asked.

"Not sure, but I believe it's got something to do with the material that Eacher is trying to distribute."

"Yes, but we didn't create it, and you and I aren't exactly on board with it."

"No, but it's menacing nevertheless." She said. "Where have we put the flash drives that he gave us?"

"I've got a copy on my computer, and we've now got maybe six of them that I know of."

"Well, I've got two of my own that you're probably not counting," Rose said. "What should we do with them?"

"Honestly? I'd like to listen to it in great detail." This is a hard admission for him to make. He has been a trusting government supporter and hasn't changed his opinion or concerns about climate change. Still, he's curious why the government is so committed to suppressing Eacher. Whatever happened to Freedom of Speech?

"Me too. Bart gave his life supporting this guy's cause. I'd like to better understand why." Rose said.

"So, where can we hide this material, so it doesn't get our house toasted?" Paul said. The idea that they could be next is something that haunted him in his dreams earlier in the day.

"First, get it off your computer; that's too obvious a place to store it. Next, let's keep these disks together for better accountability. We don't want any one of them accidentally left lying around. Let's put them in your hiding place in the back bedroom for now." She said.

"Agreed. Can you collect any copies that Kirk, Clare, or Windy have?" Paul pulls out his computer and turns it on.

"I'll ask them when they wake up. We'll consider the hiding place our special library. We can't discuss this material online or mention it to anyone outside our family."

"Agreed," Paul said. "Want to listen to a podcast?"

"Not now. Let's give it some time to let all this blow over."

"Oh shit. You're right. Now that those Feds know that some people in the area have been exposed to Eacher, they might get aggressive; his ideas are a virus they might want to stamp out."

"Yes. You're right. I'll secure these right now along with my computer." Paul pauses for a second and notices the sweltering heat building on the porch. "God, it's going to be another hot day."

"Morning," Kirk said, coming out on the porch.

"Morning," Rose replied.

"How you guys holding up?" Kirk asked.

"About as well as can be expected. Rough day yesterday." Paul said.

"Yes, but I woke up a while ago with something bothering me," Kirk said.

"Yes?" Rose asked.

"What is it that we didn't hear during the fire?" Kirk said.

"I don't know. Popcorn?" Paul said, not sure what point Kirk was trying to make.

"Kind of. Do you remember the meeting at our house?"

174

"Yes." Paul replayed the discussion in his mind, and then it hit him. "You mean the dynamite?"

"Yes, and the ammo. As the house was burning, we didn't hear any explosions."

"Do you think the Feds took it?" Rose asked.

"No, I don't believe they would have thought to look for it. It must still be there somewhere." Kirk said.

"You're right. If we find it, what should we do with it? Will we be exposed if we bring it here?" Rose said.

"Let's take a look," Paul said.

***

That evening, just after dark, Paul and Kirk walk to Bart's house. Everything appears pretty much as they had left it. Some unrecognizable metal shards are sitting on the slab, which they believe are the residual steel skeletons of various appliances and fixtures. The fireplace still stands without any adjoining walls. Very little else is left.

They walk to the barn, and the door is unlocked. It has stalls that once held horses, and a diesel tractor is still sitting below a hay loft. They look around with a flashlight.

There is a small room with a lock on the door that has been busted off. Most likely, this is a room that once held the horse harnesses and tools.

They continue to search around the barn. The brothers inspect the loft and find nothing. They scan the floor for trap doors but don't see any. There are no more apparent areas where something could be stashed in the central portion of the barn. Paul pulls the entrance to the small room open and walks inside, and Kirk follows him.

The shelves contain open toolboxes and various automotive fluids in half-empty containers.

Kirk taps the plywood of the cabinet, and discovers a section that looks unfinished.

Paul opens the doors next to it on both sides, and this section seems hollow. Paul continues to focus on it and discovers a small piece of metal just below the counter top. When he presses it, a hidden door swings open. Inside are metal boxes and a wooden crate. "Holy Shit," Paul said. "We've found his arsenal! Now what?"

They remove the items and take inventory. There are about a dozen boxes of ammunition of all caliber, a wooden case of dynamite, something labeled C4, and several steel ammo cans full of various items. The total weight is too heavy for Paul and Kirk to carry home in a single trip. The ammunition is primarily stored in boxes placed within gallon-sized plastic storage bags to keep it air-tight.

"Most of this stuff is illegal for us to own," Paul said. "Why again would we want to bring it to our place?"

"Well, if it were mine and I could find a place to store it without causing notice, it seems like it could be useful to have," Kirk said.

"Useful for what?"

"I don't know. You have a right to defend yourself, even if the government doesn't agree." Kirk said.

"Is it really defensive when we have dynamite and explosives? I would think of them as something that could be used for an offense of some type." Paul listens closely to see if he can hear other noises around the barn. He also wonders if someone might have planted a listening device in this barn.

"Look, we need to get out of here. No telling when someone is going to return to this property. If we're still here and someone shows up, these materials will be hard to explain – even if they're not ours.

If we just leave them out in the open, there is no telling who will get them. If we bury these materials here, we'll probably never be able to retrieve them. That is, if we ever wanted to."

"You know, I'd doubt we'd ever want to retrieve them. So, I'm okay with simply burying these items as long as we do so away from the house. If we can remember where we buried them, we might have the option to return and get them. It's dangerous to have them on our property." Paul said.

Kirk can't argue with this reasoning. He grabs a shovel that they find in the barn. The two carry part of these materials from the house to the fence. They deliberately choose a location only about two hundred feet from the main road but out of sight of the road and the barn. It is dark, and many pine trees block the light from the moon.

Paul turns on his flashlight to provide some light.

Kirk starts digging. He has to cut through some thick tree roots which takes a little time. Once through, he continues deeper. The dirt about a foot down has a pungent smell that makes it hard to breathe. He then encounters a clay layer that takes a while to penetrate.

Paul makes several more trips to the barn. He carries the rest of the ammunition, explosives, and other associated materials to this location. He also brings a large piece of canvas on the last trip. They set aside a small handgun in a plastic storage case and a portion of the ammunition that Paul could use. In addition, they keep a few gun cleaning toolkits.

They take turns digging, and the final hole is about five feet deep. Paul sets the canvas on the bottom, and they pile the various items on top. When done, they fold the stiff fabric over the materials, throw the dirt they removed back in the hole, and step on it to pack it down. They mark the location by stepping off the distance and using the compass on Paul's phone to note the azimuth from a recognizable post set in concrete visible from the road.

The two then walk back along the road and are prepared to dart into the woods if they see any headlights. Thirty minutes later, they are back home.

The memorable part of this explosive storage story isn't whether what they are doing makes any sense. It's a big step from anger to stockpiling explosives. Storing these resources feels empowering, even if they aren't on their property. Had Bart not been killed, they would not be following this path.

They bring everything into the barn when they return to the house. Rose hears them return and walks into the barn.

Paul and Kirk are startled when she announces her presence with "Nice arsenal, cowboys. You guys planning on going to war?"

"Oh, these are just some goodies we found in Bart's barn," Paul said.

"Any luck finding the dynamite?" She inspects both of them in the limited light. "Why are you covered in dirt?"

"Well, let's just say we found some other firecrackers," Paul said.

"And you buried them at Bart's place." She said.

"What?" Paul asked.

"I'd have known if you had buried it here. Please tell me exactly what you found and how much of it." She starts looking at the items laid out.

Paul goes through a description of the items they buried.

Rose nods like she understands exactly what they are describing and knows how to use it. "Look, we don't want that stuff here, but it's reassuring to know we have access."

"Reassuring?" There are times like this when Paul doesn't understand where Rose finds her tenacity. They now have a few more bullets, yet Rose is already contemplating what she can do with the explosives they buried at Bart's farm.

Rose gives them an explanation of her interest in these munitions. "Look, we're all a lot more on our own these days. You can't get a sheriff, an ambulance, or a fire truck to show up when you need them. The feds may have even declared war on us, given recent events. If we ever deal with bad guys, we'll have a few more resources to defend ourselves."

"So, you're okay with our having access to those explosives?" Paul starts moving the ammunition into storage containers in their barn.

"Damn right. Hopefully, we'll never need them." Rose picks up the small gun and starts loading the magazine with ammo. "This one is mine."

"No problem, here's a cleaning kit for it. Time for bed." Paul said.

Together
SEPTEMBER, THE LOST WOODS

Eacher has been on the road for two months after their last get-together. He has returned to the Lost Woods to assist Irene with her debate preparation.

They had stayed in touch and spoken with some regularity for a while, and then he could not reach her. He doesn't even know if she's here at this time.

Eacher is aware of a number of the challenges she has faced in her outreach program. Irene knows about the close calls that Eacher faced in Arkansas.

When he checks with Dora, she tells him that Irene's guest room is adjacent to his in a separate building from the one they had stayed in before. This information is exhilarating for him.

Shortly after Eacher locates her room, he knocks lightly to see if she's in. Her door opens just a bit, and she speaks to him from the other side. "Eacher, is that you?" She asked faintly.

"Yes, would you like to come to my room or somewhere else so we can start your debate preparation?"

"You can come in, but please talk to me first," Irene whispers.

"Ae you okay?" The sound of her voice is profoundly different and nothing like the spirited woman he knows. He pushes a little more firmly, testing to see if the door will open further. He feels a determined resistance from the other side to stop him from entering. He takes a step back.

"Can we talk about what happened?" Eacher asked softly.

"This country is not a safe place to travel alone."

"I know what you mean," Eacher said instinctively, but he didn't. Yes, what they were doing was dangerous, but what exactly had happened to her. Eacher's concern and anxiety rapidly increased, and he felt his pulse racing.

"The problems started just after we finished at the ranch and after a few friends and family visits. I struggled to find friendly forums where I could casually talk to people. A woman alone on the road these days sends the wrong message. I initially tried to stay in more populated towns, but the only people that were easy to interact with were getting tanked in saloons."

"Are you okay?" Eacher is less interested in hearing the story than hearing how it ends.

"No."

"How can I help?" Eacher whispers. He pushes gently on the door once again, and this time it swings open without further resistance. He enters to see Irene facing the far wall with her back facing him. A single bedside light is on. "I'm here."

"I feel you." She said.

"He's at a loss of words, tears welling down his face. He is content to simply be on this side of the door for the moment. He gently closes the entry door behind him and waits for her to speak again.

"I was driving on a country road by myself when a gang saw me drive by. Those monsters pursued me, and I used my acceleration to outrun them. I also hit the smoke and left them in a cloud behind me. Everything worked as hoped. However, they managed to catch up with me later in the day when I had parked my bike in a secluded part of the woods to camp. When they noticed that my bike had a biometric device that prevented it from operating without my index finger, they removed that finger. They violated me in every way you could imagine. One guy with a skull tattoo on the front of his upper neck seemed to direct most of the violence. They left me naked, raw, and bleeding. They took everything and left me dead in a ditch. Mike had installed an emergency locator under my skin, and I pressed that button before passing out. I woke up here several days later."

Eacher thinks to say something, but words seem too angular and invasive. Tears well up again, and he collapses to his knees. "Irene, why wasn't I with you? I would have died rather than let them do that to you."

"Yes, you would have died, and I would have had an even greater loss," she said.

He stood up. "May I?" was all he could muster.

"Maybe," she said barely audibly.

He gradually advances to where she stands. He places his hand on her shoulder. She tilts her head to touch it with her cheek and then flicks off the light switch by her bed; this leaves the room in darkness. He uses his hands to softly massage both her shoulders. Initially, she shrinks away from his every touch.

He tries to avoid her skin, which seems to relax her slightly, and allows him to envelop her with his arms around her robe. After a short while, he brushes her hair away from her face. As she brings her hand to meet his, he can feel the nub of her index finger, and he shudders involuntarily when he notices it.

"I had no idea." He said. "No one let me know you were here."

"I wasn't ready for visitors." Irene choked back a sob.

He stays there, holding her in the darkness. He tries to reassure her by holding her as tenderly as possible, but she is too tense. He simply says as many reassuring things as he can think of.

She slumps to the floor, and he follows her, trying to cradle her. Soon she falls asleep in his arms, and he lies next to her, trying not to awaken her. After a while, he gets up to go to the bathroom. When he returns, he can hear her breathing on the mattress. He dares not approach her on the bed in the dark and quietly returns to his room.

***

The next day, he was told she did not want to see him. It hurt not to be able to be part of the healing she needed, but he wanted to support the distance she wanted.

He received a second text message asking if he was willing to meet with the new climate skeptic fellows. They were available at 10 am if he was interested. He replied that he'd be there.

Eacher walked into the same classroom where he had seen Mike's hologram. Two men and a woman were in the room, along with Dora. Eacher sat there just listening to the discussion for a while.

They gathered some observations regarding how adaptation was better than mitigation. The economic consequences might be local, and there would be some benefits. This was a moot point for the United States; the damage had already been inflicted and had been profound.

They wrapped up their discussions and turned their attention to Eacher.

"Is there anything you wished you'd have known when you sat where we now sit in this program?" One of the men asked.

"Well, yes. I can reassure you that Mike is not using this program to execute you. That was a nagging doubt when I was in your position."

There was a chuckle among the group at this response.

"Is there any advice you'd be willing to share?" The woman asked.

"Honestly, I don't know what benefit we're serving trying to educate the public. In general, the masses are not particularly aware that they need to be schooled, and there's little they can do about it."

"Please stick to the questions," Dora asked.

"Program design is something you should bring up with Mike if you have any issues."

"You're right. I'm sorry. I would guess that there is value in working together. The two of us that graduated from my program worked independently." Eacher said. "I'm not saying it will be any worse for men or women, and I was lucky to escape a few times."

"Was all the training useful?"

"The physical fitness part of this training made me think I was younger. Even so, I never lost sight of the reality that it put me at risk of serious injury. Most of us are old, and I don't know how many effective years we still get. In my case, my memory is not what it should be. Perhaps we are near the end of our shelf life; there's a limit to how long we can be useful."

The program participants sat quietly while they contemplated his words. Dora seemed to note how much his thoughts had dampened the enthusiasm that was in the room when he first arrived. "Eacher, anything else you want to share?"

"No, I would simply say that the jury is still out. I'll probably never know if anything I ever do makes a difference. As climate critics, we're accustomed to not getting respect or equal consideration. Even so, what you're now being asked to do is probably more demanding and more perilous than anything you've ever done. Think carefully about why you want to do it or why you'd want to continue doing it. I'll leave my contact number with you so that you should be able to reach me if you ever need assistance."

Dora wrapped the class up and sent the students to their following requirements. She asked Eacher to stay in the room a little longer; he agreed.

She closed the door, hit a switch and took a seat to the side. Mike's hologram reappeared in the center of the classroom.

"Eacher, good to see that you are still doing well. Sorry to hear about Irene. You're close to her, aren't you?" Mike said.

"Yes, it breaks my heart to see her in such pain. Thank you for assisting with her rescue, by the way." Eacher said.

"It was the least I could do. Fortunately, we were able to locate her." Mike said.

"Yes," Eacher said.

"By the way, I've got a debate obligation that I committed to on behalf of our program here. Whether you realize it or not, other people contribute to funding what we do. I need that debate to happen so they'll keep funding their share."

"Irene is no condition to debate," Eacher said.

"I agree," Mike said. "Is there any chance we could persuade you to take on this challenge? You and Irene both had a similar qualification level. If you agree, that will take her off the hook, and I could even provide her a portion of the check I had promised her for doing it in the first place."

"That's the least I could do, I'm sure she won't object. Is the debate still scheduled for the same date?"

"Yes, it's still next Wednesday; I don't have any flexibility on that detail. Do you think you can get ready in time?" Mike asked.

"I don't think I need much of a review, but this is such a short notice."

"So, is that a yes?" Mike asked.

Eacher mulls it over in his mind for a minute. "Yes, I'll do it. Just make the entire check out for Irene."

"Agreed. Please give her my regards. I'll have Dora arrange a tailor to measure you for a suit. Let us know if there's anything else you need to prepare."

"Dora has all the other details?" Eacher asked.

"Yes, she'll get you lined up. Sorry, I need to run. Bye."

With that, Mike's hologram disappeared, and Dora handed Eacher a notebook with the rules of the debate and an appointment with the tailor.

Debate

Eacher is sitting in the backstage area of a small auditorium on the campus of the Lost Woods. His makeup was applied in a preparation area, and he now wears a new linen suit. Having not worn a tie in years, he feels awkward wearing one now, but he admittedly looks more professional.

He is positioned on one side of the stage. When he looks to the other side, he can see his old nemesis, Professor Baker, relaxing behind the curtain.

They are supposed to walk out on the stage in ten minutes and assume their positions behind the two podiums.

Professor Baker is about ten years older than Eacher. Not only had he been the department head until just a few years ago, but he also served in officer roles on several national committees. Also, he had been further recognized as a national science advisor to the current administration. His curriculum vitae features ten pages of peer-reviewed papers.

Had Irene been debating, she had few similar qualifications. It's a similar mismatch with Eacher's background, but at least he knows more than a little about Professor Baker.

The same thing could now be said in favor of Professor Baker, who knows quite a bit more about Eacher than he would have known about Irene. If Professor Baker got to choose his debate opponent, it would be Eacher.

Until now, Eacher had assumed that Professor Baker had gone through the same ordeal that Eacher and Irene had faced in Shreveport. Maybe that wasn't the case at all. Perhaps they only brought him into that room to give him the benefit of the discussions with Irene and Eacher. The terrible thought occurs to him that the attack against Irene might have been deliberate. It resulted in Eacher walking into this forum with almost no debate preparation.

The stage director motions to him with two fingers – indicating that he will walk onto the stage in two minutes. Eacher taps his wireless microphone attached to his lapel to confirm that he can hear the sound in his earpiece. The stage director now gives him the signal to walk on stage.

Professor Baker emerges simultaneously from the other side and both assume their position. Eacher feels the top of the podium just to reassure himself that he's not dreaming.

Now that Eacher can see Professor Baker clearly in the studio lights, he notices how terrific his suit looks. He frequently wore a custom-made suit of Australian Merino Wool and the one he's wearing today looks brand new.

A debate moderator sits in front of them. Dressed in a beautiful red dress, open at the neck, he recognizes her as a news anchor from a major television network. Behind her is a set of high-quality video cameras that can be switched during the presentation to change the perspective. This is truly a professional setup. A television screen on the far studio wall shows what the viewers see as the cameras switch back and forth. Eacher is glued to that screen. It zooms in on the moderator as she asks the first question.

She faces forward. "Hi, my name, of course, is Maryam Napper." She then turns her head to the left, and a camera on that side catches this movement. "Professor 'Chuck' Baker, can you please tell us something about your personal qualifications to be on this stage?"

Chuck takes the next three minutes to answer the question related to his background in detail. It is a sobering reminder of his extensive credentials.

"The same question to you, *Mister* Eacher," Maryam pronounces this title as if he's just some random participant. She really ought to at least address him with has academic title.

He ignores this affront. "Well, I have a Ph.D. in geology with a focus on ancient climates, and I've taught at the college level for more than thirty years."

There is a pause as Maryam expects him to speak a little longer. The camera swings back to her, and she is caught focusing on her fingernails. She looks surprised and then quickly reads the text on her monitor.

The next question deals with the 1.5 degrees that the IPCC established as the dangerous temperature threshold. Chuck answers that he was on the committee that created that standard, though he does not clarify how they determined it. He believes that irreversible climate harm will take place beyond that safe limit. Maryam nods her head as if she's impressed with his scientific standing.

Eacher spent his time explaining why that standard had neither an economic nor scientific basis. He also pointed out that temperatures were several degrees above that safe limit a hundred and twenty thousand years ago during the previous interglacial.

Maryam has no idea what he is talking about, and her face momentarily shows confusion. The camera switches to Chuck, who looks incensed by these remarks. The camera then returns back to Maryam, who reads on.

"*Mister* Eacher, would you consider Net Zero policy a failure?" Maryam said.

"Absolutely." Eacher raps the wood of his podium for emphasis. "The United States unilaterally pursued net zero while China, India, and most of the developing world ignored it. That alone confirms that we didn't consider the larger picture when we inflicted these policies on ourselves. Net Zero was justified based on flawed climate science; real science is determined by experiment and observation, and the IPCC's supporters did their best to dodge both. Their energy solutions were even more problematic. The rush to abandon reliable energy solutions destroyed our economy and turned this country into a banana republic." Eacher continues on a bit longer before Maryam cuts him off.

"Professor Baker, your turn?"

"You see, these are the idiotic observations of a teacher that didn't even earn tenure when he had the chance. Of course, Net Zero has been a success. We are all doing exactly what Net Zero was designed to accomplish. First and foremost, the United States releases considerably less carbon dioxide than we used to. We now mostly grow our food locally, don't eat much meat, and use very little fossil fuel. Our major conveyances are electric scooters that are very efficient and don't burn much energy. While China and India are not yet on board, they must follow our lead in time. God bless the United States of America."

The camera moves from Chuck to an American flag hanging on the wall, and patriotic music starts playing softly in the background over the overhead speakers.

"Thank you, Professor Baker. Can you also describe some of the advantages of solar energy?"

"Well, certainly. It doesn't pollute, doesn't cost us any money for fuel, and certainly doesn't emit any carbon dioxide. People might complain because the output varies with the sun and the clouds, but that's considerably better for the environment than fossil fuels."

Chuck continues on for another two minutes on why solar energy is so crucial to the world.

"Mr. Eacher. Same question. Your turn."

"Are you kidding me?" Now it's Eacher's turn to look emotionally distraught, and his angry face fills the camera screen. "There is something called the Energy Returned on Energy Invested ratio. This metric tells you that most of the residential solar panels above a certain latitude can't even produce as much power as they cost over their lifetimes. If an energy source does not provide net energy, it's a complete waste of resources. It doesn't matter that you might save money using it because the government subsidized your cost or that there is a market for renewable energy credits. We waste our resources and despoil our environment chasing such low density, inefficient, and non-dispatchable energy systems."

"That's enough!" Maryam says these remarks in a slightly awkward way, suggesting that someone is coaching her on the proper emotional tone.

Chuck and Eacher respond to a few more questions, then the discussion turns to wind energy. Chuck pointed out that their production costs had fallen below those of fossil fuels, nuclear, and even new hydroelectric power systems. He raved about how these clean energy systems had been a God send.

Eacher responded that Professor Baker was living in an alternate universe. He explained how a much more expensive and unreliable intermittent generation approach replaced a highly efficient and low-cost fossil fuel system. Not only did electricity prices soar, but the reliability of the previous electrical system disappeared. All of this was driven by political mandates, not economics. The new design used just as much fuel, ten times as much concrete and steel, and didn't reduce carbon dioxide emissions. Now that all the backup systems are gone, the system has been gutted. He then turned to face his opponent. "The sweet part of that deal was that the utility operators made an attractive return when they paid for all the grid modifications. Professor Baker, aren't you a director on a utility board?"

"That's not true!" Chuck shouts.

"Then you're not a utility board director?" Eacher asked.

"No, I am, but we simply approved what the government required us to do. You can't blame those system changes on the board."

The moderator touches the microphone in her ear and then interjects. "That's enough!"

The debate continues for the next hour. Chuck's answers to every question align with the IPCC's narrative, and Eacher's do not. Maryam then announces that they've reached the last part of the debate. "For this last question, you are allowed to ask one question of your opponent, who will have sixty seconds to respond.

Professor Baker, could you ask your question first."

"You failed to acquire tenure at our university, and I understand that you then taught at a community college. Can you explain what you've done to support or oppose Net Zero during your illustrious academic career?"

"You've used your question for what is essentially an ad hominem assault!" Eacher asked in disbelief.

"Is that *your* question?" Chuck asked.

"No, of course not. You've touched on a sore point. As you know, I *didn't* get tenure in your department. Not enough research funding and too many papers were blocked by a system that was more 'pal' review than peer review. Since moving on, I've mostly maintained a low profile. The reality is that there's little that I've personally done to counter Net Zero or even slow it down." Eacher glances up in time to see Chuck on the television monitor with a satisfied smirk on his face.

"Thank you, *Mister* Eacher," Maryam said. "Your turn to ask a question of Professor Baker."

"Professor Baker, the IPCC claims they are trying to eradicate poverty. How is that possible when they won't allow the most impoverished countries in the world to get financial assistance to build fossil fuel power plants?"

"The United States has demonstrated that running an electrical grid solely on wind and solar power is perfectly acceptable. Why can't those impoverished countries simply follow our leadership on this? Why would those in serious poverty be interested in pursuing fossil fuels with all their noxious side effects? Once we completely get rid of those energy sources, we'll discover that nature is truly nurturing and well-suited for the future of all life on this planet." Chuck said.

"You are aware that most people died before they reached the age of thirty before fossil fuels?" Eacher asked. "The world is wild and dangerous unless we take action to protect people from those risks. Condemning those in greatest poverty to continue to live without much access to energy is inexcusable."

Chuck really looked indignant at this response that was outside the debate instructions. "I don't want to condemn them. I simply want to assist those in need with renewable energy; you're the one that claims that this approach is inadequate." Chuck said.

"Thank you, Professor Baker and *Mister* Eacher. We're almost done." Maryam said. "Could you both remain on stage for a few more minutes so that we can get a little more footage?" She then walks onto the stage. She asks both to shake hands with each other, and they comply. Eacher tries to smile, and Chuck sneers at Eacher as if he's disgusted by his presence.

Next, Maryam assumes a place between the two debaters with Eacher to her left. Maryam raises Eacher's right arm into the air – as if he had just won a prize fight.

Eacher looks and feels ecstatic, and Chuck seems bored. Maryam then lowers his arm and repeats the same motion with Chuck, and he appears triumphant, and Eacher looks crushed. She then drops his arm, thanks both contestants, and leaves.

"Do you think she actually understood anything we said?" Eacher asked.

"Nah, why would it matter if she did? She's easy on the eyes and did a good job reading the questions." Chuck said.

"So, none of this has been broadcast yet?" Eacher asked.

"No, of course not. Didn't anyone tell you that a studio will edit and broadcast the footage later?"

"Well, I wasn't aware of that, but that would explain why they declared each of us the victor. They can choose the appropriate segment when they determine who won."

"Seriously?" Chuck said. "There's only one way they could score the outcome, and it won't be in your favor. Good day." With these remarks, he leaves while Eacher is still standing there.

Eacher thought that Chuck's victory claim was a particularly moronic thing to say. If anything, Eacher was convinced that he introduced more factual information and materials that the viewers would have probably never heard before. Most of the story is simply never available to the average Joe, and getting the chance to listen to Eacher's perspective might open some eyes.

Broadcast

Eacher has spent more time with Irene and has been in no hurry to leave. While walking around the property outside, she wears a veil to cover the injured portions of her face. Her strength recovers quickly in his company.

On the third day after the debate, he is told that their program will be televised at 8 pm that night. Eacher is nervous about the potential outcome but genuinely excited that the general public will view some of his remarks. He sends a text message to Paul and Rose to notify them of the time slot and channel so they won't miss it.

Irene and Eacher sit next to the television in her room, waiting for the program to begin. Only thirty minutes are scheduled for the broadcast, so he knows that some of their material got cut.

The show starts with a ten-minute commercial for the climate change narrative. It's an abbreviated portion of the broadcast that Eacher had seen in the hotel in Shreveport.

Then, after a commercial interruption, it flips to the debate stage. Both Eacher and Chuck can be seen from a high camera angle. Then the camera focuses on the moderator.

"Nice looking moderator!" Irene said. "She must be what, about twenty-six years old?"

"Ah, that didn't matter. Maryam's reading skills seem fine." Eacher said.

Irene laughs at these remarks.

The first question is the one on qualifications. They play both of those responses in total, meaning that Chuck gets ninety percent of the time allotted for that question and looks vastly more qualified and better dressed than Eacher.

The next question was the 1.5-degree question. Chuck indicated that he had been on the committee that had determined this standard. The show then goes to a commercial break.

When the show returns several minutes later, it zooms in on Eacher's face. He points out that China, India, and much of the developing world did not participate in Net Zero. Then it ends with Chuck explaining why Net Zero had been good for the United States. One last scene shows them raising Chuck's arm triumphantly, and the camera locks in on Maryam's backside as she walks off the stage. The credits roll quickly, and another commercial begins. A different show starts a few minutes later.

Eacher sits there stunned. Basically, nothing controversial that he said made it into the show. The only remark he had been allowed to utter was what sounded like an attack on China and India.

Had the debate really been judged on the merits of the discussion, he thought he might have won.

"What's it mean?" Irene said.

"It means they mostly edited me out of the debate," Eacher said.

"Yeah, that would be my take, but why?"

"I don't know. I'm guessing the people we thought were on our side aren't."

A text message arrives on his phone, and he is asked to meet with a reporter the following day to talk about the broadcast.

Eacher replies to the request that he's available. The plan is to interview him in the same space used for the debate a few days before.

Paul and Rose called him to ask him what happened and wondered why he didn't learn more during his course.

He points out that what was played was nothing like the actual discussion.

"Oh," is their surprising response, and they quickly hang up.

Eacher suddenly feels sick and asks Irene if she'd mind if he goes to his room.

She is feeling tired and agrees to allow him to go. Before he can go, she catches him with these words, "you do understand that this changes nothing," Irene said.

"How so?" Eacher said.

"I love you," Irene said.

"You climate modeler!" He kids her in just a slightly elevated tone.

She grabs him and motions him to the bed. She then lays down beside him and puts her arms around him. "I think it's best if you sleep here tonight."

"That's okay as long as sleep is the only thing on your mind." He quips.

"Not a chance," she said as she pulled her gown over her head.

"Why are you interested in me?" Eacher asked. "I'm an idiot on television!"

"Yes, but you're my moron!" She said. "Also, had I gone on stage, I'd be the one with a challenged public image."

***

The next day Eacher returns to his room early to prepare for his interview. He puts on his suit and tie and heads to the meeting place.

The reporter is already there. She is occupying the moderator's desk and appears to have the support of a small camera crew. It's Connie, the same woman who had given them their graduation exam. Eacher almost pivots and leaves the room when he recognizes who it is. For some inexplicable reason, he doesn't.

"Would you mind standing at the podium when I ask questions?" She asked.

"Okay, I'll bite. I mean, after all the editing done to our debate, it's remarkable that I'm even here." Eacher said.

"We don't need to do this if you don't want to." She said.

"Well, what have I got to lose at this point?" Eacher asked.

"Since you're not wearing a microphone, I've asked them to turn on the microphone on that stand."

"Yes, that should work."

"I researched you online and came across some interesting biographical information. My first question is whether you were ever hospitalized for mental illness?"

Eacher tapped twice hard on the microphone, which resounded loudly throughout the room. "I'm sorry, I'm not doing this. Thanks for your time." Eacher quickly left the auditorium.

Eacher hears his phone vibrate while pacing the hallway and looks at the text message. It is Chuck apologizing for the editing process. He indicates that had he known that it was going to be that one-sided, he never would have participated in the first place.

Eacher texted him back. "Me either."

Eacher next texts a message to Dora, "Can we meet?"

She quickly responds back. "Sure, my office, now?"

"Okay, on my way," he texts back.

When he arrives a few minutes later, she is already there. "How'd your interview go?"

"Did you know it was the same woman that gave us our graduation test?"

"Oh, you're kidding me!" She said. "That's unfortunate."

"Have you seen the tape from the debate?" Eacher asked.

"No, I watched the debate, and I thought you did a reasonable job."

"Well, take a look at what was broadcast," Eacher said quietly.

"Okay, I'll bring it up." She said.

She then enters her password into her computer and downloads the file. When it starts playing, she fast-forwards through the commercials. She then listens to Chuck insulting Eacher and then his various remarks.

"Well, that's unrecognizable from what I heard at the debate," Dora said.

"You're not just saying that?" Eacher said.

"We spend a lot of time on these materials, and this is nothing like what we covered. I'm going to have a talk with Mike about this. How can we ask you to share information with the world if it only leads to these embarrassments?"

"Thank you," Eacher said. "Is there any chance you can get me a copy of the unedited debate? I'd really like to watch it."

"Sounds like a fair request," Dora said. "I'll check with Mike."

"Good to hear. I'll be heading back today," Eacher said.

"Thanks for letting me know."

At Risk

Eacher returns to Irene's room. She meets him with a kiss when he walks in the door.

"What was that for?" Eacher asked.

"Are you kidding? We slept together last night!" Irene said.

"Yes, but that was all that we could do. I apologize if I couldn't rise up for the occasion. You know, I was really depressed from the debate."

"Oh, don't worry about that. I'm post-menopausal. I'm not sure I could have been available, but it was special just to be with you. It snapped me out of my darkness."

His phone vibrates. He looks at his text message. Dora tells him that he is not allowed to have a copy of the original debate video. It's the property of the production company.

"Damn it. The Lost Woods studio won't share a copy of the unedited debate footage with me. For a minute, I thought Dora would give me a copy, but I guess Mike wouldn't let her share it."

"Are we talking about the same Dora? She's no friend of mine, I assure you. I wouldn't trust her as far as you could throw her."

"Really, that's harsh!" Eacher said.

"I don't think so. This whole debate thing has opened my eyes. Remember how you used to joke about whether Mike wanted to kill us after we signed his liability release?"

"Oh, come on. Why would Mike pay all this money to train us as climate skeptics if he really had no need for us?"

"He needs us. Think about what just happened with the debate. How many people would be willing to play stooge for a media blast like that? Someone made money on the content that was nationally broadcast."

"Stooge?" Eacher whispered.

"Maybe only for the material that the public got to see. Someone around here thinks of climate science as entertainment. Why do you think those people wanted to interview us in Shreveport?"

"I don't know, but that was strange. Something to do with the debate, I think." Eacher said.

"Bingo. They were handicapping the participants, and there must have been a betting line among their affluent clients. We might have also presented to some of the bigger betters at their ranch. I'd bet money that the real debate was broadcast to a select group the night it was made. Who knows, you might have actually won that event."

"I think you're being a little harsh on these guys," Eacher said.

"Nah, something is going on here that neither of us understands. It's a front for something larger than what we've seen." Irene said.

"What do you think it is? I don't know yet, but I'm hoping to learn more. They don't watch me closely as an injured old woman," Irene said. "I'll see what I can learn."

"Well, don't take any chances. It's not worth it. If anything happens to you and I find out that Mike or Dora had anything to do with it, I'll come back here and go postal on these guys."

"Eacher, don't think like that. We're not the bad guys here; we're not the ones playing these high-level games causing so much destruction. Let's be a positive force for change."

"Busted," Eacher said. "We need to operate from the higher ground somehow. By the way, I'm heading back to my house for a quick trip. Hope to be back here in the next week or two." Eacher said.

"Take care of yourself," Irene said, giving him a long and soulful kiss.

"So good to see you back to normal. You're still beautiful, you know." Eacher said.

"You've shown me that there can be both life and love after being violated. My challenge will be to not slide backward while you're gone." Irene said.

"Please call me if you ever need someone to talk to!" They kiss again and hug, and he returns to his room.

Eacher grabs his bags and returns to the garage where his scooter is parked. He drives to the gate, scans his identification, and exits.

He rides cross country for about an hour along minor two-lane roads, which are not the normal roads he travels on. He can't get the thought out of his mind that Irene might have been deliberately attacked. If that were true, he also might be in danger. His concerns don't dwell on his recent debate embarrassment but on the possibility of sharing his remaining days with Irene.

The breeze keeps him calm, and the weather seems less blistering than a month earlier. He passes through some unfamiliar small towns and clumps of forest interspersed with many small farms with workers toiling in the fields.

While passing a bar, Eacher glances to his left just in time to see a bunch of bikers mounting motorcycles and moving onto the pavement. They would have overtaken him had he been on a standard scooter. He wants to stay clear of them and rockets forward when he triggers his acceleration capability. Intent to put some distance between himself and those behind him, he crests a hill but immediately loses speed.

He realizes that those bikers behind him will be on top of him in a few minutes. He immediately pulls off the road onto a small trail in the woods. He's confident that they could not have seen him take this path from their position below him. He rides about three blocks into the woods, turns off his bike, and hides it in some bushes. He then quickly jogs up a small hill with his bag. This allows him to look down at where he stashed his bike from a hidden vantage point.

All the bikers take the same turn that he took and arrive at his location within a few minutes. He watches as they all stop right next to where his bike is hidden. They dismount and start searching for it. One guy with a skull tattoo on his upper neck uses a phone application and quickly locates it.

Learning that Eacher is not with the bike infuriates them, and they take out their anger on his scooter. They stomp on the tires, kick the fenders and rip the seat off. They then throw everything into the gully. They continue to search a little bit longer in the vicinity, but the effort seems half-hearted. Eacher crouches low and out of sight, and he doubts they can locate him.

They mull around a while longer, perhaps expecting him to return. But after some discussion, they take off back in the direction of the highway they had come from.

Eacher waits until dark to return to his bike. He is pleasantly surprised to notice that they hadn't taken his advanced battery; that would have been worth a lot of money. While the scooter is in bad shape, it's actually operational; it's as if they want to tempt him to drive it again.

He leaves the bike in the gulley while he works on it. He twists off a few broken wheel spokes. The wheel wobbles precariously, but he's willing to test it.

He presses out the fender so it won't rub on the tire. He then places his bag where the seat used to be and sits awkwardly on it. Before cranking on the bike, he has second thoughts about doing so.

He then pulls out his electronic bug detector from his bag. He scans the bike and notes a GPS locator device mounted below the running board. He pries it off with a screwdriver and takes a picture of it. He leaves it on the ground exactly where his bike was thrown.

He scans his map to see if he can exit this trail away from the road he came in on. He learns that there is another highway about two miles farther down this trail. He keeps his headlight off and slowly drives the bike. He reaches the other road in about fifteen minutes. Taking it would add another thirty miles to his trip, but it's a safer way to go.

After the first thirty minutes on the asphalt road, he stops worrying about being followed. He turns his headlight back on and continues driving the rest of the night.

New Neighbors
OCTOBER, ARKANSAS

Kirk learns from Paul that new people are living on Bart's property, and it's a disturbing thought given recent events there.

Rose sends Paul and Kirk to that location to introduce themselves and learn more about the newcomers. They ride over together on a single scooter with Paul driving.

When they arrive, Kirk notes that all the rubbish and debris left on the exposed concrete slab Bart's house used to sit on has now been cleared. The previously free-standing chimney was also knocked over and now forms a jagged line of fire brick leading away from where it once stood. Both efforts were intelligent moves to make this property safer for the residents.

Several kids are running around near the fence. When they see Paul and Kirk, they run into the barn. When Paul parks their scooter, two men walk to meet them.

"Greetings," Paul said. "Welcome to the neighborhood."

"Good to be here." The taller man said."

"You guys related to Bart?" Paul asked.

"Bart, who?" The taller man said.

"The older gentleman that used to live here," Kirk said.

"Never met him." The shorter man said.

"So, what brings you to these parts?" Paul asked.

"We had to leave the city. It was getting too vicious, and we couldn't grow enough food. One of our friends mentioned that this place was vacant, and we immediately arranged for a moving truck to drop us off."

"Yeah, those moving vans are a trip!" Kirk said. "What a sweet deal they have with the government."

"So, you're buying this place from one of Bart's relatives?" Paul asked.

"Mister, you haven't introduced yourselves." The taller guy said.

199

"I'm sorry. That was rude. I'm Paul, and this is my brother, Kirk. We live on a farm down the road with our families." Paul casually motioned down the road in the direction they'd come from.

"So, you're our welcoming committee?" The other guy asked.

"Not exactly. We just want to know who you were. Did you speak to any of the relatives in Bart's family?"

"No, can't say that we did." The taller guy said.

"You spent all that money to move here, and you don't know what plans his relatives have for this property?" Paul asked.

"Mister, I'm afraid that's none of your business. This place is vacant, and we're living here, and I don't see where that should be a problem for anyone." The large guy said.

"Can you share your names with us?" Kirk asked.

The large guy introduced himself as Tony, and he introduced the other guy as Rusty.

"Are there many of you here?" Paul asked.

"That's not exactly your business now, is it?" Tony said.

"You guys familiar with farms?" Paul asked.

"What's it matter. We'll grow our own food here and give ourselves a chance." Tony said.

"Got it. But, you understand that winter is coming." Paul said.

"Was that a reference to Game of Thrones?" Tony said. "I saw that. You ain't got any White Walkers around here, do you?"

"Nah, seriously, in a month or two, it's going to be freezing living in that barn, and you won't be able to grow much food until next spring," Paul said.

"That's really none of your business. We're survivors." Tony said. "By the way, are one of you guys married to a Chinese woman?"

"That would be me," Kirk said.

"Well, nice to meet you. Sounds like quite a woman." Tony laughed.

"Curious how you heard that," Kirk said.

"Not important," Tony said.

"Good luck, and let us know if you need anything," Paul says. With this last remark, Paul motions to Kirk and they both hop on the scooter and return home.

Kirk and Paul discuss this development with Rose and Windy. Based on Paul's analysis, this new group doesn't have permission to live where they're now staying. Neither Paul nor Kirk believes that they've brought much food with them and have no idea if they have the funds available to buy it. Also, Paul doesn't think they understand how problematic it will be to live in that unheated barn in the winter. If they needed help, they didn't ask for it.

The conversation then turns to the explosives that Kirk and Paul buried on the edge of Bart's property. It is disturbing to have them located on property now controlled by unfriendly and possibly hostile people. Rose wonders where they might store those items on this property.

Windy isn't really on board with this idea. "So, what you're telling me is that we will bring explosives to this property that would get us all arrested if they are discovered?"

"That's the basic idea," Paul said. "They might come in handy if things get rough."

"Really, that's our excuse? Only soldiers are allowed to use guns in China. You don't think we're asking for trouble?" Windy said.

"Windy, you've got to trust my family on this. These explosives and ammunition could allow us to fend for ourselves if attacked. If we don't get them now, we might never be able to get them." Kirk said.

"Why not just leave them where they are?" Windy asked.

This was actually a reasonable idea. "We could," Paul said. "We run the risk of others getting control of them, and it would be harder to get to them if the new neighbors put a fence up or if more tree roots grow across the area where we put them."

"You're right. That's an option." Kirk said.

201

"Windy, you don't need these weapons until you really need them. I'm a bit troubled by where they are." Rose said. "You and Kirk are just visitors. If we ever get caught with this stuff, just say you don't know anything."

"I'm still not comfortable," Windy said. "Are you sure they won't just blow up if they're on our property?"

"No, I've done a little research, and I think there's only a minimal risk of that happening. We can further familiarize ourselves with what we have after bringing it here, and we should ensure that we can at least handle it safely." Rose said.

"If the three of you are okay with this, then I won't try to stop you," Windy said.

"Good to know," Paul said. "What about the root cellar?"

"The what?" Kirk asked.

"The old root cellar. There used to be one on the property, and I'm just trying to remember where it was. It might be a good place to store the explosives away from the house." Paul said.

"I like that idea," Windy said.

Rose searches her memory. "Wait a minute. I remember. It's about fifty feet from the back porch. The access panel has been buried for a while, but I'm sure we can probe the soil with a stick and find it."

"Kirk and I will try to locate it," Paul said.

Paul and Kirk use a long wooden dowel to probe the ground to locate the root cellar. They contact something solid within ten feet of the location that Rose suggested. They remove the dirt and pull a handle to open a steel panel on hinges.

Though the root cellar probably hasn't been used in a long time, it's still intact. Kirk is surprised that Paul and Rose weren't using it for possible tornado protection. When pressed on that question, they both thought that the hiding place in the back bedroom was a better option. Kirk quickly replaced a few wooden stair boards that had rotted. The root cellar is sufficiently functional to use as their storage location.

After checking the expected weather and everyone's resolve, they committed to retrieving the explosives that night.

Rose does most of the planning and gives everyone their instructions after dinner. Clare is not aware of what's going on and goes to bed early after working in the fields most of the day.

The group meets for "Operation Sparkler" at ten o'clock. The weather is overcast with very little chance of rain; it looks like it will be a little darker than normal this night. The four drive two scooters to a place several blocks short of the property and then store them in the woods in a low area not visible from the road. They then move slowly together in the dark, where Paul and Kirk had buried the materials.

As previously arranged, Windy is to serve as a lookout focused on noise from the barn area, and Rose is to serve as a lookout for the road. They each have a red-lensed flashlight that they can use to flash warnings. When the girls both position themselves as agreed, Paul and Kirk quietly locate the exact spot to dig. The dirt is still somewhat loose, reinforcing the idea that they are at the correct location.

Kirk digs first. Paul shines some light with a low flashlight setting from his phone. Kirk uses the shovel to quietly move each spade to a spot downhill in the direction of the road. He makes some serious progress moving the soil quietly, then hands the shovel to Paul, who continues to work on the hole.

In about an hour, the shovel strikes the canvas. Kirk and Paul move the rest of the earth from the cover. They roll the loose ends to the side of the hole, and Paul remains in the pit handing Kirk each item one at a time. He quietly stacks each piece to the side at the surface.

When every single item is out of the hole, Paul folds up the tarp and hands it to Kirk. He then takes turns with Kirk carrying the items to the scooters.

It is very dark, and they are afraid to make much noise or to use a light while walking. Kirk grabs the crate of dynamite and moves it carefully to the road and then to the location where the scooters are. Paul stays at the hole. Kirk gets a bit disoriented in the dark on the way back, but Paul makes a low coyote sound and gets him back to the hole. On the next trip, Kirk stays at the hole, and Paul takes a burlap bag of various cables, detonators, and a couple additional ammo boxes. Once Paul deposits these items at the scooters, he returns.

On the last trip, they each load up the remaining materials and the folded-up canvas and slowly take these pieces back to the scooters. It's dark, but they can stay close most of the way.

When they make their way back to the hole, they lose their way a bit, and while slowly searching for it, Kirk falls into it. The fall scares him more than it hurts him, and without thinking, he cusses louder than he should. Before they can begin to push the dirt back into the hole, they hear a husky voice shouting from the direction of the barn. "Who is that?"

Windy flashes her red-lensed flashlight in their direction, and then Kirk sees it getting closer. It's dark, and he hears a branch snap, and she then groans.

Kirk climbs out of the hole and heads toward her. He finds her and then holds her hand to guide her back to the road.

"Who's there?" A loud voice booms again. This time the volume is louder; someone is walking in their direction.

Kirk leads Windy along the road and then turns to where they left everything, lying on the ground out of sight. Rose and Paul join them a few minutes later, and they all hug the ground.

A shotgun blast goes off some distance away — so it's clear that whoever is looking for them has a weapon. Rose, Windy, Paul, and Kirk remain in place. A light briefly shines on the trees behind them, and then it's dark again. Whoever is holding that flashlight is walking along the road and sweeping the woods with it.

The searcher apparently can't make out where they are.

After a while, they hear the footsteps pass down the road again in the direction of Bart's property.

They wait another hour. Kirk walks down to the road and then walks along it a while to see if he can see any movement, and he can't.

He returns to the others, and they slowly walk the scooters to the road together. They load the crates and other materials on the floorboards of the scooters, and then Rose and Windy each drive those motorbikes back home. Paul and Kirk discuss whether they should return and try to fill the hole.

The bottom of that hole is barely covered with any fill material and would look like an open grave if it weren't so dark. Paul and Kirk decide not to risk going back to Bart's farm. While Paul carries the shovel, the two brothers walk to their home. They walk cautiously and slowly along the edge of the road so that they can immediately run into the woods if necessary.

***

The following day, Rose inspects all the items, with Kirk and Paul standing by to answer any questions about what they might know about these materials. The ammunition seems well protected in plastic bags, but the dynamite appears old. Some of the sticks exude brownish liquid drops that she is very nervous about.

They move the ammo and other stuff into the root cellar, close the tornado door, and throw dirt over the top. The land looks recently disturbed, so they move an old heavy farm implement over it.

Windy is still anxious that these explosives are now on the property. In her mind, it seems they are asking for trouble. She quietly shares her concerns again with Kirk. He listens to her arguments but insists on allowing Rose and Paul the final decision. The new neighbors make everyone nervous.

"Did you carry a gun last night?" Windy said.

"Why do you ask?" Kirk asked.

"Did you?" She asks this question both firmly and quite seriously.

"No, I didn't."

"Did Paul have one?" She asked.

"I don't know. Maybe. I suppose I didn't expect to actually run into anyone."

"See, that's the kind of thing that really bothers me." She said, looking at him in frustration.

"How so?" Kirk asked.

"You don't think that's a pretty important detail that we all should have known about?" She asked.

"You mean whether we had a gun with us?" Kirk asked.

"Yes."

"You're right. Rose should have clarified that detail."

"So, you don't really know the answer either?" Windy said.

"No, I don't."

"Well, in that case, I'm less concerned about it. I felt you kept me out of the loop on some important details."

"We were all in the dark. I assure you. Guess we need to get more skilled at managing that coordination."

"Fair enough," Windy said.

"How's your arm doing?"

"Just a little bruised, but not too bad."

"Glad to hear." Kirk looks at her with his head slightly tilted to the right. "Are you sure that our little adventure last night didn't actually turn you on a little? We were at risk of being discovered in the darkness by some random stranger with a large, dangerous weapon. Isn't that your kind of fantasy?"

"Interesting thought." She said, smiling. "You been a good boy?"

"I could be."

They kiss, and she takes him for a short walk on the property.

He likes that she's taking charge.

She chooses a place not far from the highway where they might be in view if a vehicle were to drive by and the driver was looking in their direction.

Kirk barely notices the dirt that soon covers his backside in the ensuing enthusiasm.

Her appreciation for the outdoors is increasing.

206

Persisting
THE LOST WOODS

Eacher arrives at his house only to find that his back door has been kicked in. The door still sits on its hinges, but the door frame is broken and no longer allows the deadbolt or passage lock to hold the door closed.

Someone has rifled through everything in the house – which wasn't much. Mostly there were a couple of tables, a few chairs, and a few organizing pieces.

The walls are mostly bare. The futon has been sliced open – as if someone was looking for something. The one bookshelf was thrown over, and all of Eacher's books are in a pile. The clothes from his dresser and the closet are scattered on the floor.

The real damage was done to his food storage shanty. Numerous glass food containers are shattered on the ground, and his tools are scattered outside in the weeds. Whoever did this to his house must have been riding scooters, and had they had better transportation, they would have at least taken this food with them.

He quickly picks up the tools he can locate and returns them to their place. While doing so, he notices that the corn and other vegetables planted on his fields by his neighbor this season are doing fine. His rental portion of that effort should provide him enough provisions to last a few months.

Eacher immediately returns to the road and heads over to Paul and Rose's house.

It's mid-morning, but he finds everyone still asleep. It's uncommon for farmers to sleep late on a weekday when their crops are in the field.

He sits on the porch and waits for someone to wake up. Just before lunchtime, Paul comes outside.

"Morning."

Eacher said. "Long night?"

"Eacher, how long have you been here?"

"About an hour, I guess. Everything okay?"

"Quite an evening. We now have explosives on our property."

"Sounds serious. You guys okay?" Eacher asked.

"Yeah, suppose so. It got a little more exciting than we thought it would be."

"No injuries?'

"None, but it was pretty scary at one point."

"Rose did the planning?" Eacher asked.

"Of course. Not sure what I'd do without that woman."

"Yep, she's a keeper, for sure. Hey, I meant to tell you, someone broke into my house while I was out of town."

"I'm sorry to hear that. Did those vandals steal your food?" Paul said.

"Worse than that, they ruined most of it."

"Damn, what a shame. Someone doesn't like you much."

"You're the one with the explosives." Eacher said.

"True. We took advantage of an opportunity to upgrade our defenses."

"In my case, I seem to be having some difficulties with people related to that program I participated in."

"Rose won't be surprised. Remember, she suggested that something seemed odd about that training."

"Smart lady. I was a bit slow to figure it out myself." Eacher said.

"How can we help?" Paul asked. "Need any dynamite?"

"Not at the moment. But I do need to get my bike fixed. Know any reliable junk yards in the area?"

"Yeah, Windy and Kirk just visited one they liked. It's the one not far from Renfro's restaurant."

"Oh, I know the one you're talking about. I'll head over there and check back later today."

"What happened to your bike?"

208

"I'll update you later," Eacher said.

***

Eacher parks his scooter in front of the junkyard. He then approaches a small, grimy-looking one-story building and knocks on the office door. Dusty is sitting inside with the screen-less windows open. He waves Eacher inside.

"I'm looking for some assistance with my bike."

Dusty takes one look at it out the window and starts laughing. "Who'd you piss off?"

"That's not important. Have you got some time?"

"Sure, walk it in the gate."

They leave his bike just inside the property, and Dusty walks him to the scooter section of the junkyard. He grabs some fenders from a stack of twisted metal parts. He removes a seat top from a bike with a badly bent frame. He brings those pieces to Eacher's bike and grabs a toolbox out of his office. His repair efforts don't take long. When finished, he stares at it curiously. "You've got a really strange scooter. Where did you get these modifications?"

"I had a friend that added them for me," Eacher said.

"Are you sure he's a friend?"

"I thought so. What's wrong?"

"See that controller there?" Dusty points to the end of the device that gives his bike additional acceleration. "That's actually something that can be controlled from a distance. If you were using it and someone triggered it, you wouldn't get any acceleration."

"Can you remove it?"

"Yes, nothing to it," Dusty said. "Also, it looks like your bike had a special GPS locater attached to it, but I don't see it anymore."

"Well, I pried that off with a screwdriver."

209

"That's one way to do it. You might have also detached it with an Allen wrench, but it looks like part of it is still attached."

"Can you remove the rest?"

"Better yet, I can replace it with one that can be accessed with your phone," Dusty said. "Here, I'll show you how it works." He then opens his own phone that displays a map showing the location of several vehicles.

"You sure this won't be too expensive?" Eacher asked as he set the application up on his own phone.

"Not compared to all the fancy gear that you have here. Is that a smoke generator? I've never seen one on a scooter before." Dusty said.

"Yes, it was a gift."

"Do you mind if I remove the remote activator for it as well? It works the same way the accelerator control works; it can be triggered from a great distance."

"Yes, by all means. Please de-trick this damn bike."

Dusty quickly removes it and sets it to the side. "Sounds like you've got some rich friends with a sense of mischief. Wait for a second. Didn't I see you on television about a week ago?" Dusty said.

"Maybe," Eacher said. "It was a bit of a smackdown that I hadn't expected."

"Well, that's what I thought when I saw it. Your opponent is the same guy that did this crap to your bike?"

"Maybe not him, but perhaps friends of his."

"Well, with friends like that, who needs enemies?"

"Agreed." Eacher said. "By the way, what's the deal with that large truck in your garage? Are you in the monster truck business?"

"Well, in a way. We modify gasoline engines to run on natural gas, and it runs about the same, and the fuel is a lot cheaper and a whole lot easier to get."

"Do you rent these?"

"Well, this one belongs to a customer, but I might persuade her to let you use it for a small fee. Any interest?"

"Maybe. Let me check on a few details first."

"Well, let me install that GPS device, and we'll get you out of here in no time. Also, I'll add your scooter location to my phone, just in case you ever lose your bike and phone together. Just call me if you need to know where your scooter is."

***

Eacher stays with Paul's family for the night. They update him on the entire explosives retrieval story, and he compliments them on their courage and planning. Eacher asks to see their new munitions, and they escort him to the root cellar.

Eacher has actually recently been trained to employ dynamite and detonating cords. The program rationalized this training as a sort of confidence-building exercise, but it's now actually coming in handy. He demonstrates how to wire the blasting caps and connect all the explosives. They offer him a few sticks of dynamite, just in case he needs them, but he politely declines. It's nice to know that the offer still stands if he changes his mind later.

***

Eacher speaks with Irene on her phone. He updates her on all that has happened to him since they last saw each other. She suddenly goes quiet when he describes the GPS and remote operation functionality installed on their scooters. Eacher intuitively understands why she's concerned; they've both reached the same conclusions.

"Eacher, I don't feel safe here anymore. I can't help but think I was deliberately attacked on the road by people following orders from Mike or Dora. Can you come to get me?"

"If I leave now, I can be there tomorrow. Are you able to ride on the back of my scooter?" Eacher asked.

"I'll have to be. I'm no longer comfortable being here."

"Did you learn something new that you're not telling me about?" Eacher asked.

"We can talk about it after you pick me up,"

***

Just after lunch the next day, Irene packed a small travel bag and walked to the back gate. Eacher texted her and advised her he'd be there around four pm.

She waits in the woods just inside the gate but out of sight of anyone entering the compound. A vehicle enters the gate and then takes off towards the campus. She sneaks out of the gate before it closes without crossing in front of the camera. She believes she's been able to avoid alerting anyone at the Lost Woods that she's left their facility. She walks a short distance on the other side away from the perimeter road and then waits in a shaded area out of sight. Irene texts Eacher with her location.

He finds her a few hours later and then carefully assists her in mounting the scooter. He remounts the bike just in front of her. She wraps her arms around his waist, and the two of them try to put as much distance as they can from this complex.

The funny thing is that they never even discuss where they are heading for the next several hours. Irene's house, Eacher's house, somewhere else? Eacher doesn't care. He's exactly where he wants to be – traveling somewhere with Irene. Hopefully, she'll be a part of his life going forward. All he knows for sure is that he is finished as a climate warrior.

He took a chance and it didn't work. No need to persist.

Employment
ARKANSAS

Paul is watching today's economics broadcast in the classroom where he tutors.

There are only about six students in the room for the lecture; most leave immediately after class ends. A student that he recognizes approaches him.

"Professor, may I ask you a question?" Dwayne asked.

"Sure," Paul replied.

"Can you explain the concept of a discount rate to me?" Dwayne pulls out a notebook and pencil so that he can take notes.

"Hope so." Paul then takes the next ten minutes to walk him through some finer points of why discount rates are helpful.

Dwayne seems to follow the discussion and then surprises Paul with these comments. "By the way, I was looking at the Stern Review; the appropriate discount rate for long-term projections is essentially zero."

"The Stern Review? How did you ever hear about that?" Paul recognizes it as one of the documents on Eacher's disk. It was a document used by the United Kingdom's Treasury Department. It argues that society should spend unlimited money trying to aggressively reduce carbon dioxide emissions immediately for some distant future benefit decades from now.

"Well, I was at a friend's house and got a copy of his flash drive. He said that he got it at some party."

"Really, that's strange," Paul remembers the specific file he's referencing. "I'm afraid I don't know much about the document you're describing."

"The discussion dealt with politicians using extremely modest discount rates to value things," Dwayne said.

"So your confusion is whether it is appropriate to use such a low discount factor in that analysis?"

"Exactly."

"Well, I'll say that you impress me by understanding that such questions exist. The short answer is that discount rates have value in calculating tradeoffs like the one you describe. What do you think it means when the report uses a discount rate close to zero - especially when this analysis compares cash flows over the next hundred years?"

"Well, it means that the guy that did the analysis thinks that ten thousand yuan today is almost the same as ten thousand yuan a hundred years from now." Dwayne said.

"Yes. It also means that we are willing to spend a tremendous amount of money today in exchange for benefits that would only be received by others in the distant future. It presumes that we understand who will be around a hundred years from today and that we understand their preferences. We pretend to understand their level of wealth and the level of technology available to address concerns a century from now. It's a very unrealistic assumption."

"So, you've seen this Stern Report?"

"No, but the general economic idea we're talking about is straightforward. I suspect that if you use a higher discount factor, say something like six percent. This analysis no longer passes a cost-benefit test. In that case, it might not make sense for us to undertake the recommended actions." Paul said.

"So, you agree that we should never have invested so much money in wind turbines and solar panels in recent years. Such investments don't pass a reasonable cost-benefit analysis." Dwayne said.

"Hold on, that's not what I'm saying, but it does pose an interesting question. Would we be better off had we not made those investments? Might it have made sense to think twice about the steps our nation took to eliminate carbon dioxide emissions? The rush to abandon fossil fuels and implement wind and solar energy systems has already consumed massive resources, leading to a much less reliable electrical grid. Are we really doing anything useful for future generations? I was on the front lines protesting for Net Zero like everyone else. Yet no one ever mentioned that a small discount factor was being used to rationalize these projects; it's an obvious overreach. As an economist, it makes me uneasy when political leaders use such unrealistic assumptions."

"Well, thank you for your thoughts," Dwayne said. "I really enjoy your assistance and look forward to our next discussion." He puts his notebook into his computer bag and looks like he is about to leave the classroom.

"Okay, please understand that my thoughts are not the official position of this college and are simply designed to help you understand some of the finer points of this material." This is a standard disclaimer that many teachers throw into their classroom explanations.

Dwayne walks toward the door. Paul watches him leave with mixed emotions. It was a strange discussion and nothing like any interaction he'd ever had with other students. In addition, for the first time, Paul is now aware that some really peculiar economic assumptions are being used to rationalize important official government reports. That is not an indicator that these reports are credible or based on reasonable and objective assumptions. He is now determined to go over Eacher's flash drive to read this document in greater detail.

He is also curious how this student got access to Eacher's data. More strangely, the student actually cares enough to want to understand it further. This seems like a very improbable development. Today's students generally don't question global warming theory. The national education curriculum treats it as rock solid science, and teachers are explicitly directed not to examine it. Something seems off, but he doesn't dwell on it.

When Paul returns to his cubicle, he finds an official email on his computer. He is being notified that his job has been terminated, and there is no explanation. This is something that Paul has long feared.

Lots of kids are choosing not to go to college. His class size has fallen considerably since last spring. Understanding how a college education will justify the cost in this altered world is challenging.

In addition, what value is a local teacher's aide when all the students can simply have their questions answered from an online call center in God knows what country?

Paul sits at his desk, staring blankly at the computer screen.

A second email explains that his access to the computer system will be terminated at midnight. He needs to turn in his desk, office, and building keys by the end of the day. He locates a cardboard box that will fit on his scooter and a large plastic garbage bag to protect it from the weather on the drive home; he starts packing his personal stuff.

He is crushed. How will his family get by without the income from his job? He's worked at this campus for many years and has never received any type of negative evaluation before. He returns home and is sick to his stomach from worry. He doesn't feel like explaining this development to anyone. He apologizes and goes to bed early.

***

The next day, Rose shakes him awake.

"Time to get moving. You're going to school today, right?"

"I lost my job."

"What? How? Why?"

"I don't know, but it seems like a case of mistaken identity. Some kid got a flash drive at Bart's party and asked me some questions. I couldn't tell if they sent me a termination notice because of my part in that discussion or because I've long been a friend of Eacher."

"That's nuts!" Rose said. "We're Net Zero supporters."

Paul then told her the rest of the story about the student with the strange questions.

Rose listened closely and agreed it was an atypical discussion with the student. She finds it ironic that Paul had done nothing irregular but was now suffering the consequences of simply listening to an alternate viewpoint.

Over the next few days, Paul is thoroughly depressed. With none of his immediate family working, money will be more of an issue. They don't have enough savings to even pay their annual property taxes.

Engaged

Rose is well aware that whatever safety net she and Paul once had is gone, and they are on their own. Windy and Kirk give them some money.

Rose asks Paul to dial down the electric circuit breaker panel software. The only thing done regularly is pumping water for the house, charging the phone batteries, and running the LED lights. Even plugging in the scooters is less critical since they have little need to make any trips to town.

They finish their fall harvest and bottle everything they can for the winter.

A few nights later, they hear noises outside the house. Paul cracks the front door with a shotgun at the ready and then carefully moves toward the barn with Rose behind him with her small pistol. Whoever it was had already left, and a chicken and a number of their vegetable bottles were missing.

Rose guesses that the new neighbors are trying to solve their food problems. If so, Rose wonders if they even realize this is where Kirk and Paul live. Rose and Paul guess that the family on Bart's land does need supplies for the winter and also fear that this visit may be the first of many.

Rose broadcasts this break-in to the neighbors by text message. Many of them are aware of the new people on Bart's property; there are rumors of people roaming around the area on horseback.

Rose hosts an online meeting to talk about a joint defense. The neighborhood watch group elects to do almost nothing at this point. They do increase the collective awareness of what is going on. Everyone on the call promises to keep the others informed.

They move as much food into the house as possible into the hiding place in the back bedroom. There is not much they can do to further protect the chickens; only a few are left, and the egg supply is sparse.

The young chicks acquired from neighbors will take some time to mature.

Paul and Rose try to figure out how to harden their property to make it more resistant to incursions. They lock the gate at night with a padlock and then reinforce the fence around the property the best they can. Rose and Windy

---

tie together some tin cans with rocks as warning devices if anyone tries to open the barn door at night.

The first community alarm sounds with the neighbors to the east. Rose and Paul take the guns, and Kirk carries a machete.

Clare and Windy are left at home.

They advance in the direction of the adjacent farm slowly and carefully. They get there after the raiders have departed. The residents complain about the loss of some food supplies.

These neighbors got a shot off at the visitors. However, that was only after they were already moving down the road on horses with their plunder. The riders returned fire, showing them a hole in the door frame where a bullet had lodged.

The next night, a different family is hit, and this one does not fare as well. They don't learn of the attack until the day after.

By the time they arrive, the occupants are dead from wounds that appear to have been inflicted with knives. They find no food anywhere on that property; this makes them believe that it was carried off by the attackers.

Two weeks later, they got word that the people living at Bart's place had relocated to this ranch house. They can't blame them for taking advantage of the situation to get a winterized cottage. Still, everyone on the local defense team is convinced that they are the ones who killed these neighbors in the first place.

They call the police hoping they will investigate, but they never return their call or show up.

After Tony and Rusty's crew have moved into the new farmhouse, another group of people shows up at Bart's place in a moving truck. This time, they elect not to meet their newest neighbors.

Rose quips that the Feds are somehow involved with these relocations.

Paul won't even guess on that topic but agrees that the trouble with the neighbors started after the party at Bart's house.

***

The defense team has started monitoring the house where Rusty, Tony, and their families are staying. The Internet is unreliable in this region, so there is no assurance it will work when they most need it. Someone flew a small drone into a tall tree near their compound, and it came to rest on a branch overlooking the property. The camera can be turned on and off remotely as needed, allowing the battery to last longer.

That night, two men and two women leave their house around midnight wearing dark clothing riding on two horses and are clearly armed. All the lights at this house are out. Fortunately, it's a cloudless night, and the moon is bright enough for better visibility.

Some images of the group moving are texted by phone to the group distribution list, and Rose gets the message.

Rose wakes up Paul, Windy, and Kirk. Paul takes the shotgun, Rose brings her pistol, Windy has a steak knife, and Kirk has two sticks of dynamite and some matches. They quietly and carefully move to the barn.

A few minutes later, they hear the fence rattling and the sound of horses just outside their gate. Cappy barks furiously from inside the house. The fence shakes as if they are frustrated that it won't open. Rose notes that this farm must have been their intended target for the evening. They then hear the sound of horses growing fainter as they continue down the highway.

Rose sends a text message to the group, letting them know that the intruders just passed their house after testing the fence.

They wait another hour and hear some gunfire. A text message describes an attack at another nearby property.

While the horse-mounted group thought they had the element of surprise, the farmer and his wife were waiting for them. When the front door was forced open, they were standing at the ready with weapons and started firing back. Blood is on the doorstep, but there is no other sign of the intruders.

Kirk volunteers to stand on guard the rest of the night and is armed with Paul's shotgun and the dynamite. Everyone else goes back to sleep, though it's a restless night after the battle.

The next day most of the neighborhood militia meets at the attacked farm. They compare notes; Rose describes how the intruders could not get through their locked front gate and believes that the attackers do not have access to bolt cutters.

Rose and Paul then distribute dynamite sticks and ammunition to anyone that wants some. They do not mention that they have other explosives. Most farmers agree to accept their offer and pass out about half a case of the dynamite and about half of their ammo. Spike wants some explosives too. They give him the dynamite he requests but require him to promise that he will not use it to attack the wind turbine he hates.

***

The next few nights are quiet. Someone provides a text message about a visit to Tony and Rusty's house. Apparently, only Tony is available to come out of the house. Tony is annoyed and claims to know nothing of the horse-mounted raiders.

The report also notes that children looked out at the visitors through the window. The visitor asked if they needed any help with their food supplies, but Tony insisted they did not.

Paul and Rose change their mind and decide to check on the newcomers at Bart's place. The new residents indicate that they don't know the previous residents and confirm they brought a lot of canned food and seeds.

This reassures Paul and Rose that they are probably no threat to the group. As winter approaches, this new family is still challenged by their living situation in an unheated barn. Rose gets their contact information and promises to keep them updated if they hear of any issues in the neighborhood.

So the group focus remains on Tony and Rusty's farm. The little drone continues to operate much longer than anticipated. Rose theorizes that they have flown it back to its original location to periodically recharge.

Recognition

Eacher and Irene decide to go to Eacher's house. Even though she knows it's been ransacked, she's ready to assist. They drive a circuitous route on the way home and take a couple of days to return.

They fish in some lakes along the way and sleep under the stars beside a campfire. The weather is beautiful, and the leaves are changing. It's hard to recall the hot sticky days of summer or worry about the upcoming requirements for winter. They pass numerous small farms where workers are on their knees attending to their crops. When they stop to rest, he tells her he's given up on the climate skeptic role.

Irene suggests that he can still make a difference.

He disagrees but is careful to voice his concerns delicately. She listens intently as he expresses his deeply-rooted frustrations.

"By the way, are you aware they actually use that religious facility at the Lost Woods?" Irene asked.

"Is that true? I never saw it get used."

"I didn't either during our program. But, during my convalescence, the Lost Woods staff wasn't spending much energy trying to keep track of me. There really is some type of organization that is operating from that facility. It's like a secret society, but religious and spiritual overtones are involved. I've nicknamed them the Cabal. There are some attendees, but others access the services remotely over an encrypted system."

"That's strange. Did you get to attend one of the events?" Eacher asked.

"Yes, I was walking outside and noticed some activity. I found a secluded spot where I could listen and observe.

"What were they saying?"

"They are concerned about protecting the Earth. They see humanity as a lethal virus and want to safeguard the planet from us." Irene said.

"How do they do that?" Eacher asked.

"The world is expected to reach ten billion people by the end of this century. That will be ten times the population two hundred years earlier. Birth rates fell, but that was offset by longer life expectancies."

"Medicines, energy, clean water, and ample food have contributed to those quality of life improvements," Eacher said.

"Yes, these people are convinced that the world can't sustain those population levels. They fear there will be trouble, especially if mankind allows more energy per person. They believe that doing so will rapidly exhaust the planet's natural resources and condemn humans to perpetual poverty for the rest of our existence." Irene said.

"This doesn't sound all that remarkable. There have been numerous dismal economic predictions that mankind's population will outgrow its ability to feed itself. In that case, war, starvation, and disease will force the planet's population back to lower levels. Those predictions have been overblown and wrong for the past sixty years. What has this got to do with us?"

"Well, remember you've always asked me who's behind the curtain on Net Zero?" Irene said.

"Yes, the climate change justification is so weak. There must be another reason our government's forced a drastic transition on this country."

"Well, I think we've met the people calling the shots," Irene said.

"What was that? I don't follow."

"Well, think back to our discussions last spring. If more carbon dioxide is really a concern, why didn't the government pursue nuclear power? I mean, it's a reliable energy source that doesn't produce any carbon dioxide." Irene said. "It's certainly no more expensive than wind or solar power."

"Probably because all the activists would show up and use the courts and protestors to delay the completion process until the project was no longer economical," Eacher said. "I remember that Brenda was bullish on nuclear power."

"Many are. Yet few plants have been built since the 1970's," Irene said.

"But, how does what you describe fit with Net Zero?" Eacher asked.

"Well, think about the last decade. We trashed our economy and crammed unreliable electricity down the throat of our citizens. We made it nearly impossible to get fossil fuels, which cut the transportation legs of our economy. How would life have been different had we gone with nuclear energy?" Irene said.

"We'd all still be accustomed to reliable electricity. That alone would have kept a lot of businesses intact." Eacher said.

"So, there's some chance our economy might have survived the transition?"

"Yes, reliable and affordable energy would have made a profound difference. It's what we were all getting from fossil fuels before they took those away from us." Eacher said.

"We both know that didn't happen, so what happens twenty years after all these wind and solar installations get installed," Irene said.

"Well, when most of them wear out and will need replacement. Had our politicians installed the nuclear plants, those might have lasted another hundred years." Eacher said.

"Given the low financial capability of our country and associated destruction of our economy, what are the odds that we'll actually be able to replace those worn out wind and solar facilities? Irene said.

Eacher paused to think about the consequences. "There's a greater chance that we'll simply have to find a way to do without." He said thoughtfully.

"Yes, I think so too. I don't think China will sell us anymore if we haven't the financial capacity to service that debt. Do you now see the problem?"

"The Cabal is trying to push our society back into a mode where we don't use much energy," Eacher said.

"You got it!" Irene said. "Contrast that notion with a world where energy is plentiful and affordable for most. Even those currently in the greatest poverty could have the chance to improve their situation and choose to have fewer kids. It's a better world where globalization and technology continue to thrive."

"Oh my God!" Eacher said. "The Cabal is focused on a drastically different vision of the future."

"Their elite members would be the only ones left with comfortable access to energy. They're not against energy. How could they be? Energy is wealth. They object to too many other people with access. That's why high energy prices don't generally bother the richest among us; they can afford to pay those prices." Irene said.

"Irene, this is really scary if it's true," Eacher said.

"Think about the materials they allowed you to share with the nation during the debate," Irene said.

"The only thing they quoted me was that China and India weren't following the Net Zero path," Eacher said.

"Think about it; the Cabal especially hates China. They pulled a billion people out of poverty and built an energy-sufficient society. Public transportation supports vast numbers of apartment building complexes."

"You really think that's possible?" Eacher asked.

"Their members were far happier with China before their economy took off and almost everyone was poor. China is now building a country designed to provide comfortable energy access to its citizens. They are using fossil fuels for the transition and nuclear energy for the long term. You ever hear of a nuclear energy protest in China?" Irene said.

"No, can't say I have," Eacher said. "So you don't think that China has been behind the badly conceived decarbonization schemes that have gutted the developed economies?"

"You can't blame them for our gullibility. China has done a competent job of looking out for themselves." Irene said.

"So how would China feel about the Cabal?" Eacher asked.

"I'm not sure where China stands, but I've got my suspicions. Let's talk to Windy about that." Irene said.

The Leap

Irene returns with Eacher to his house. They enter warily and conceal their scooters, so they are not visible from the street. They don't plan on staying long; they are apprehensive that the feds know where he lives.

They do their best to quietly put everything back in order inside the house. Some furniture is not fixable or maybe just not to Irene's taste, and it ends up in the woodshed.

They text Paul to see if they can stop by.

When they arrive late in the afternoon, they notice that Kirk, Paul, Rose, and Clare are all out in the yard. They knock on the front door, and Windy comes to meet them.

"Eacher! You're back!" Windy said.

They exchange greetings and Eacher introduces Irene.

"I've heard a lot about you!" Windy said.

"She's heard about you too. Would you mind if Irene joins you in the house while I visit with Paul?"

"Not at all. I could use the company. Irene, please come in. I'm making dinner." Windy said.

Eacher watches them walk to the kitchen porch, and he heads to the garden. Windy cooks on the grill on the back porch as she updates Irene on their hostile neighbors. Windy also advises her of her intentions to return to China soon.

Irene speaks about her recent ordeals but doesn't share many specifics. She wears a glove that conceals her disfigurement. She then casually mentions the group she ran across at the Lost Woods and their hatred for China.

"Which one?" Windy asked. "There seem to be a lot of groups with a negative impression of my country. It's like an officially sanctioned narrative about China is being fed to outsiders."

"I've seen my share of dangerous narratives," Irene said. "The group I'm talking about is some sort of billionaire's club determined to consolidate most of the energy in this country for themselves. I've nicknamed them the Cabal."

"Ah, yes. We've heard something about such a group in China. Aren't they also big Net Zero supporters?" Windy said.

"Really? You've heard of them? That's remarkable!" Irene said.

"Not really. Many groups hate China, and some have taken a few swipes at us. This particular group doesn't like that our country believes in providing our citizens sufficient energy access."

"All this is new to me. Can you tell me more?" Irene asked.

"Well, people have the wrong impression of China. They think that if the rest of the world goes over the cliff with Net Zero, we'll have access to a larger share of the world's resources. It doesn't work like that. We still need a lot of energy imports and world-class suppliers; if the rest of the world goes missing, we've got a severe problem. Previous Chinese dynasties often deliberately isolated themselves from the rest of the world, which just didn't work out well. We don't seek isolation. We want to be part of a global system where technological innovation comes from many parts of the world. We're better off when the rest of the world keeps up or catches up." Windy said.

"Well, that's certainly not what I've read in the news," Irene said.

"Well, consider your source. How much of what you've learned about the issues with climate science came from the media?"

"Point taken," Irene said. "Can I ask you an odd question?" Irene said.

"Go ahead."

"Well, if China had a way of reducing the influence of this organization in the United States, would they be interested?" Irene said.

"Maybe. I know some people that know some people." Windy said.

"What are you thinking?"

Irene gives her some background on what they've learned about the Cabal. She describes the debate that Eacher went through and how they edited it for their purposes. She admits that the United States seems to be in an economic death spiral. Still, if they could simply pull the nose of the plane up a little, they could keep it from auguring even further into the ground.

"So you're wondering how you could somehow influence the national election," Windy said flatly with disbelief.

"Kind of. We're sure this Cabal is a big supporter of our current administration. If we could find a way to publicize where the Cabal and the President are trying to take us, it might give the other candidate a chance." Irene said.

"Sounds unlikely," Windy said.

"Without help, it's not remotely possible. With the right assistance, perhaps it could work?"

"What are the chances that you could provide something that compelling? You don't have much time." Windy asked.

"Better than you'd guess," Irene said. "The Cabal leaders are getting overconfident and a little sloppy. I think there's a chance that we can come up with a real zinger!"

"Do you have anything right now that you can share with me? It will help me reach higher-level officials." Windy said.

"I've got some video that I took on my phone. It's low quality but will give you some sense of what I'm talking about."

"All right, share what you have, and let me send some emails," Windy said. "I'll let you know if I hear something back."

***

Irene and Eacher eat dinner with Paul's family.

They learn about the deadly battles in the neighborhood and are concerned for their safety. They offer to help, but Paul insists that their assistance is unnecessary. Rose offers to let them stay for the night since it's a long way home, and it might be better to return to Eacher's house during the light of day.

Eacher and Irene discuss the idea and accept the offer. They insist on sleeping in the barn, and after a persistent effort to get them to stay in the living room, Rose relents. Having a roof over their head will be a slight step up in luxury from their recent nights spent under the stars.

They lay out the blankets and pillows Rose shared on a rough wooden floor in the barn shed. They then take a seat on two small stools near their bedding.

"Irene, what did you learn from Windy?" Eacher said.

"You're not going to believe it," Irene said.

"Try me," Eacher said.

Irene then updates Eacher on her discussion. There is a chance of China assisting if Irene and Eacher can come up with anything genuinely compelling.

"Wow. Just in time for the election!" Eacher said. "I've still got Jenny Almond's contact information."

Irene ponders something quietly. "We might have more bullets than we realized." She said. "You've got connections with a Presidential candidate who is ready for a change. Windy might have some valuable Chinese connections. The two of us have a pretty good idea of the type of footage we need."

"Yeah, but how exactly might we solve that part of the puzzle?" Eacher said.

"I'm pretty sure we can't just show up at the Lost Woods and ask for a brochure," Irene said.

"No, it's not going to be that simple,"

"But there's another vital component here that we haven't really brought up. Our country is so much weaker than it once was. Those drastic changes in circumstances have radically weakened the ability and willingness of most of us to take a chance on anything. So many people are living hand to mouth these days, it's difficult to recall what it was like. This might be the last chance to rally people in a different direction."

"People have been so deadened by all this that many have simply tuned the world out," Irene said.

"Jenny is trying to get the word out, but she's just not being heard."

"Yes, but the reality is that this is about the destiny of our country. Are we better off with a few prosperous elites and the rest living in poverty?" Irene looked at him with a determined look.

If we can get that message out, we might make a difference in the outcome." Eacher placed his hands over his eyes, and he was undoubtedly winding down for the evening.

"If we do this, we'll be risking our lives," Irene said. "Are you sure you're willing to take this on?"

"Yes, if we miss this window, there may never be another one," Eacher said.

"Anything else?" Irene said.

"The money available to fund the media has disappeared in this country. There are only a few starving news services that are begging for income. You feed them a real story; we may be able to focus this nation's attention in a way that hasn't been possible since Pearl Harbor. Maybe we can even get China to pay for some advertising."

"Interesting notion. Find the exposé and turn the key." Irene said.

"Perhaps it's an idea that's ripe?" Eacher said.

"You've got a lead on how to get what we need?" Irene asked.

"Maybe," Eacher said.

"Seriously? What are you thinking?" Irene said.

"Look, I can't justify putting you in harm's way again," Eacher said. "If I tell you what I'm thinking, would you consider staying here and allowing me to go to the Lost Woods alone?"

"Not a chance. I need this. If we go down, let's do it together." Irene said.

"Are you sure? It just seems so ill-advised. Winter is coming, and neither of us has enough food set aside. Shouldn't we really use what little time we have left to look out for our immediate needs?" Eacher said.

"This is everyone's window of opportunity," Irene said. "If I've got to beg or go hungry later to survive the next few months, I'll do it.

It's now or never!"

"Who's to say that the transition we might enable would be any better than the one the Cabal has chosen?" Eacher said.

"The difference is that we're thinking of others less fortunate, and they aren't. Now would be an optimal time to focus on a more inclusive energy transition!" Irene said.

"No regrets here as long as we're a team," Eacher said.

"Let's do this," Irene said.

Termination

It's been five days since the last encounter with the gang attacking their neighborhood. A warning message goes off on Rose's phone, and she immediately wakes up and reads it. The text reports three people on two horses on the prowl. The night is overcast and darker than the previous night, so the message is less clear on what is happening. Rose forwards the text message to Eacher and rouses Windy and Kirk.

The four of them move to the barn with their weapons, and Eacher and Irene are ready for them when they arrive. Rose quickly sets out the defense plan and gives Eacher and Irene some dynamite. They all head into position.

They hear the horses walking toward them on the pavement about ten minutes later. Then, the chain securing the front gate fell to the ground. "They did have bolt cutters!" Rose whispers to Paul. The rusty hinges on the front gate groan loudly as it swings open.

Cappy hears the sound at the front gate and furiously barks inside the house. None of the lights in the house come on though he continues to bark and claw at the front door to get out.

They listen closely to determine if the horses entered their property or the riders dismounted. They hear the sound of a foot in a stirrup, and then the horses continue down the road. They all stay where Rose had positioned them and continue to wait. Rose sends a situation update on her phone to their neighborhood watch list.

About a half hour later, they hear gunshots. There are some initial blasts in rapid succession. There are a few retorts shortly after, a few explosions, and a few individual shots. Then there is a small muffled explosion in the direction of Spike's property. They wait for the horses to pass by on their way home, but they do not.

Rose gets a report of the night's events. The gang of three is no more. The visitors expected the occupants to be well-armed and ready for them, but they were surprised by the dynamite. When they reacted to it, it exposed them to gunfire. Two raiders are now sprawled dead on the soil in their front yard. One of the women attackers is gravely injured but still alive. The horses have been captured without injury.

Paul and Rose jump on scooters and drive to the attacked farm. Everyone else is encouraged to go back to bed.

When they arrive, they notice a fallen tree across the entrance to the farm. It looks like one of their sticks of dynamite was used to keep the invaders from escaping back to the road.

In the porch light, they notice bullet holes around the door frame and holes in the window glass. There are sheets over two bodies. An injured woman is reclining against the side of the front yard porch under the occupants' watchful eye.

"You okay?" Rose recognizes her as the leader of the fed group that searched their house.

"Do I look okay?" The woman is more than a bit irritated but sounds clear-headed.

"Actually, you look like shit. You've been gut shot." Rose doesn't see any wounds other than the one in her stomach.

"It feels like an ovary exploded."

"That must hurt! Your name is Layla?"

"How'd you know that?" There is a lot of blood on the dirt around her.

"You gave us your card when you visited."

"Who is that with you? I don't recognize him?"

"That's my husband, Paul."

"Paul, nice to meet you." Layla coughs up some blood and grips her abdomen in pain.

"The pleasure is mine." Paul has always had a low tolerance for blood, and he walks over to sit next to the neighbors.

Rose takes a backpack that has been lying on the ground. She quickly rummages through it to ensure it doesn't contain any weapons. She then uses it as a pillow to prop Layla up into a sitting position. "How's that feel?" Rose said.

"Why should you care?" Layla coughs again.

"I hate to see anyone in this kind of pain," Rose said. "Do you want any water?"

"Better not. Doctors may have to operate." Layla grips her waist again. "Do you know if they called an ambulance?"

"I don't know. Let me check." Rose walks over to the occupants and quietly asks. "Any calls for an ambulance?"

"If you're going to call one, can I shoot her one more time? Those bastards were trying to kill us earlier." The man of the house spits in Layla's direction. "Good thing that we were ready for them."

"Look, we can't stop the internal bleeding. If this attacker doesn't get medical help really fast, she will not make it. Tell you what, let me call one." Rose said.

"Go ahead. I won't stop you." The farmer said.

Rose walks back over to Layla. "Nope, it doesn't look like anyone called an ambulance. You want one?"

"Damn!" Layla grimaces at the thought, and this knowledge seems to deflate her a bit.

"Can you *please* call an ambulance?"

Layla's voice trails off with these remarks.

Rose pulls out her phone and hits a few digits. "We've got an emergency. Need an ambulance. Gunshot wound." Rose gave the address and put the phone back in her pocket.

"Thanks," Layla said.

Rose didn't mention that the ambulance they called for Bart didn't show up until the next day. "You guys ever find Eacher?"

"He was there the day that we searched your property. I'm sure of it." Layla seems to be seeking confirmation from her on this detail.

"Yeah, he was there hiding with my husband." Rose is now betting that Layla doesn't survive the night, and it's a gamble to encourage her to talk by trading information with her. If Rose is wrong and Layla lives, she and Paul might be at risk.

"I knew it! I should have looked myself. We did hear that he made it to the party." Layla closes her eyes and recoils from the pain.

"Why were you after him?" Rose watches her response.

"Those were our orders." She said. "Also, we quickly figured out this was a nice neighborhood where we could move our families. Chasing Eacher let us get a closer look."

"You were after our land?"

233

"The cities are falling apart. Residences are just a door lock or window pane away from anyone that wants what's inside." Layla pauses to catch her breath.

"You don't really work for the Feds?"

"We did until recently."

"What happened?" Rose asked.

"You just kicked our ass." Layla closes her eyes again and then falls off the backpack. She lies on her side in the dirt.

"Do you need me to adjust your position?"

"No, this feels better." Drool is coming out of her mouth with whatever is in her stomach; she seems to have little energy to even spit.

"Are there any more of your people coming this way?" Rose places her hand on her side to reassure her that she's still there.

"They'll find softer targets elsewhere." Layla is breathing hard as if she can't catch her breath.

"So they aren't coming here?" Rose wishes she could save this question for another day but doesn't think Layla has one coming.

"Nah, no word from us means stay away."

"So, you're not really looking for Eacher?"

Layla coughs in considerable pain. "Not recently."

Rose wipes her face with a wet cloth.

"The government thinks he might be telling the truth?" Rose looks at the color of Layla's face. She's not wearing any makeup, and her skin is turning grey before her eyes.

Layla reaches up and squeezes her forehead between her thumb and fingers. Speaking seems to be distracting her from the pain. "That has nothing to do with it." Layla returns her hands to her waist, trying to cover the hole where she's bleeding.

"Then why set Bart's house on fire?" Rose places a towel between Layla's hand and her wound.

"We didn't mean to. We wanted to keep it." Her voice is becoming weaker, and she is trying to adjust her position.

"And yet you moved from there?" Rose said.

234

Layla takes a moment to respond to this question. She's clearly fading. "For a while."

Paul walks back over, trying not to notice all her body fluids soaking into the ground.

"Did you guys have anything to do with me losing my job?"

"Why would we? Who are you again?" Her tone is irritated but without any force. She closes her eyes, and her face relaxes.

Rose puts her face close to Layla's. Her chest stops moving, and she feels for a pulse but can't find one. She walks over to the residents to let them know she's dead.

The resident offered Rose a plastic tarp to cover the body. Rose repositions Layla and then covers the body from head to toe.

She and Paul then say goodbye.

They return home on their scooters.

***

The next day Rose calls the neighbors and confirms that an ambulance showed up in the morning. The emergency staff confirmed that there was nothing they could do and left. She sends Kirk and Paul over to assist with burying the bodies.

Rose updates Eacher and Irene on their conversation from the night before, and they head back to Eacher's house. Rose lets them keep the dynamite she had given them the night before.

Rose sends a text message to the local militia. She outlines most of her final conversation with Layla, suggesting that the regional threat is over. Had the neighborhood been unable to augment their collective defense with Bart's stash or stay in mutual communication, the result might have been very different.

Layla's crew had been well-armed and skilled in violence.

Rose arranges to visit the farm where the attackers had been living recently. Three people ride on two horses on the road in front of their farm, and Rose follows on a scooter. She arrives shortly and takes the lead to knock on the door.

A young boy comes to the door in pajamas, half asleep, and Rose asks him if any adults are available. The child looks and then returns to let her know there are none. After some questioning, they learn that Rusty is now buried in a fresh grave in the backyard.

Rose enters the house and looks through the drawers to see if anything explains who these people are. Much of the material she uncovers comes from the original occupants. Rose stacks that material in one pile on the table. Then, she finds a trunk that apparently belonged to the newcomers. She finds some audio-visual bugs similar to the one placed in their home. In addition, a receiver allows someone to monitor the output. A moving receipt also shows a company paying for their move to this neighborhood. Rose places the invoice and the devices into her backpack and returns home.

The new family at Bart's place is offered the chance to move to this winterized farmhouse. They accept. They also agree to raise these kids. No one expects any relatives to ever turn up to claim them. They can use the horses to pull an old wagon in Bart's barn to move their stuff.

A week later, another group of people shows up without notice at Bart's place. Rose and Paul visit and confirm that they have adequate supplies for the winter and are relatives of a family that lives in the area. They share this information with the local neighborhood group.

***

Paul and Rose make it a point to drive by the wind turbine near Spike's house; the blades on the one nearest to his house are not turning. This seems odd since it is a windy day, and the other wind turbines nearby are rotating at considerable speed.

Rose and Paul were never quite able to confirm exactly what happened. Even so, that particular wind turbine near Spike's house suddenly experienced a terminal issue with its gearbox. It is the kind of device that two sticks of dynamite could effectively disable if one wasn't afraid to climb several hundred feet up the ladder to reach it.

Rose stops by Spike's cabin to ask him if he might know what happened to that wind turbine. He denies that he was the source of the problem. Rose asks him if he can give the leftover dynamite back. He apologizes that it has been used for other purposes related to the battle. He declines to go into any further detail on the matter.

However, he offers to share some deer meat sausage with Rose, and she readily accepts his generous offer. He seems to be in a better mood than the last few times she's seen him.

The Plan
EACHER'S HOUSE

Eacher and Irene formulate a plan. The risk is unavoidable, but the remote possibility of success pushes them forward.

Windy's return call to Irene assures them that the Chinese are interested. Even so, they won't commit until they see precisely what Irene and Eacher can produce. Their time window before the election is closing rapidly.

Irene calls Dora and takes the time to explain why she left the compound on short notice and without warning. She dared not relay her concerns that she and Eacher were targeted using the GPS devices they had installed on their scooters. Dora does not sound overly concerned with her absence but does try to press her to learn where she is staying.

Irene tells her she's traveling for the next day or two but will be at her own house by the end of the week.

Dora thanked her for the update.

Eacher raises the idea of contacting the newest climate skeptic students currently at the Lost Woods. Irene considers it but doesn't know enough to trust them with their plans.

Eacher agrees with her analysis.

"Did Jenny suggest the date?" Irene asked.

"Sort of.

There's some evidence that the President will be in the right part of the country around that time." Eacher said. "There also appears to be an unexplained hole in her schedule that evening."

"That's the best we have. If Madam President doesn't show, we'll have to try to locate some sort of video library on location." Irene said.

"Trying to locate electronic files at a hostile location would be a Kamikaze mission. If it comes to that, let's simply consider abandoning the assignment." Eacher said.

237

"You're probably right. That place is well secured, and most doors are locked or opened with biometric devices that would announce that we're there." Irene said. "If we end up that desperate, let's reconsider whether it makes sense to try and contact one of those climate skeptics on location."

"True, but our most important advantage is that they don't know that we know the Cabal exists," Eacher said.

"We still might be able to catch them by surprise and get out before they know what we've done."

"Let's hope it doesn't come to that," Eacher said.

"Oh, by the way, Windy mentioned that they had recovered some listening devices and receivers. They were in the drawers of the group that had been attacking their neighborhood. Those hostiles are now all dead, by the way."

"I'm sorry to hear about the deaths but glad that Paul and his family are now safer. Do you think they might let us use their new toys?"

"You're right. We could put those to work," Irene said.

Observing
ARKANSAS AND THE LOST WOODS

Eacher and Irene stop by the Stewart house. Paul and Kirk are on a walk, but Rose and Windy are home. Rose is still running on adrenaline and gives them a complete account of how their neighborhood dealt with the well-armed invaders.

When she finishes, Eacher informs them of the upcoming trip to the Lost Woods.

Windy wishes them luck and offers her hope that everything goes as planned. She's not feeling well and returns to her bedroom to rest.

Rose insists on getting a full update on the plan and more background on the Cabal.

Irene takes the lead and lays out the situation, plan, and contingencies. She then covers what she knows about the Cabal.

Rose offers some insightful suggestions and volunteers to loan them the listening devices and receivers.

Irene goes over the details again and addresses how they will be incorporated into the mission.

Eacher listens attentively as these two women sift through all the operational specifics.

Rose retrieves the promised electronics from her desk and gives them to Eacher. He places a receiver in an envelope, includes a note, and then leaves it with Rose.

Rose then loans them her small handgun and gives them a box of ammunition. They still have the two sticks of dynamite she had given them recently.

Irene and Eacher head back to the Lost Woods.

Eacher and Irene take turns driving most of the night and the following day. Once again, their miracle battery has saved them a lot of refueling concerns. They arrive at the Lost Woods just before sunset.

They wait for someone to enter the gate, speed behind them, and enter the facility before it closes.

They conceal the bike in the woods inside the complex not far from the entry gate.

They walk through the woods in the dark to the compound. After not seeing anyone in the area, they sneak into the Temple. Irene shows him where the lecturer stood previously.

It's in the central area along the back wall. Eacher places an audio-visual listening device on a wall that faces where any speakers will likely be standing. There is no podium at this location, so he imagines that the speaker is somehow set up with a wireless microphone. He didn't know how long their device would broadcast, but Rose had fully charged it and thought the battery ought to last a week or two.

Irene and Eacher return to where they had stashed their scooter and equipment. There is obviously no activity on location this evening, and they quietly discuss how long they'll stay if nothing happens. They find a well-concealed spot where they spread their blanket and sleep together under the stars.

They lay low the next day. They try to stay out of the sun and eat some food they brought. They find some potable water in a local stream. There is a bit of janitorial activity in the Temple, and they observe it from Irene's hiding spot.

On the third day, traffic into and out of the gate picks up. A catering truck shows up and delivers food which they both take as a positive sign. From a safe distance, they note some official-looking people in dark suits systematically combing through the complex.

They return to watch the gate, and a modest amount of traffic comes through.

Eacher and Irene then eat the last of their rations and sneak closer to the Temple in anticipation of a service.

Screened by the woods, they return to Irene's vantage point, where they can observe activity at the Temple. A few hours later, they are rewarded for their efforts when a column of people in long blue robes open a door and then walk into the room in a straight line.

Another individual walks out of a different door built into the wall where Irene had seen the speaker before. This person walks to the front of the group and then lowers her hood. It's Dora.

Eacher starts recording from the small audio-visual device they had placed. Both Irene and Eacher listen through Bluetooth ear devices.

Dora launches into some remarks. "To all of you watching this presentation remotely, thank you for your time and continued support. We continue to move toward the next national election in the United States. Our candidate for President will almost certainly win a second term. And when she does so, we'll help her tighten the screws on Net Zero even further. Electricity is not necessary for a good life. Hot water, refrigeration, and air conditioning are all luxuries the planet can't afford. Help our President hold the line on these principles. I will stop speaking now and let our special guest explain what's in store next term."

The rear wall door opens, and a figure walks to the speaking area. It's the President of the United States. She follows up on everything Dora described. In particular, she confirms her administration's efforts to relocate the population from cities to small farms, the reduction in national energy usage, and their dedication to further eliminate fossil fuels and commercial fertilizers. She thanks Dora by name and promises to make China the world's pariah for failing to pursue Net Zero. The President then extends her appreciation for the generous financial support given by those present and those watching from a distance.

Dora gives a few parting words.

Eacher pulls his phone out of his pocket to check the time. The flashlight feature automatically illuminates, which lights up his face and reveals their position. He plunges it back into his pocket. He looks toward the Temple, where Dora is pointing up in their direction to the security staff. Against the Temple's light, he observes many people outside the building heading their way. He suspects that some of them are special agents for the President.

Eacher and Irene stand up, hold onto their gear and move into the woods. It's dark, and there is little visibility. Eacher says, Mayday-Mayday as they follow the trail back to their scooter. Irene grips the back of his shirt in the darkness.

Flashlights now shine all around them. An elevated overhead searchlight kicks on and bathes the area in even more light as it moves back and forth across the compound. The additional illumination assists Eacher and Irene in seeing where they are going and allows them to move faster.

They find where they had left their scooter, and Eacher slips their gear into his bag and throws it over his shoulder. The two quickly mount the scooter and speed toward the front gate.

He does his best to shield her from the branches slapping him in the face, and she does her best to protect him from the bullets that are barely missing them. Irene wraps her arms around his waist with surprising calmness, perhaps for the last time.

Several bullets slam into nearby trees not far from them.

Suddenly a giant monster truck comes barreling through the fence and stops next to them. Rose yells, "get in," from the driver's window. Paul jumps out of the passenger door, takes a shooting stance above the truck's hood, and fires several rounds at the lead pursuers. Kirk gets out to direct Eacher and Irene into the back seat opposite the gunfire. Paul dives back into the cab as Windy fires a few rounds out her window behind Rose. Everyone's ears ring from the concussion of those shots.

The second Paul is inside, Rose buries the gas pedal, and the truck plows through the fence not far from the first hole she had made. She heads away along the perimeter road at considerable speed.

242

They race back to Rose and Paul's house and make good time despite the numerous potholes.

The truck has stacks of scuba tanks filled with natural gas in a wooden rack behind the pickup truck's cab. Each canister is connected to the fuel system through a manifold arrangement. This system allows them to avoid stopping to change the tanks, and they make good time. It takes about eight hours to make it back to the Stewart residence.

As they arrive home, it's almost sunrise, and a soft orange hue just above the ground gives way to yellow rays that push the blue sky higher on the horizon.

Eacher and Windy go inside to transfer the recorded material onto her computer.

Windy loads these files to the designated website using her Chinese Satellite Internet connection.

Eacher later sends an email to Jenny letting her know they've transferred their video to the Chinese. Later that day, they post the same material at an Internet link that Jenny provides them.

Transitions
ARKANSAS

Windy notes that after the leaves change color and the weather cools, the windows allow a fresh breeze to cool the house. Everyone works together to bottle vegetables for the winter and do their best to prepare for the upcoming wintery weather. Kirk and Paul cut logs with hand saws and axes. Windy caulks the windows and doors and tightens the insulation throughout the house.

There is a family discussion about whether it makes sense to attempt to utilize the sludge in the septic tank for fertilizer. Paul points out that doing so could trigger issues with amoebic dysentery.

Rose recommends that they defecate in the outhouse and use the night soil directly. Paul promises to do more homework on these ideas, since commercial fertilizer is too scarce.

Paul researches potential jobs, and Windy tries to assist. His primary objective is to find a remote position that will allow him to work from home. This would be convenient, but the competition for such jobs is fierce, and the resulting pay would likely be modest.

He's competing with an international labor force, often willing to work for a few yuan a day. This work takes a lot of time and keeps Windy in the shade on most days.

***

Just after this discussion, Windy starts preparing to return to China.

Kirk seems a bit conflicted. "Why don't we wait a little longer before we head back?"

Windy knows Kirk would like to help his brother's family but comprehends what both would be giving up by not returning to China. "No, I think we've stayed long enough."

"When?" Kirk asked.

"Now." Windy replies.

"It might be tricky to get to Houston."

"Yes, but I don't know if it will ever get easier."

"Got it," Kirk said. "I'll travel with you to Houston." He heads off to assist Paul with something.

Windy is interested in something other than the kind of labor available on this farm. One year in the fields would age her ten years. She has to get away while she can still benefit from the escape.

She hoped Kirk would return with her, but his answer didn't promise that result. She is prepared to go home without him.

Windy phones Gus, who indicates that he can stop by within a week but is unclear on the specifics.

She agrees that the deal terms will remain the same as the last trip.

Windy updates Kirk on her call to Gus. They both pack their suitcases and prepare to leave on short notice.

***

Windy finds Clare sitting in the living room doing homework. "Got a minute?"

"Sure," Clare said. "I've heard you're leaving."

"Yes, we're just waiting for our ride."

"It was an eye-opener to have you here. You're much different than most of the women that live around here."

"You mean because I'm Chinese?"

"No. I mean, because you think differently."

"How so?"

"Well, you've figured out this whole Net Zero thing is a mistake."

"Your parents don't share this opinion?"

"None of the parents around here do, and none of the kids do either."

"Everyone is entitled to their perspective on the matter," Windy said.

246

"Maybe. You're the only one I know that voices a different one."

"I come from a different country. We made different decisions."

"Will China follow a Net Zero path?" She stares hard at Windy when she asks this question.

"No, probably not. There is even less reason to be confident that there are valid climate concerns now than when the US launched itself on this path."

"You're confident that's true?" She runs her fingers through her hair, and they get hung up on some hair knots. She removes her fingers from her hair.

"Yes. A country with a higher standard of living for its citizens is better prepared for the future."

"So, the US is in trouble?" Clare looks particularly distressed by this last comment.

"Look, I don't see how you go from where you are now to where we are in China. We use a lot of energy and manufacture a lot, and it's a good life. Since I've been here, I've learned a lot about how not to implement an energy transition."

"How did this happen to us?" Clare looks like she might cry.

"I can only speculate on what I've heard or suspect is true. Perhaps those Net Zero enthusiasts meant well, but their policies have done more damage than carbon dioxide could ever do."

"I've got nothing to compare this to," Clare said. "I've been taught all the wonderful reasons why we followed those policies."

"Do you believe them?"

"Would if I hadn't learned that China and India ignored it and are doing much better. Why would our government do this if the other large carbon dioxide emitters didn't agree to do it too?"

"Now, that's a great question. Keep asking it." Windy said.

Clare paused as if to give that recommendation some time to sink in. "Should I go to college?"

"What do you want to do?"

247

"Does it matter? I will be farming this land for the rest of my life."

"Learning is always important. If you don't enroll in college, keep studying anyway. There's a good chance that someday, it will matter. Don't give up on what will happen in the coming years."

"It seems like your country is the one with an exciting future."

"We'll see about that," Windy said. "I wish you and your family the best. Stay in touch? I'm just an email or phone call away."

"That means a lot to me. I'll miss you!" Clare said.

The Return
GULF COAST

They lose track of time as trying days run into each other. Each move takes them back and forth between Louisiana, Arkansas, and Texas. Some days they'll end up closer to Houston, and the next day finds them farther from their destination.

Windy naturally takes on the role of move manager, leaving her out of the heavy lifting and putting her planning and organization skills to good use, orchestrating others.

Gus has dropped three people off and picked up two others. It's icy in the back, and they cloak themselves with furniture blankets when riding there. They still have one more day before they must be in Houston to catch the boat, and Gus assures them they'll make it.

They run low on fuel and pull into a gas station along Interstate 20 in Texas.

They passed this area the day before, and this particular gas station looked normal.

Today is a different story. Someone assaulted the convenience store, and glass shards cover the floor. Through the window gaps, they see bare shelves, and they keep their distance.

Had this been the work of a passing gang, Kirk would have expected to see garbage and empty bottles thrown around the store and the lot, which is not the case.

Perhaps the corporation that ran the gas station pulled all their merchandise? Someone cleaned out this place.

Gus tests a diesel pump to see if he can still pay by credit card, but the electricity is off. They start to pull away when someone comes racing after them, and Gus slows down to hear what he has to say.

"Can you take me with you?" He yells as he jogs next to them.

Gus stops.

"Why are you here?" he asked.

"I was the clerk." He said.

"What happened?" Gus looks at him warily.

Kirk alerts to a skull tattoo on his upper neck.

"This morning, a truck pulled up, and some criminals just took over the convenience store. They smashed cameras and then loaded everything in the store on their truck. As they left, they busted the glass." He said.

"How did you get here?" Gus asked.

"I had a scooter, but they took that with them." He said.

"Where you going?" Gus asked.

"Home." He said. "Right now, I just want to get away from here."

"I'm sorry we can't help you," Gus said. The truck accelerated out of the lot, and a few minutes later, they were back on the Interstate, heading to the gas station at the next exit.

"Why'd you do that?" Kirk asked.

"I didn't trust him. I don't think he is who he claims to be."

Gus then tells Windy and Kirk about his observations on what is going on with the gas stations. The loot at these gas stations isn't the food; it's the gasoline and diesel. Clerks comply, or they get shot. The ones that comply get beaten up as a courtesy; otherwise, they look guilty of the robbery. This guy looks like he hasn't suffered enough. Also, he seems a bit rough for a store clerk.

Gus finds an open gas station at the next truck stop and fills his fuel tanks.

As they leave, Kirk notices the guy who claimed he was a clerk earlier show up on a motorcycle with several others also on motorcycles.

One of them walks over to another truck that is still filling up. That guy takes out a long knife and punches through the front tire of that truck.

Gus quickly drives out of the truck stop and slowly heads to the feeder road; he hits his horn twice, an agreed signal. One of the passengers riding with him heard the horn blasts and came sprinting out of the restroom holding his pants up with his hands. Gus slows down enough for him to climb onto the driver's sideboard. He holds on to the mirror as Gus pulls onto the feeder road and accelerates onto the Interstate.

The bikers behind them quickly jump back on their bikes, speeding after Gus's truck.

As they close in, Kirk reaches into his bag and pulls out a stick of dynamite with a fuse. He waits until they get a little closer, lights it near the end of the fuse, leans out the window, and tosses it above the truck. It lands right in front of the motorcycles and explodes.

The lead biker loses control of his bike and lays it down on the highway. The other cycles change direction quickly to avoid him, and they leave the road in the direction of the woods to the right.

They all stop following Gus's truck.

Kirk breathes a sigh of relief. It was the only stick of dynamite that he'd brought. Had he missed, they'd have been defenseless.

He looks over at Windy, who has reached into her bag and now holds a stick of dynamite that she's ready to pass to him. She learns fast.

Gus stops a few miles later to allow the passenger, still standing on the running board on the driver's side of the truck, to return to the cargo area. Gus only slows down again when he reaches Houston.

***

As Gus pulls into the port terminal area, Windy and Kirk are still sitting in the front of the truck.

"Just drop us off over there." Windy gestures toward a bus stop not far from the entrance to the port facility.

Gus pulls the truck over. Gus and Windy jump out of the cab, and each grabs their suitcase from the back. Two other riders in the rear head to the cab.

Windy returns to the driver-side window. She steps on the running board and hands Gus a dynamite stick in a paper bag. He places it in a canvas bag under the passenger seat, to the surprise of his new passengers.

He thanks them for assisting with the outlaws. He promises to pick them up again if they ever need another ride in this part of the country. He drives off slowly and waves out the window as he leaves.

There are the usual bums living around the port terminal, and Kirk thinks he might even recognize one or two from the last time they were here. He and Windy each pull a tattered suitcase and start walking towards the entrance; they blend in with the locals in their moving clothes.

They look pretty shabby and don't draw much notice from the vagrants in the yard this time.

"Can I help you?" An employee asks them when they enter the ticket area.

"Maybe," Kirk said. "Our boat doesn't leave until tomorrow, and we need a place to stay tonight."

"Which boat is yours?"

"It's the Mulan," Windy said.

"Ah, you guys are heading to China?"

"Yes, we have tickets already. Do you know if they'd let us stay on the ship tonight?" Windy asked.

"Probably so." The porter said. "Your boat is the fifth one on the right, and it's been here unloading for a few days. Go talk to their ticket desk upstairs."

They carry their luggage to the ticket purchase area. One person is sitting at the counter for the China Star passenger service.

Windy asks him something in Chinese. He responds and starts entering information into his computer screen and responds to her.

She turns to face Kirk. "My ticket is good." She said. "It was an open round trip ticket that they will honor. Yours was a one-way ticket from China?"

"I'm sorry, I should have mentioned that." He said. "Do they have any room for me?"

Windy proceeds to engage the clerk in a discussion about a ticket. "Yes, they have room, but it's going to cost us another five thousand yuan to get you on this boat."

"Windy, do we still have that kind of money? It's been an expensive trip."

She completes her discussion with the clerk. She then directs Kirk to chairs in the back of the room with their suitcases in tow.

"Kirk, we need to talk."

"Yes."

"Why didn't you buy yourself a round-trip ticket before we left China?"

"Well, it occurred to me that we might want to stay in the United States."

"But you reserved a round-trip ticket for me?"

"Yes, you control our finances, but you let me reserve the tickets in this case. I always knew that you were going to return to China."

"Given what we've encountered here, that was a reasonable assumption. Why did you think you might not be returning with me?"

"Windy, why aren't you pregnant? I did my best to make it happen."

"You're changing the subject, but that's a reasonable question. I'm still on birth control."

"Think you might have mentioned that?"

"Would it have made any difference in the number of times you wanted to have sex?"

"It was a bit sobering knowing that what we were doing wasn't just for fun. I'm a little intimidated about the idea of having kids."

"You are? You never mentioned that before."

"Look, you're an intelligent, beautiful woman, and our kids would likely have those advantages. It's such a big commitment, and a child would require a lot of attention."

"And you don't think you'd be able to provide it?" Windy asked.

"I'd do my best, but it's been so nice to have you all to myself – at least when you're not traveling for business."

"After being here for six months, do you still feel like you might want to stay?"

"Look, I get it. This place is in bad shape."

"It would be hard to argue otherwise," Windy said.

"I still recall what it was like before I left. Take my word; the United States used to be very different."

"Oh, I've heard plenty of stories, and I'm pretty sure you're not exaggerating how things were."

"I'm not," Kirk said.

"So, you now want to go back to China?"

"I don't know. Do you want me to go back with you?"

She was quiet for what seemed like a few minutes. Finally, she whispers. "I'm not sure either." She pauses again. "You've been a different person around your brother and his family, and we've both been able to contribute to the work required. What are you going to do in China?"

"You're giving me a job interview?" Kirk asked in a surprised tone.

"What are you going to do in China if you return?"

"Well, I've been tutoring students in English, you know that."

"Yes, but who needs English these days? You've struggled to find students the last few years."

"True."

"You've tried to learn Chinese but haven't gotten very far."

"Yes, it's an exacting language. Even if I try harder, I'm not confident I'll ever be fluent."

"Without it, you can't contribute much in China these days."

"Agreed."

"Tell you what; I know you can't make your mind up on whether you want to be in the US or China. You're faithful to your family and want to be loyal to me."

"You know me."

"I also know you won't be happy in China any longer. Sure it's nice to live a more affluent lifestyle. Even so, you'd be worried about what's happening here with your brother and his family."

"Well, this trip has opened my eyes."

"Your family is here, your heart is here, and your future is here. Mine is not."

"Are you sure that I can't convince you to stay?"

"Not a chance. Everyone has to pull their weight on that farm, and I'm not going to destroy my face in the sun just getting by."

"So, what's your perspective? You're the intelligent one."

"It's time we go our separate ways."

"But, I love you." When he shares these words with her, he tries to look her straight in the eyes, but she evades his efforts.

"Is love enough? There's no way I could live here; this is too primal."

"You managed to adjust here. You were adapting well. That stick of dynamite you had in the truck was amazing! I didn't know you had it in you!"

"You're right. It's possible to survive here – at least for a while, but I don't want to." Windy said.

"It would be nice if Eacher and Irene could make a difference. Even so, if by some miracle that happens, it could be decades before this country gets its act together."

"Okay, let's forget the idea of your living here. I'm trying to figure out if you want me to return to China with you.

"Listen. You're a good guy, and I've enjoyed our time together. In a different world, we have a future together somewhere. However, my future is in China, and yours is not."

"You sure? I'm not giving up on you. I love you and want to spend the rest of my life with you?"

"Where?"

He didn't answer immediately. He gazes directly into Windy's eyes. "Where ever you are, I need to be."

"Are you sure? I can't have you second-guessing yourself for not staying with your brother's family."

"What can I do here? If I return to China, I can get a job somewhere, and we can transfer some money to them on occasion."

"Really, what will you do in China?"

"Man, aren't you taking this job interview too far? Okay, here's what I'm thinking."

"Yes?"

"That one-child policy left China with too many old people. In addition, a few deep-pocketed English-speaking people and foreign companies have moved to China. There must be something useful I can do! There must be a real chance to find meaningful work in China. If I get too depressed again, there's medicine for that. We can make it work as long as we're together."

"You don't want to stay here and help save the United States?"

"Nope, our citizens screwed themselves." This observation sounds more indifferent than he had intended but consistent with an inescapable truth. The challenges now facing this country are mostly self-inflicted, and humanity's future will not depend on anything done in this part of the world.

"And that's why you want to return to China with me?"

"No, not at all. I love you and want to help you raise a family. If we didn't do that in China, your relatives would never forgive us." He's searching her face trying to read what she's thinking. He doesn't want it to end like this and dreads how this conversation seems destined to wrap up.

"You'll help change diapers?" She stares directly back into his face, and their eyes meet.

He pauses at this remark and notices a certain twinkle in her eye. "What are you telling me? Are you…"

"Suggesting that I was on birth control was to test you. I'm about two months pregnant."

"You wouldn't have told me if we had gone our separate ways? What a disturbing idea!"

"No, I didn't want you staying with me for the wrong reasons. I can handle the worst case."

"No, you've seen the worst. I want to be with you wherever we want to be.

"What about the baby?"

"Now that it's real, it feels less scary than I imagined. You just gave me an important job." Everything is happening so fast. He struggles to catch his breath.

"Are you sure?"

"Absolutely!" He feels excited in a way that he hadn't anticipated. He's about to become a father! He then remembers the challenge at hand. "Uh, can I talk you into buying me a ticket for the trip?"

"You'll have to work it off." She said.

"I can hardly wait! Ready for a foot massage?"

"No, you don't understand. I can get you a ticket for a thousand yuan, but you'll have to be a waiter for most of the trip."

"What? The deal's off. I'm calling Gus back!"

"Just kidding. Don't be so dramatic. Grab the suitcases, and I'll buy the ticket." She starts walking back towards the ticket counter.

"Let's do this." He says as he catches up with her. "It's time to get you home."

Newsworthy

Newsworthy

WINTER, ARKANSAS

Shortly after Windy's video is uploaded, it is all over the Internet. Recent polls suggest that Jenny might only lose by thirty points.

Eacher is ecstatic and greatly encouraged that Jenny will be able to make an important statement.

Jenny asks Eacher to be her advisor, and he agrees to the position as long as Irene is also given a similar role. Jenny immediately accepts this condition. These positions allow both Eacher and Irene to join Jenny's election campaign on the road. They tell their stories about their recent adventures and respond to energy and climate questions.

Their video went viral and received ten million views in the first week. The media questions the authenticity of the material released, and the President publically claims that the person in the video is an imposter. That denial drives even more publicity. Her integrity becomes one of the most significant election issues as various facial recognition software experts confirm her identity in the footage.

Jenny's persistent jabs have the President on the ropes. She argues that if the plans set out on the tape were implemented, most people in the country would be put one more step closer to perpetual slavery.

This theme resonates throughout the country, especially in the cities. The urban vote becomes the backbone for Jenny's election success. Jenny gets elected President, and her party captures both houses of Congress.

No one is more surprised than Jenny and the others in her party. The idea of winning was such a long shot that no one in her party developed plans to run the government. In addition, the county is in such poor economic shape that the government has little access to any resources.

Mike calls to congratulate Eacher and Irene on their contribution to the new President's campaign. He was shocked by the posted video and also learned that there were gangs connected to the Lost Woods. He has now taken action; Dora and her associates have been terminated.

He apologized for any problems that happened. Mike indicates that he's on board with the country's new direction.

Given that Mike lives outside the United States, it's plausible that he didn't know what was happening. At the same time, it's also equally possible that Mike was the mastermind and simply terminated some staff to shift the blame.

Winning the election seems to have been the easy part. It remains to be seen whether Jenny and her associates will be able to make a difference.

General Comments

"**My opinion** wasn't based upon the decades of scientific study that I never conducted, it **was based on the feeling that the information was wrong, incomplete, biased, and overly politicized by groups whose general purpose in life is to dismantle western free-market economies.** Moreover, I think the movement to be a believer in the global warming theory has become overly confused with the desire for a cleaner, healthier environment. **It's as if many well-meaning people can't simply embrace the idea of clean air and water without having a catastrophic reason for doing so.** I think the desire to live in a world with blue skies, clear water, beautiful untouched forests and fields and to be free from terrorist intimidation needs no added incentives or invented hyped-up rationale."

MARC J RAUSCH

If you've made it this far and not just peeked at the back of the book, you ought to have gotten a taste of what Marc is describing.

Admittedly, the chosen Net Zero path in this novel is ludicrous.

True democracies allow those citizens in the yellow vests to have their say. Governments tend to reconsider suicidal programs that harm our interests, diminish our energy security, and threaten our collective well-being.

However, don't yet dismiss this story as pure fantasy. Please note that substantial progress on this plan is underway. Academia accepts a dire climate narrative. The media incessantly proclaims any unordinary weather event as a sign of human-induced climate change. Hollywood consistently champions these concerns. You can't fault the average person for simply assuming that all this consistent messaging is valid.

261

As evidence of the other actors in motion, recognize that recently, oil, natural gas, and coal prices have hit very high levels. There are sufficient reserves of fossil fuels; even so, activists and Net Zero enthusiasts have deliberately conspired to withhold an adequate level of capital, permits, leases, infrastructure, and social license. Why invest in making automobiles more efficient when Europe and California have already banned combustion engine vehicles within the next thirteen years? How do fossil fuel companies rationalize capital investment when the market insists they will be stranded soon? Fossil fuels provide eighty-four percent of our current global energy use. Why is it credible that wind and solar power, which account for only 5% of global energy, is the anointed solution? The certainty of these particular renewable solutions is more than a little suspect. Countries and regions chasing this dream have seen dramatic increases in their electricity rates and face regular blackouts.

It's not a question of whether this story could happen; it's already well on its way. The open question is how long we persist collectively along this path. We should come to our senses and tone down the hatred against fossil fuels, nuclear energy, and other reliable forms of energy. The remainder of this section's material is my tribute to a few that have brought considerable clarity and balance to the ongoing discussion.

"Herein lies the moral danger behind global warming hysteria. Each day, 20,000 people in the world die of waterborne diseases. Half a billion people go hungry. A child is orphaned by AIDS every seven seconds. This does not have to happen. We allow it while fretting about 'saving the planet.' What is wrong with us that we downplay this human misery before our eyes and focus on events that will probably not happen even a hundred years hence? We know that the greatest cause of environmental degradation is poverty; on this, we can and must act... Climate change is a norm, not an exception. It is both an opportunity and a challenge. The real crises for 4 billion people in the world remain poverty, dirty water and the lack of a modern energy supply. By contrast, global warming represents an ecochondria of the pampered rich."

PHILIP STOTT

Richard Lindzen, GWPF 2018 Lecture (Extract)

"*So there you have it. An implausible conjecture backed by false evidence and repeated incessantly has become politically correct 'knowledge,' and is used to promote the overturn of industrial civilization. What we will be leaving our grandchildren is not a planet damaged by industrial progress, but a record of unfathomable silliness as well as a landscape degraded by rusting wind farms and decaying solar panel arrays. False claims about 97% agreement will not spare us, but the willingness of scientists to keep mum is likely to much reduce trust in and support for science. Perhaps this won't be such a bad thing after all – certainly as concerns 'official' science.*

There is at least one positive aspect to the present situation. None of the proposed policies will have much impact on greenhouse gases. Thus we will continue to benefit from the one thing that can be clearly attributed to elevated carbon dioxide: namely, its effective role as a plant fertilizer, and reducer of the drought vulnerability of plants. Meanwhile, the IPCC is claiming that we need to prevent another 0.5°C of warming, although the 1°C that has occurred so far has been accompanied by the greatest increase in human welfare in history. *As we used to say in my childhood home of the Bronx: 'Go figure'.*"[1]

RICHARD LINDZEN

---

[1] Richard Lindzen, Global Warming for the Two Cultures

Richard Lindzen, The Imaginary Climate Crisis (Extract)

"In punching away at the clear shortcomings of the narrative of climate alarm, we have, perhaps, missed the most serious shortcoming: namely, that <u>the whole narrative is pretty absurd</u>. Of course, many people (though by no means all) have great difficulty entertaining this possibility. They can't believe that something so absurd could gain such universal acceptance.

Consider the following situation. Your physician declares that your complete physical will consist in simply taking your temperature. This would immediately suggest something wrong with your physician. He further claims that if your temperature is 37.3C rather than between 36.1C and 37.2C you must be put on life support. Now you know he is certifiably insane. The same situation for climate (a comparably complex system with a much more poorly defined index, globally averaged temperature anomaly) is considered 'settled science'."

RICHARD LINDZEN

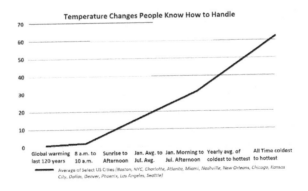

265

Figure: The total change in the mean [temperature] is much smaller than what we experience over a day, a week or over any longer period.

"And, in case this situation isn't sufficiently bizarre, there is the governmental response. It is entirely analogous to a situation that a colleague, Bruce Everett, described. After your physical, your physician tells you that you may have a fatal disease. He's not really sure, but he proposes a treatment that will be expensive and painful while offering no prospect of preventing the disease. When you ask why you would ever agree to such a thing, he says he just feels obligated to 'do something'. That is precisely what the Paris Accord amounts to. However, the 'something' also gives governments the power to control the energy sector and this is something many governments cannot resist."

"Our task is to show the relevant people the overall stupidity of this issue rather than punching away at details. In focusing on the details, we are merely trying to showcase our own specialties. My use of the word 'merely' is probably unjustified; the details can, in fact, be scientifically important. However, we are not considering either our target audience or the intrinsic absurdity of the issue. It is likely that we have to capitalize on the insecurity of the educated elite and make them look silly instead of superior and virtuous. We must remember that they are impervious to real science unless it is reduced to their level. When it is reduced to their level, it is imperative that we, at least, retain veracity. Whether we are capable of effectively doing this is an open question."[2]

[2] Richard Lindzen, *The Imaginary Climate Crisis - How Can We Change the Message?*, Irish Climate Science Forum

Quotes Too Good Not to Include

*"They [the environmentalists] should tell us how it really is. I am afraid they are not so naïve as they pretend to be, they probably only do not want to reveal their true plans and ambitions. **To stop economic development and return mankind centuries back.** In that case, with such ambitions and plans, technologies are unimportant."*

*"The **existing and functioning technologies have never been abandoned before they were genuinely replaced by better ones**. There arises for the first time in history the threat that the old technologies will be abandoned before new technologies become available."*

*"There is **no known and economically feasible method or technology by which industrialized economies can survive on expensive, unreliable, clean, green & renewable energy**.*

*"It is evident that **the environmentalists don't want to change the climate. They want to change us and our behavior. Their ambition is to control and manipulate us.** Therefore it shouldn't be surprising that they recommend preventive, not adaptive policies. Adaption would be a voluntary behavior. "Our" voluntary behavior. Which is not what they aim at. The capacity to adapt is arguably the most fundamental characteristic of mankind and **our adaptive capacity is increasing all the time** with the development of technology."[3]*

VACLAV KLAUS

---

[3] Vaclav Klaus, for*mer President of the Czech Republic, Debunking Global Warming*

Contemplating the Big Picture

Here's a drawing from 1956 by Marion King Hubbert.

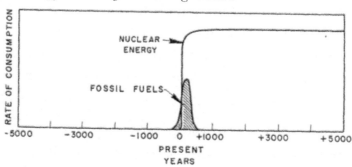

Relative magnitudes of possible fossil-fuel and nuclear-energy consumption seen in time perspective of minus to plus 5,000 years. [4]

Here's the way I'd slightly modify that drawing today:

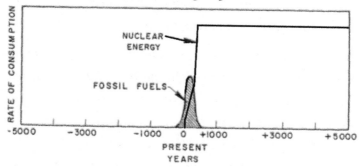

---

[4] Figure from Hubbert's 1956 paper, *Nuclear Energy and the Fossil Fuels,*
https://mkinghubbert.wordpress.com/2009/03/08/hubberts-early-take-on-nuclear-energy/

268

References

Non-narrative Viewpoints on Climate Science and Energy

Berry, Ed. 2020. <u>Climate Miracle: There is No Climate Crisis. Nature Controls Climate.</u> Montana, Ed Berry, LLC.

Crichton, Michael, 2004. <u>State of Fear</u>. New York, NY. Avon Books.

Christy, John. 2019. *The Tropical Skies: Falsifying Climate Alarm*. London, United Kingdom. The GWPF Note 17.
<u>https://www.thegwpf.org/content/uploads/2021/02/Christy-2019A.pdf</u>

Collins, Gabriel and Michelle Foss. 2022. *The Global Energy Transition's Looming Valley of Death*. <u>https://www.bakerinstitute.org/research/global-energy-transitions-looming-valley-death/</u>

<u>Curry, Judith. Climate Etc.</u>

Epstein, Alex. 2022. <u>Fossil Future: Why Global Flourishing Requires More Oil, Coal and Natural Gas – Not Less.</u> New York, NY. Portfolio Penguin.

The Global Warming Policy Foundation. <u>www.thegwpf.org</u> London, United Kingdom.

Darwall, Rupert. 2013. <u>The Age of Global Warming: A History.</u> Padstow, Cornwall Great Britain. T J International Ltd.

Foster, Peter. 2020. <u>How Dare You!</u> The Global Warming Policy Forum.

Goreham, Steve. 2012. *The Mad, Mad, Mad World of Climatism; Mankind and Climate Change Mania.* New Lenox, Illinois. New Lenox Books, Inc.

Happer, William. 2011. *The Truth About Greenhouse Gases*. London, United Kingdom. The GWPF Briefing Paper No 3.

Idso, Craig. *CO$_2$ Science.*

Irish Climate Science Forum. Lecture Series.

Klaus, Vaclav. 2008. Blue Planet in Green Shackles - What is Endangered: Climate or Freedom? Competitive Enterprise Institute.

Koonin, Steven E. 2021. Unsettled: What Climate Science Tells Us, What it Doesn't, and Why it Matters. Dallas, Texas. BenBella Books.

Laframboise, Donna. 2011. The Delinquent Teenager Who Was Mistaken for the World's Top Climate Expert. Toronto, Canada. Ivy Avenue Press.

Lawson, Nigel. 2008. An Appeal to Reason: A Cool Look at Global Warming. Overlook Duckworth. Woodstock, NY.

Lindzen, Richard. 2018. *Global Warming for the Two Cultures.* London, United Kingdom. *2018 Annual The GWPF Lecture.* https://www.thegwpf.org/content/uploads/2018/10/Lindzen-AnnualGWPF-lecture.pdf

Lindzen, Richard. 2022. *Assessment of the Conventional Global Warming Narrative.* https://www.thegwpf.org/content/uploads/2022/09/Lindzen-global-warming-narrative.pdf

Lomborg, Bjorn. 2020. False Alarm; How Climate Change Panic Costs Us Trillions, Hurts the Poor, and Fails to Fix the Planet. New York. Basic Books.

May, Andy. 2020. Politics and Climate Change: A History. United States of America. American Freedom Publications LLC.

Mills, Mark. 2019. *The 'New Energy Economy': An Exercise in Magical Thinking.* https://media4.manhattan-institute.org/sites/default/files/R-0319-MM.pdf

Mills, Mark. 2022. *The Hard Math of Minerals.* Mills, Mark. 2019. *The "New Energy Economy": An Exercise in Magical Thinking.* https://media4.manhattan-institute.org/sites/default/files/R-0319-MM.pdf

Mills, Mark. 2022. The Energy Transition Delusion: A Reality Reset. *The "Energy Transition" Delusion | Manhattan Institute (manhattan-institute.org)*

Moore, Patrick. 2021. Fake Invisible Catastrophes and Threats of Doom. Comox, British Columbia, Canada. Ecosense Environmental Inc.

Moore, Patrick. 2019. *The Power of Truth.* https://www.youtube.com/watch?v=UWahKIG4BE4 .

Moran, Alan as Editor. 2015. Climate Change: The Facts. Quebec, Canada. Stockade Books.

Nakamura, Mototaka. *Confessions of a Climate Scientist.* https://c-c-netzwerk.ch/images/ccn-blog_articles/717/Confessions-Nakamura.pdf

Net Zero Watch. https://www.netzerowatch.com/

Nova, Joanne. https://joannenova.com.au

Plimer, Ian. 2014. Not for Greens; He Who Sups With the Devil Should Have a Long Spoon. Australia. Connor Court Publishing Pty Ltd.

Ridley Matt. 2015. *The Climate Wars' Damage to Science.* Quadrant Online. https://quadrant.org.au/magazine/2015/06/climate-wars-done-science/

Robson, John. *Climate Discussion Nexus.* https://climatediscussionnexus.com/

Sangster, M. J. 2018. The Real Inconvenient Truth; It's Warming: But it's Not CO_2. Lexington, Kentucky.

Shellenberger, Michael. *Why Renewables Can't Save the Planet,* https://www.youtube.com/watch?v=N-yALPEpV4w , TEDxDanubia.

Shellenberger, Michael. 2020. Apocalypse Never; Why Environmental Alarmism Hurts Us All. New York. Harper.

Solomon Lawrence. 2008. The Deniers. The United States of America. Richard Vigilante Books.

Soon, Willie. 2019. *GlobalWarming Fact or Fiction.* https://www.youtube.com/watch?v=1zrejG-WI3U

Spencer, Roy. *Latest Global Temps.* https://www.drroyspencer.com/latest-global-temperatures/

Spencer, Roy. 2010. <u>The Great Global Warming Blunder: How Mother Nature Fooled the World's Top Scientists.</u> Encounter books. New York.

Springer, Fred S. Third Edition 2021. <u>Hot Talk, Cold Science; Global Warming's Unfinished Debate</u>. United States of America. Independent Institute.

Svensmark, Henrik. 2019. *Force Majeure – The Sun's Role in Climate Change.* The Global Warming Policy Foundation. (Note: Cosmic Rays)
https://www.thegwpf.org/content/uploads/2019/03/SvensmarkSolar2019-1.pdf

Tisdale, Bob. 2015. <u>On Global Warming and the Illusion of Control – Part 1 – A Comprehensive Illustrated Introduction to the Hypothesis of Human-Induced Global Warming.</u> Available online at no charge.
https://bobtisdale.files.wordpress.com/2015/11/tisdale-on-global-warming-and-the-illusion-of-control-part-1.pdf

Vinós, Javier. 2022. <u>Climate of the Past, Present and Future.</u> Madrid, Spain. Critical Science Press.

Watts, Anthony. *Watts Up with That?* https://wattsupwiththat.com

Net Zero and Absolute Zero References

These references are provided to assist you in understanding where certain governmental organizations believe they are heading.

Biden, Joe. April 22, 2021. *FACT SHEET: President Biden Sets 2030 Greenhouse Gas Pollution Reduction Target Aimed at Creating Good-Paying Union Jobs and Securing U.S. Leadership on Clean Energy Technologies.*

IEA. May 2021. *Net Zero by 2050; a Roadmap for the Global Energy Sector,*
https://www.iea.org/reports/net-zero-by-2050?mc_cid=565ffdf6d5&mc_eid=ab5a382900.

UK FIRES. November 2019. *Absolute Zero Energy Emissions 2050, University of Cambridge* https://scote3.files.wordpress.com/2020/06/absolute-zero-digital-280120-v2-uk-fires-report.pdf

Acknowledgments

I'd like to acknowledge the assistance of Louis Pelz and John Kemp. Mark Sooby, Jim Kelly, Sam Burkett, and Leo Giangiacomo also weighed in with encouragement. Linda Williams and Phillip Hotchkiss provided extremely detailed and useful editorial suggestions. Katie Cape, Matt Bridgeman and Michelle Miranda also contributed. Particular thanks go to Steve Bach, David Hale, Magdaline Cardimitropoulo, Bob Forbes, John Stein, and Bill Fullerton, who took considerable time to convey their perspectives in a later draft.

A special thanks goes to my partner. Not only did she assist me with her literary observations, but she introduced me to her love for China during a number of short trips there.

Many Chinese students have studied English in school. They appreciate our styles, brands, and technology and we have benefitted from their manufacturing wizardry. Why is it now, with so many social and economic linkages possible favoring closer ties between China and the United States, that both of our governments seem determined to put us on opposite sides of the next cold war?